"Tom Pitts' H̲u̲s̲t̲l̲e̲ is the kind of in-your-face street level noir that American crime fiction hasn't seen in a long, long time. Frankly, not many writers have either the balls or the talent to pull it off. Pitts has both in spades. Bold, honest and daring."
—Todd Robinson, *The Hard Bounce*

"Tom Pitts is part of a rare and dying breed, a self-taught, instinctual writer whose tight, pitch-perfect prose was honed the old-fashioned way by reading and walking the seedy alleys of life. HUSTLE is quick-paced and dark, at once sad and funny as hell, with a Jim Thompson-esque cast of characters and echoes of Bukowski in its poetic sensitivity. Pitts' own experiences on the streets of San Francisco make HUSTLE a novel unlike any you've read before. I love this book."
—Ro Cuzon, *Under the Dixie Moon*

"What makes HUSTLE such a remarkable book—and Tom Pitts such a formidable writer—is the juxtaposition of literary tradition versus street ethos. HUSTLE pushes boundaries and challenges the peripheral but not at the expense of story, which zips along the dirty streets of San Francisco to tell a terrifying tale, the likes of which, I promise you, you've never heard before. This is in-the-trenches, first-hand, in-your-face reportage, from a guy who knows what it takes to survive those streets. Unflinching and without apology."
—Joe Clifford, *Junkie Love* and *Lamentation*

"HUSTLE is a smart and deceitful novel that can't wait for you to judge it. It presents itself with a raw, unadorned prose, but it's way more than meets the eye. Tom Pitts is a wicked storyteller. He barely arrived in the publishing game, but expect him to become one of these cult authors with a rabid fanbase."
—Benoit Lelievre, DeadEndFollies.com

"HUSTLE in an insane mind-fuck."
—Liam Sweeny, *Welcome Back Jack*

HUSTLE

ALSO BY TOM PITTS

Knuckleball
Piggyback

TOM PITTS

HUSTLE

DOWN & OUT
BOOKS

Down & Out Books
3959 Van Dyke Rd, Ste. 265
Lutz, FL 33558
www.DownAndOutBooks.com

Cover photo by Mark Krajnak
Cover design by Dyer Wilk and Eric Beetner

ISBN: 1-943402-19-1
ISBN-13: 978-1-943402-19-9

For Cheryl, always.

FOREWORD

Tom Pitts' *Hustle* is, quite simply, one of the very best novels I've read in a long, long time. There's just no other way to describe it. Years from now, I'm convinced it will be viewed in the same light as the early work of Charles Bukowski—as a ground-breaking classic. To be honest, there is no one to compare Pitts to with this book.

Perhaps the best comparison—not in the writing, but in the revealing of an underworld lifestyle—would be to Robert Beck's seminal classic, *Iceberg Slim*. The difference is, Pitts doesn't attempt to portray his protagonist as heroic as Beck does, but more along the lines of Jean Genet's character Divine in his brilliant *Our Lady of the Flowers*. But, while both of these writers and both of these books use the settings of the underworld of sex-for-pay and/or aberrant sex-for-pleasure, there is a significant difference in *Hustle*, in that Pitts' protagonist, Donny, isn't portrayed as a man who sees himself as a maverick or a rebel, raging against the system and defiantly proud of his rebellion, but simply as a human being to whom drugs have reduced to an intolerable lifestyle which he is unable to escape, although the entire book is about his struggle to do so. Both Iceberg Slim and Divine embrace their lifestyles, but Donny does not. That is the difference and why, even though there are similarities in settings and lifestyles, Donny is more akin to Bukowski's Martin Blanchard than Divine or Slim. And yet, he isn't like Blanchard either. The thing is, he's an entirely different character than just about anyone in literature. Donny shares similarities with other literary creations, but in the end, he is a whole new creation. And, because of that, *Hustle* is a whole new category of noir.

i

And, while Donny doesn't see himself as heroic, of course he is. He's a survivor and that is the best proof of heroism that exists. He's proactive on his own behalf to escape the hell that he's in and against more terrible odds than Hercules or Atlas ever faced and what makes him extremely likeable is that he doesn't see himself as heroic in the least.

Hustle is going to be seen by its critics as both remarkable and abhorrent. Often both by the same critic. It's going to offend some crime writers I suspect, because compared to their own work, which of course they will in their own minds, they're going to realize that their efforts—compared to Pitts'—are more along the lines of *The Hardy Boys Have Adventures in Sugar Creek*. In other words, there are many pretenders and posers writing crime and noir novels, who have little or no experience with the element they are writing about. Pitts knows his milieu and better than anyone I've ever read. His novel rings loud and clear with hard, honest truth. He knows these guys and he doesn't judge. Readers looking for the comfort of stereotypes are bound to be disappointed. Like Bukowski's Martin Blanchard, he allows his characters to have souls and, indeed, insists on it.

Pitts told me that there was some pressure on him to edit some of the rougher parts to make it more palatable for readers. In his words, "They're trying to have me soften it a little, I'm trying to hold fast." Please do, Tom! If any of this gets "softened" it will only prove that as a culture, we have, indeed, become so PC'd we've lost our souls. To "soften" this book would mean literature has lost to moronic politics. And we'll all be the poorer for that.

—Les Edgerton,
author of *The Rapist*, *The Bitch*, and
The Genuine, Imitation, Plastic Kidnapping

CHAPTER 1

It seemed like it would be fun. Everyone referred to it as a party. *Hey, you wanna party? Do you like to party?* The drugs—the things he really loved—were called party favors. It made it all seem that much more normal, like they were flappers from the roaring twenties asking who was going to bring the champagne. *You got party favors?*

Donny's first time was for the party favors—just went to some shitty hotel with two guys. Donny only had to be with one of them. The big guy said the little guy couldn't get it up, that he was too high. But he was wrong; the little guy got it up. The little guy only watched, but came three times. Maybe he didn't like the idea of someone else touching his dick. Donny couldn't blame him. Should have seen his friend.

It was easy, or at least it got easier, so Donny returned to the corner. Down on that corner, everybody knew each other. Everybody was into each other's business. The boys depended on each other for information. Information was survival. They all knew the regulars, the older men who would cruise the corner in their luxury cars. They got to know who was married, who liked to party, who liked it freaky, and who was HIV-positive. Some of the tricks didn't care who knew, but some liked to keep it a secret.

The HIV-positive thing never really bothered Donny much. A trick was a trick; that's what rubbers were for. They all used condoms—or said they did. Some of those freaks gave up extra money to go without, but not with Donny. He wasn't there 'cause he liked the sex, he liked the party—more specifically, the party favors. Some of those older johns, they would carry a sack of the shit just for the pick-ups. They

1

never used it, probably drop dead of a heart attack if they did. But they all knew, down on Polk Street, speed was like candy at the schoolyard.

After a few more tricks, it seemed silly to keep doing it just to smoke a little crank; might as well walk out of there with a few bucks. At least then you could buy some downtown, help you forget all the bullshit you just went through. This is how Donny met Big Rich. Big Rich could get that cheap brown Mexican dope no matter what time of the night it was.

Big Rich had been down there longer than any of them. He was bigger, tougher, and more street-worn than the rest of them, but he was still handsome enough to be desirable. His few years on the corner added up to eons of experience. He was a seasoned pro. Rich could smell vice before they ever hit the block. He'd give a high whistle whenever he heard them coming and the boys would all start moving, walking, lighting cigarettes and talking on cell phones. It's not like they were fooling anybody. Everybody in the city knew what went on down there.

Big Rich's appetite to party was insatiable. So was his need for cash. He needed speed to work and heroin to live. He'd already burned through the regulars. He knew how to size up the fresh meat. He could tell by the make and model of the car—even just the headlights—if the guy inside was real money or just flash. It was Big Rich who showed Donny how to steal from the tricks. He taught all of them the finer arts of being a hustler.

"In the car, that's easy," Big Rich said. He was on the corner proselytizing the new boys. "Then you just tell 'em you want to see it, all of it, get 'em to pull their pants down all the way. After you start, just go through their pockets while their pants are sittin' around their ankles."

"Multi-tasking," someone joked.

"Exactly," said Rich, serious. "But if they wanna do *you*, then it ain't so easy. Better to tell 'em that you don't feel safe on the street, tell 'em you got busted in a car just last week, it'd be better if you go to a room."

"That way you know if they have any more than what they're willing to spend on you, if they're serious," said one of the boys, eager to be part of Rich's sermon.

Donny just listened, took it all in. To him, Rich seemed like one of the good guys, like he had their best interests at heart. They didn't have pimps down there; Rich was the closest thing they did have—someone who was looking out.

"Once you're in the room, it's easy," continued Rich. "If they got party favors, y'all know how to palm 'em, or just get greedy and suck 'em up. Start smoking and blow it straight up into the air. Shit, once they've paid for a room, they got their name on the register downstairs and they don't want any trouble. Believe that."

"What about the money?" asked Donny.

"Oh, c'mon. You know, you tell 'em you like it clean, get 'em to go into the bathroom, wash it off. When they do, you grab what you can. You know this shit."

It was true; Big Rich had been schooling Donny from the first week he was on the corner. He looked out for Donny. The first time the two of them met, they went together to do a show for some old fucker who just wanted to see them get hard. They did their thing. The old guy did his. All by himself. Then he left the room. Maybe he had some shame issues. Guilt, regret, whatever. Big Rich and Donny stayed in that room for two days, even ordered room service. Finally, the drugs ran out, and so did they.

The cops rolled on the corner and broke up their little pep talk. Just a black and white, probably didn't even notice them. But even the sight of a police car got them nervous. Everybody walking, talking, acting like they belonged somewhere else. Of course, none of them did.

After the crew had scattered like frightened pigeons, Big Rich and Donny stood alone on the corner.

"Got any smokes?" Big Rich asked.

"Nah, none."

"Hungry?"

"Always," Donny said. It wasn't always true, but he'd be a fool to pass up any offer of a free meal.

"Let's go get a slice from the Arab. I wanna talk to you about somethin'."

The two walked down Polk Street and Rich bought them both a slice from the Arab. The Arab was the owner of Alzer's Pizza on Polk. Even though his name was emblazoned above the door, the boys referred to him only as the Arab.

"For here," Rich told the Arab.

"To go," replied the Arab. Alzer hated these boys in his place. They were bad for business. He knew they shot up in the bathroom; he was the one who had to clean the blood off the walls.

Donny and Rich took their slices, packaged in white cardboard to go containers, and sat down anyway. They picked a spot near the front window. There, they could watch the street and not be easily heard.

"I been thinking," said Big Rich, "about the long haul. Y'know, ripping these assholes off for drug money ain't too satisfying. We get maybe two days well out of it and we're back to sucking dicks."

Donny nodded and chewed his pizza. It wasn't too warm and it wasn't too good. Alzer had probably given them the stalest slices in the shop. He'd had better pizza out of trashcans.

"Thing is, we go to these guys' houses all the time. Steal a few nick-knacks, shit we can pawn before they know it's gone. It ain't nothin' really. These are million dollar houses we're sittin' in. Sick fucking perverts who make more money than God. They don't know how lucky they are."

"And...," Donny said with his mouth still full of pizza.

"And we can help 'em appreciate how lucky they are."

Donny still didn't see what he was getting at.

"We pick one of these old fuckers, someone with a wife, a family, you know. Shit, he don't want to turn his world upside down. Someone who's got so much dough that it won't hurt to pay us off. And keep paying us off. Like a weekly paycheck, so we can stop this bullshit we're doing out here." Big Rich pointed to the traffic outside the window.

Donny had heard his friend go down this path before. There was nothing new about blackmailing johns. It was the second oldest profession in the world.

"I thought you said it was a bad idea. That it never worked out."

"Aaah," Big Rich held up his finger, "this time we do it right. We get inconvertible evidence. So it's not just my word against theirs."

"Incontrovertible," said Donny.

"What?"

"Incontrovertible. That's the word."

"Bullshit, that's not how you say it."

"It is. Convertibles are cars."

"Shut the fuck up, Donny. You don't know. This is my plan and I've been giving it a lot of thought. We just find the right guy, in the right circumstance, and then we get it on film. That's it. We tell him we're gonna expose him, put it on YouTube or some shit and let the money roll in."

"You got it all figured out, why don't you do it?"

"Because, Donny, I need someone to hold the camera."

Rain had started to fall when the boys left the pizza shop. It was only a spit, but enough to make them not want to go back to the corner.

"Let's call the man," Big Rich said.

"I only have eleven dollars," said Donny.

"I thought you said you didn't have any money?"

"Not *food* money," Donny said.

"That's okay. I can get a front from Hector. I don't owe him anything."

Donny was relieved. The habit that he'd acquired from daily use of heroin had shown no signs of slowing down. Nowadays it seemed he only had a few hours before he was going to feel sick. He could already feel the irrepressible yawns coming on and the rain was not helping with the chills.

"Let's go back to my hotel room. I got a bag of fresh works," Big Rich said. He pulled his cell from his jacket and stepped under an awning while he scrolled down to Hector's number. He spoke into the phone with a serious look on his face. After he finished, he turned to Donny and said, "Twenty minutes."

They marked the time walking back through the Tenderloin streets until they reached Big Rich's place on the worst part of Eddy Street. Deep in the Tenderloin, the streets were lined with vagrants despite the weather. Old men sat slumped, piled in rags, looking like heaps of garbage. Women with stringy whiskers on their chins talked to themselves as they pushed carts filled with garbage only they valued. Every few feet there were drug dealers offering pills of every variety, most of which, Rich and Donny knew, were a rip off. All of these cast offs were out there no matter what time of day or night, lining the sidewalks. Human waste.

The rain had picked up now. Heavy gobs pelted them as they both stood facing the door of the old hotel, waiting for the man behind the front desk to recognize them and buzz them in.

The door buzzed and they walked into the tiny, dank lobby. The small Indian man behind the desk said, "Ten dollars."

"C'mon," said Big Rich. "We're only gonna be here a minute. You know, Donny. He's here all the time."

"Guest deposit, ten dollars," the man said.

"We're just gonna go up and get my wallet," Big Rich said.
"Last time," said the desk clerk, "Last time."

The boys were buzzed in through the inner gate that separated the lobby from the stairs and bolted up, two steps at a time.

They got to the room and Donny was hit by the familiar funk of his friend's filth. There were pizza boxes and empty fast food containers piled high on the old dresser. The bed was unmade and the sheets were speckled with blood from Big Rich cleaning his rig after using it. On the nightstand beside the bed stood a dirty glass of water on a patch of black, the dark carbon smudge from where Rich's spoon sat when he cooked his dope.

Donny ignored the blood on the sheets and plopped down. It was dry blood after all.

"Be right back. Don't touch nothin'," said Big Rich as he checked the time on his cell phone and slipped out the door.

Donny nodded and stayed sitting on the bed. He pulled out his own cell to see how long it would take his friend to return. He sat waiting, wishing he had some drugs of his own. He reached into the breast pocket of his denim jacket and pulled out a glass stem with a blub on the end. He examined the bulb. It was cloudy and white. He held a disposable lighter to it and rotated the bulb around. Barely a puff of smoke. He sucked it in and held it.

He tilted his head up expecting to blow out the smoke and nothing came out of his lungs at all. On the ceiling he saw more blood spatters. There was so much blood up there it looked like a Jackson Pollack painting. Donny knew how it could be, the rig getting clogged, blood coagulating; you gave it a little pressure to squeeze out the goop and squirt, there it went, half your shot was on the roof. The shitty coke they got from the Mexicans was the worst. It'd gum up your works in a minute if you didn't find a vein. And no one wanted to squirt out any of that shit.

Donny sat wondering if Big Rich would have the sense—and the gall—to ask for a half-gram of coke from Hector, too. A speedball would really brighten up this rainy day. Hector carried both, but he was the toughest one to get credit from. All these assholes knew that if they said no, you'd do what you had to do to get the money and you'd call them right back. Junkies were incredibly creative when it came to finding money. The dealers gave only a little credit to keep you regular, so you wouldn't call the next Hector.

Donny heard the key in the door and checked his cell phone. Eight minutes, probably a record for Rich making it back in time.

"Quick, huh? What did I tell ya?" Rich said smiling. He reached into his jeans and pulled out a small balloon and began to bite at it with his teeth.

"How much?" said Donny.

"A full gram. I only paid him twenty. Not bad, huh? Hector's got the shit right now."

"You get anything else?"

"What do you mean, anything else? You mean coke? No. Hector won't front coke. He'd have to front it all day long."

As happy as Donny was to be getting well on someone else's dime, it was tough to hide his disappointment. He wanted to feel this shot, he wanted to get high.

"Aw, poor Donny. Tell you what, I got a bit of that raw crank left from Dupree, we'll put that in the spoon, okay?"

"Yeah," Donny said. He liked to shoot the raw speed better than the glass anyway. It gave a better rush in the vein.

When the boys were done they sat cross legged on the bed smoking cigarettes and sharing an ashtray between them. Now was the time for grand ideas, for false promises. They were warm and high and far from the corner. The subject, as always, came back to money.

"So, Rich," Donny said. "I know you wouldn't have brought up that YouTube thing earlier if you didn't already have someone in mind."

"Yeah, so?"

"So, who is it? Is it someone I'd know, like, a trick I've already had?"

"You don't know him, Donny."

"You sure? Is it somebody that comes by the corner?"

"You don't know him, Donny." Rich sounding more firm this time.

"I'm not gonna steal your idea, if that's what you think."

Rich leaned in, lowering his voice even though there was no one who would be listening. "I'm not worried about that, Donny. I just know it 'cause of the kinda shit he likes. He doesn't like to come by the corner—too dangerous. Doesn't want to be seen. That's why I think he could be the perfect guy for this." Big Rich was nodding his head and raising his eyebrows at the same time. His look said, *See, I've put some thought into this.*

"He's some kinda lawyer. A fuckin' big wig. He's married, lives in a big ol' house in Pacific Heights. I seen a picture in his house of him and the mayor. He's got something he doesn't wanna lose, Donny. He's perfect."

"What kind of lawyer is he?"

Big Rich smiled and said, "A *rich* one."

CHAPTER 2

Gabriel Thaxton sat behind the wheel of his Bentley Continental. It was an ostentatious choice for a vehicle, to be sure, but it set the right tone for the associates at the firm. The radio was off and the windows were rolled up. It was silent in the car. He sat looking up at the old, brick, multimillion dollar monstrosity he lived in. It was also ostentatious; too big for him to live in at his age, too many stairs, but it also set the right tone for his neighbors. He'd lived in Pacific Heights for most of his life, having acquired the house just two years out of law school. It was a mansion, a brick and mortar estate. He stared at it. He watched the sun move the house's shadow across the lawn, onto the driveway, and finally, he waited till its darkness consumed him in his car.

He'd worked late at the office, even though he didn't need to. In fact, he really didn't need to go into the office at all these days. He had no upcoming cases, no prospective clients; the firm was quite efficient—and just as profitable—running itself. As long as his respected name was at the helm of the brand, the firm was going to prosper.

Thaxton, Spreckle, and White had been doing business in San Francisco for close to forty years. The three partners had built their reputations as risk-taking, media-savvy, criminal defense attorneys who weren't afraid to take on cases the public viewed with distaste. In the mid-eighties, they took on several capital cases that became the focus of national news. Vilified by the public and the press, the firm's client base exploded after three of their capital cases ended in acquittal. Since then, he'd been the go-to guy for high profile criminals of every variety.

In recent years, he'd begun to feel the weight of his contribution to the world. Gabriel wondered what kind mark he'd left. Contemplation only served up guilt. It was a feeling he never experienced early in his career. In the eighties, and even on into the nineties, he was invigorated by the job, his successes. But now, he couldn't avoid that ominous feeling that there would be a terrible price to pay for the legacy he'd left behind.

He wanted to go inside and pour himself a single malt scotch and forget about everything, but the house was no longer a home, no longer the sanctuary it once was. He'd let his base desires, his weaknesses, take a forefront in his life, and, in doing so, had let an evil into his house. He couldn't face going in.

Gabriel put the key back into the ignition, started the Bentley, and pulled out of his driveway. He wasn't sure where he was going. He just didn't want to be home.

The sun was dipping down and the headlights of other cars flashed on as he zigzagged through the steep streets of Pacific Heights, working his way through rush hour traffic toward Nob Hill. Gabriel thought about going for that single malt in a bar, perhaps a nice anonymous hotel bar, but he just kept driving. On some level, he knew where he was going; he just didn't want to admit it to himself. He was heading toward Polk Street, where the boys stood on the corners. He wanted to see if his newest young friend, Rich, was there. He wouldn't stop. Gabriel just wanted to see if he was out there. Catch a glimpse before he moved on with his night, a mental image, a memory he could take home with him later.

It was already dark by the time he reached the intersection of Polk and Sutter. The corner was near empty. The wind was blowing and it looked cold. Regular foot traffic: people with their collars up hurrying home from work, homeless derelicts pushing carts, transsexual hookers in outrageous clothing heading back to their roosts on the next block. No young men out there. Gabriel sat at a red light wondering why he'd bothered. He had the boy's cell number, he could easily call and set up a meeting, a date, but he wasn't up for a face to face encounter, not tonight. A horn blared from behind and startled him from his thoughts. The light had turned green while he was staring at the corner. He didn't even want to be seen down there. Embarrassed, he hooked a right and headed back toward Pacific Heights.

Donny and Big Rich woke simultaneously from a deep nod. The window of Rich's hotel room had been darkened by the night. It was cold in the room, but both of them felt warm and comfortable.

"Shit, we passed out," said Donny.

"Only for a minute."

"What time is it?"

"I dunno, but it's time we got back out there," said Rich.

"Fuck, I don't wanna go. It looks like it's freezing outside."

"It's not as cold as I'm gonna be in a few hours if I don't hustle up some dope."

"You don't have anything?" said Donny.

"We did most of it. I need a hit when I get home. If I don't get to work, I'm not gonna have a wakeup either."

For Donny, the situation was more dire. He only had eleven dollars in his pockets, not enough to cop with. Nothing else. Not a late night hit, not a wakeup, nothing. Withdrawals would set in before midnight and if he didn't get his ass in gear, he'd be fucked.

Rich got up off the bed and stretched. He walked to the shabby dresser and began to rifle through its top drawer. He pulled out bits of clothing and pieces of paper.

"What are you looking for?" asked Donny.

"Some raw. I know I left another piece in here some-where."

"We put it in the spoon," Donny said.

"Naw, that was just a teaser. I still have another chunk." Big Rich hunched over, looking desperately. He'd begun to toss items over his shoulder when he said, "Ah, here it is."

He returned to the bed with a lump of unwashed speed pinched off in the corner of a plastic baggie. Donny produced his pipe, a long glass stem with a bulb on the end where the speed went. The two sat in silence while Rich readied the pipe. When the yellowish chunk had been stuffed through the hole in the bulb, Rich held a lighter underneath, waited for that familiar bubbling sound, and drew deeply. He passed the pipe to Donny so his friend could do the same. Back and forth. Now they'd be ready for the street.

They both lit cigarettes before they left the room and then marched toward the lobby. The manager was able to say, "No smoking, no smoking!" before they hit the door.

"It's okay," said Rich, "he's used to being ignored."

The boys hit the sidewalk and headed west toward Polk Street. The wind had died down with the onset of night. Prospects were good by the time they hit the corner. There was almost no one else there. The other boys were either out turning tricks or at holed-up already, high and forgetting. Traffic was heavy and several cars slowed, but none stopped. The two stood waiting, checking the headlights on each passing car. Twenty minutes went by. No takers for either of them.

"It's the fucking internet that's killing this shit," Big Rich said.

"I know," said Donny. "Everyone makes their dates off Craigslist. We should get one of those fancy phones and take out an ad."

"Fuck that. I like to know who I'm dealing with. Some asshole answers your ad and you go meet him. Who knows what the fuck he's gonna do?"

"Yeah," said Donny. He knew that getting into cars with strangers was really no better. Freaks were freaks, and they wouldn't be out here trolling if they weren't freaks. He'd only been out on the corner for a few months and he'd seen enough to last him a lifetime. Every night brought some kind of drama, some experience he'd just as soon forget.

Twenty more minutes went by. Still no takers. Donny lit a cigarette and passed it to Rich.

"There's got to be an easier way," said Donny.

"There is, I'm telling ya. We got to look at taking off this guy I told you about."

"What's his deal?"

"What do you mean? What does he like? Company. He likes to be around me. Likes to listen to me talk."

"Talk about what?"

"Street shit, petty crimes. I make stuff up. He doesn't seem to care."

"No sex?"

"Oh, yeah, he likes me to pull out my dick, jerk it for him. He wants me to jerk him, too, sometimes. Sometimes we take a drive in his car up to Marin County. He'll ask me to pull down my pants and jerk it while he's on the freeway. Nothin' too weird. He's almost shy. That's why I figure he's good for this. He doesn't want any direct contact because he's afraid of bringing crabs or some shit back home to his wife."

"No oral?"

"Nope, not yet, but I can tell he wants to. That's how I wanna get in his house. Tell him I wanna take it up a notch."

"Where's he live?" said Donny.

"Out on Pacific Street. Where all them huge houses are? He left me in the driveway once 'cause he had to run in to piss or some shit. I walked in the house anyway. It's a fuckin' palace."

"What kind of car does he drive?"

Big Rich gave Donny a look.

"I ain't telling you."

A Lincoln Continental pulled up and Rich said, "Ah, one of my regulars." The car stopped in the bus stop across the street and the driver side window lowered just enough for the face of an older man to show. He was smiling at Big Rich.

Rich looked at Donny and said, "This guy just wants to be pissed on. Easy money, a hundred bucks. If you're still here when I get back, we'll go back to the hotel and cop. Call it a night."

Donny nodded. It was hard not to feel a little envious. *A hundred bucks for taking a piss.* Easy money.

CHAPTER 3

Gabriel was back in the driveway of his house. The place was dark except for one light in an upstairs bedroom. He sighed. He had hoped the light would be out, that no one would be home. He slowly got out of the car, locked the doors, and walked toward the huge, oak, double doors that separated him from what should have been his sanctuary.

"Hello?" he called out. He took off his jacket and hung it on an antique hat rack. He listened to his own footsteps as he crossed the marble tile of the entrance. "Is there anybody home?" He knew full well there was someone home. If that light was on, then there was someone up there.

Gabriel walked into the kitchen and opened the cupboard door above the fridge. He took out his single malt scotch, pulled a glass from the clean dishes beside the sink, and poured himself one. Three fingers deep. After a few sips, he opened the freezer and dropped a couple of ice cubes into the glass.

"*Gabriel?*"

The voice came from upstairs. He felt his heart kick up a notch. He knew there was someone else home, but hearing the voice spooked him just the same. He stared into his glass.

"*Gabe!*"

The voice, angry now, sounded closer, at the top of the stairs. He had to answer.

"Yes, dear," he said, hoping it didn't sound too sarcastic. He took one more hit off the scotch and walked out of the kitchen toward the stairs. The steps were carpeted and curved up toward the second story. An ornate gold banister curved with them. He looked up and said, "What do you need?"

"Did you bring me anything?"

At the top of the stairs stood Dustin; pale, skinny, and pockmarked. He was wearing one of Gabriel's silk robes and it exposed his pale pigeon chest. Square in the middle of his chest was a faded blue tattoo of an eagle with its talons clamped onto a swastika. It was blurred and amateurish. The tattoo was a constant reminder of where Dustin came from.

"Did I bring you anything? Like what?"

"Money, dinner, drugs—anything? I've been here all day waiting for something to happen and you drag your ass in here empty handed?"

"I had to work late. I didn't get a chance to stop by anywhere."

"You're fulla shit," said Dustin. "You can sleep down there tonight; jerk yourself off for a change."

Gabriel didn't know what to say, so he just said, "I'm sorry."

Dustin spun around, swirling his borrowed silk housecoat with him. He stomped back toward the bedroom saying, "We'll see how sorry you are."

Gabriel walked back into the kitchen. He looked at his scotch on the marble counter. He wondered how he'd let himself get painted into a corner like this, if this were some sort of subconscious payback he felt he deserved. No, he decided, what he deserved was some peace. Some pleasure. He heard the shower start upstairs and took one more hit of the scotch, picked up his keys, and walked back out the door.

He pulled out of the driveway without looking back at the house. He didn't care what Dustin would think when he got out of the shower. He'd stay away all night if he had to. Dustin was a mistake. A malignancy he should have cut out when he had the guts, the leverage. Maybe the kid would just be gone when he returned—if he returned.

It was full dark now. Past nine o'clock. The street traffic had slackened and he was back to the corner in minutes. He didn't want to go by the corner, but it lured him. It was his unconscious desire driving the car and he would have ended up there no matter what. He didn't care about being seen now, he just wanted to see the boy as soon as possible and he didn't feel like waiting. Gabriel pulled over into a driveway and dialed Big Rich's cell.

Big Rich and Donny had just finished fixing. They were high and low, lolling off the effects of a healthy speedball. The shrill electronic ring of Rich's cell phone startled them both. Rich looked at the caller ID. "It's him."

Donny smiled, but he had no idea who Rich meant. He didn't care. There were a lot of *hims*. He was settled in and didn't want to work anymore tonight. He had dope, coke, cigarettes and was warm for the first time in hours. He didn't want to leave Big Rich's room.

"Gabriel," Big Rich said into the phone. He was looking right at Donny, grinning. "No, I'm home with a friend...What are you doin'?...No, just a friend."

Donny waited. He couldn't make out what the voice on the phone was saying.

"I dunno, Gabriel. I'm kinda settled in. I don't wanna leave my friend in my room all alone. Maybe I could bring him? You'd like him."

The tiny voice buzzed through the speaker on Rich's cell.

"No, he's a few years younger than me. Maybe you've seen him on the corner...Ha, no, not like me...No, I trust him. He's a good kid, just, you know, caught up by circumstance, like the rest of us."

Donny liked that. Big Rich getting philosophical. He watched Rich play with the man on the phone. Half flirting, half playing hard to get, setting him up. Big Rich was a pro.

"I could, I guess. I gotta bring my friend with me, though. It'll be okay. You'll like it." Big Rich shot a wink at Donny and said, "Corner of Eddy and Jones. Twenty minutes." Rich hit the end button on his phone and turned to Donny. "Grab the shit and put your jacket on. We're gonna make some money."

"Shit. I really don't feel like turning any tricks. We just got here. Maybe I can just wait till you get back."

"Donny, this is the guy. The john I was telling you about. We'll do what he wants tonight. This is your chance to meet him, gain some trust. Fuck, I'm tellin' ya, I couldn't a planned it better. Grab the spoons, I got the rigs. We might not be coming back tonight."

In twenty minutes, the two boys stood dutifully on the corner, hands in their pockets, watching each set of headlights that approached.

"What kind of car does he drive?"

"A Bentley," said Big Rich.

"Seriously."

"For real, a Bentley."

Donny thought about it a minute. He wasn't even sure if he knew what a Bentley looked like. "Seriously?" His voice pitched upward with surprise.

"I'm telling you. This is the guy. He's got more money than God. Be sweet to him and we'll be fat in no time."

Donny grinned and watched the street, looking for something expensive to pull up, what his mind pictured a Bentley to look like. Like a Rolls Royce, maybe? He imagined an old car with a black-capped chauffeur behind the wheel. Donny thought about going into the liquor store and getting a backup pack of smokes, but Rich was holding all the cash.

Right on time. A sleek, black, expensive-looking car pulled up to the curb. The tinted passenger window came down and a frail-looking older man leaned his head out and said, "Gentlemen."

"That's us," said Rich to Donny. They both climbed into the car, Rich in the front and Donny in the back. As soon as they were moving, Rich said, "Gabriel, this is my friend, Donny."

Donny held out his hand, but Gabriel didn't turn to shake it. The old man kept both hands on the wheel. Donny watched the older man eyeing him through the rearview and met his eyes there.

"Where we going?" asked Rich.

"The Nikko. I've booked a room."

"Nice," said Rich.

"Well, I'm sorry about the late call. I just had to get away from the house. The room will be nice, two beds, we can order room service as soon as we get there."

The Nikko Hotel was only blocks away from the single room occupancy dive where Big Rich stayed, yet they were worlds apart. There was valet parking, and an expansive marble entrance that led into the most luxurious hotel either of the boys had ever been in. They got out of the car and Gabriel handed the fob to the valet. They strode into the lobby, Gabriel with a leather attaché case in his hand and the boys with their hands in their pockets. The Nikko was modern and expensive, the type of place most of their johns couldn't afford. Gabriel walked up to the front desk and checked in. The boys stood behind him, trying not to be noticed.

"And, Mr. Thaxton, are these your guests?" said the concierge, eyeing them suspiciously.

"No, these are my associates and they'll be staying in the room with me." Terse and quick. His tone was all business and he expected the clerk to assume the same.

"Would you like someone to show you to your room?" said the concierge, his voice now hiding any judgment that he felt.

"Not necessary," said Gabriel, pulling the cardkey from

the desk and turning toward the elevators. They were on their way.

When they reached the room, Donny and Rich flopped down on the bed like a couple of kids on a family vacation, bouncing up and down a little, feeling the springs.

"Fuckin' posh," said Rich.

"If you boys want anything to drink, feel free to grab it from the mini-bar. Later, *after*, we'll order up some food." Gabriel went into the bathroom and turned on the faucet. He splashed water on his face and washed his hands.

The room, sparse and utilitarian, had a small mini-fridge, two queen-size beds and some uncomfortable-looking, wide, brown leather chairs. Donny walked to the fridge, opened a Coke, took a slug, and then opened and poured in a tiny bottle of rum.

"You could get used to this shit, huh?" Big Rich said.

"Whew," said Donny, in response to the rum, not to Rich. Rich said, "Gimme one of them."

Gabriel came out of the bathroom drying his hands on a towel and said, "Richard, let me see it."

"Already? We just got here. Gimme a chance to settle in."

"Just let me see it, so I know that you have it with you."

Donny didn't know what *it* was. He thought maybe this Gabriel was into the same kind of drugs they were. He hoped.

Big Rich turned toward Gabriel, with his back to Donny, unbuttoned his pants and unzipped the fly. He pulled free his cock and balls and said, "Yeah, I still got it."

Gabriel said, "Can you take those off?"

"I've gotta, uh, freshen up first."

Gabriel smiled. "Be my guest."

Big Rich went into the bathroom and shut the door. Gabriel took a seat on one of the brown leather chairs. Donny sat across from him on the bed, sipping his rum and Coke from the can.

"So, Donny, tell me a little bit about yourself."

"What's to tell?"

"Well, why don't you tell me how you ended up working with Richard?"

"I met him on the corner, same as everybody."

"I guess what I mean is, how did you come to be on the corner? What happened to you that you would decide this was an acceptable way to make a living?"

"Acceptable's got nothin' to do with it. I needed the money, I guess."

"No, Donny, I mean, what happened to you? What drove you to this lifestyle in the first place? Did they beat you at home? Were you abused, sexually?"

Donny took a sip from his drink. Gabriel licked his lips.

"This is what I like, Donny. I want to hear your story. Were you a bad boy?"

Donny saw where this was going and decided to play along.

"I've been in some trouble."

"With the law?"

"Yeah, some."

"What did you do?"

Before Donny could answer, Big Rich walked out of the bathroom in his T-shirt. Just his T-shirt. He wore no pants and no underwear. Donny could smell the faint residue of the meth smoke from where he sat.

"Shit, you two gettin' to know each other?" Rich was grinning.

"Now you know why they call him Big Rich," said Gabriel.

"I've seen it," said Donny, unimpressed. "We've worked together."

"Really? Well, maybe you should make yourself more comfortable, too."

"I gotta piss," Donny got up and walked to the bathroom.

Rich whispered to him in a voice that was loud enough for everyone to hear. "It's in the cupboard."

Donny closed the bathroom door behind him, bent down and opened the paneled door below the sink. There it was: Rich's glass pipe. There was a thick layer of crystal on the bottom that made Donny smile. Big Rich had held out at his hotel. He always seemed to be able to pull some crank out of a hat. He wondered if Rich had an endless supply of the shit.

He stood up straight and watched himself in the mirror as he touched his lighter to the bulb and rotated it slowly. He watched the smoke gather in the glass and sucked it back. He blew out the smoke at his reflection. The chemical taste made him feel comfortable, right at home. He hit the pipe again, then once more, before returning it to the cupboard.

When he returned to the room, Rich had taken his place on the edge of the bed and was sitting with his legs spread wide, his cock and balls hanging over the edge of the mattress. Gabriel had moved to the small table and was sitting there with his open briefcase. Beside the briefcase was a glass of water and a blue oval pill. That, Donny guessed, was the old man's drug of choice: Viagra.

"Donny, you're back. And you're still wearing your jeans? I thought you were going to make yourself comfortable."

Donny looked at Rich and Rich gave a quick nod. Without hesitation, Donny undid his belt, unbuttoned, unzipped, and let his jeans fall to the floor. He kicked off his shoes with the tangle of his pants and shoved them with his foot to the edge of the other bed. He stood in his underwear.

"Well, at least that's a little better," said Gabriel.

"What's next?" asked Donny, not to either one in particular, just to the open air. The speed was making him anxious and he was ready to get on with whatever he had to do to earn his money.

"Relax, Donny. I just want to talk to you two boys for a while," said Gabriel. "But first, take off that ungodly underwear."

Donny looked down, wondering what was wrong with his underwear. He took them off slowly, self-consciously, feeling the old man's eyes on him. Gabriel took the pill from the table and swallowed it, washing it down with a hit of the scotch. Donny sat on the other bed, across from Rich, and spread his legs in the same fashion. Both of them now only in T-shirts, with Gabriel, triangulating them, fully dressed, waiting for his Viagra to kick in.

The small talk continued. Gabriel asked questions about their lives while he stared at their meat. After a few minutes, the old man began to massage his own crotch. He did it absentmindedly, not missing a question. Donny felt like they were being interviewed for a job. In a way, they were.

The questions got more personal, digging into their histories, uncovering painful memories. Donny could tell the more they revealed the harder Gabriel was getting. Donny was beginning to wonder if this was the whole gig, if this was all they had to do, when Gabriel opened up his briefcase and took out a white plastic lobster bib, then carefully tied it around his neck. The old man got down on the floor, grunting with stiffness and age, and sat directly between them. He opened the fly on his dress pants, took out his own cock, and started to jerk it.

"Get hard, gentlemen," was all he said.

Donny looked at Big Rich, but Rich was already doing his best, massaging his cock with his eyes closed. So Donny did the same. All three of them, now, were silent, tugging away.

Donny opened his eyes and saw the old man watching, his eyes darting back and forth between Big Rich and himself. He looked at him there on the floor, lobster bib around his neck, not caring that Donny watched him. He saw the old man's tongue flicking between his lips like some kind of hideous reptile. Donny was repulsed.

Gabriel commanded, "When you're ready, cum on my face."

Donny closed his eyes again, trying to think of something, somewhere else. His sexuality had become so confused, so oversaturated, so polluted, that he didn't know what to fantasize about anymore. He just kept pulling at his cock, hoping he could get there. Images flashed through his mind, but none of them stuck. A fast montage of pornography—unfocused, spliced, and flickering. It was useless. He thought about the girl he lost his virginity to, a junior high sweetheart named Becky. He thought about the woman across the street he used to watch mow her lawn. He'd watched her from his bedroom on sunny Saturday afternoons and masturbated while he focused on her tanned brown cleavage. These were the images that never failed him, usually. They weren't even getting him hard.

He opened his eyes to see Big Rich achieving his goal and the old man making whimpering sounds beneath him. Donny reached for his underwear and jeans and started to dress.

"So, would you boys like to watch TV while we order some food? I believe they have HBO." Gabriel was already on the phone to room service, taking the liberty of ordering for them.

"Yeah, turn it on, Donny; I gotta use the shitter again."

Donny picked up the remote and tried to figure out how to work the TV. He wanted to get back to the pipe in the bathroom too, and, as he did every time after turning a trick, he wanted a hit of dope. He watched Big Rich grab both their jackets before heading to the bathroom and said, "Save me some."

Big Rich shut the door.

While Donny waited for Rich to come out of the

bathroom, Gabriel went back to his briefcase and took out a tablet and a portable keyboard. He plugged the keyboard into the tablet and told Donny, "I'm just going to answer a few emails. You relax, son, until I'm ready again. I'm not as young as I used to be."

Donny shrugged, said okay, and pretended to be absorbed in the TV. Big Rich seemed to take forever in there, finding a vein, hitting the pipe, doing whatever the hell he was doing. Donny flipped through the channels without ever noticing what was on. From the corner of his eye, he watched Gabriel completely absorbed in his work. The old man typed quickly and lightly without pause and kept his own eyes on the tablet before him.

Donny finally asked, "Um, Gabriel," he'd almost forgotten the man's name, "what kind of lawyer are you?"

Gabriel looked up, smiled with his yellowed teeth and said, "Criminal." He said it in a tone that made Donny feel foolish for asking, then, seeing the boy's response, added, "Is there any other kind?"

Donny didn't answer. He didn't like the man's smile.

Big Rich finally came out of the bathroom. He whispered to Donny that he'd left a spoon under the sink and to be careful, cause there was blow in it. Donny knew that meant be careful not to spill it, careful to take it all, not to be careful with his life.

The evening continued in the same fashion. The boys stripping from the waist, Gabriel and the lobster bib, then the boys taking turns in the bathroom. Gabriel didn't seem to mind the bathroom trips, but eventually, when the boys began to nod uncontrollably, he said he had to head home.

"I trust that you'll be out by checkout time, Richard?"

"Yeah, of course," mumbled Big Rich.

Gabriel stopped and surveyed the room. "Oh, and be sure that there's no paraphernalia left behind in that bathroom.

Donny, it was a pleasure. Perhaps we can do this again sometime."

Before Donny could say anything, the door swung shut and he and Big Rich were alone with their drugs.

Dustin had been in his room, their room, drawing. He was waiting up, wide awake. What else would he do? He was always awake. Ever since his release from prison, he'd vowed to not spend another minute unconscious. He was trying to get back the time he'd lost.

The room was covered in paper, unfinished drawings that would remain as they were: pencil-etched visions from his darkest places. Dustin drew picture after picture of human misery, torture, and immeasurable grief. He knew he had no real talent. The drawings were just a way for him to unseat some of the sickness that lingered in his damaged head. They weren't therapeutic; they catalyzed whatever viciousness rattled his brain. He drew to validate those thoughts, bring them to the fore. They weren't art; they were wishes.

It was nearly four a.m. when he heard the car pull into the driveway. He pulled back the blind and saw Gabriel getting out of the Bentley. Empty handed, as usual. He wondered why the old fuck wouldn't just die already, but something in his head reminded him to think of the big picture. Dustin wanted everything, and he was close to getting it. He needed that old fuck alive. Dustin looked down at the drawing in his hand—a man being pulled apart by horses; drawn and quartered, he thought they called it. The horses looked child-drawn and the man's limbs were out of proportion. He crumbled up the picture, threw it to the floor with the others, and marched to the top of the stairs.

He stood there, perched, waiting for the front door to open. It did. He watched Gabriel enter, quiet as a burglar, and creep toward the kitchen. When the old man was midway across the cold tile floor, Dustin yelled, "Do you really expect me to sit up here all night with nothing?"

"I'm sorry," said Gabriel. "I didn't want to wake you. I was working late."

"I don't give a fuck where you were, just like you don't give a fuck about me."

"That's not true, Dustin."

"Bullshit, that's what you are. Fuckin' bullshit. Go to wherever you hide that shit and give me what I need. *Then* we can talk about what an asshole you are."

"Dustin, I'm sorry, it couldn't be helped. I had work to do."

"I know you were working, I checked your email, you son of a bitch. Stop holding out and bring that shit up here— *before* you make your goddamn drink."

Gabriel felt he had no choice. It was too late to put up a fight. He did what he was told. He walked through the kitchen to his office in the back and opened a closet door. In it there was a steel safe bolted snuggly to the ground. He punched in the combination and the thick steel door swung open. Inside, among papers and pictures, a small amount of cash, his passport, and an unused handgun, was a plastic box. He removed the box, opened it, and took out a plastic baggie that bulged with glassy shards of methamphetamine. Dustin's dinner.

Gabriel moved to his desk and shook out a couple of the larger pieces before returning the bag and box to the safe. The speed was sold to him by one of his former clients, a murderous biker named Bear. Gabriel felt an affinity for the biker, not because he'd helped him out of so many legal quagmires, not because they'd developed a strange friendship, but because they were both outsiders. Outside of both society and their peer groups. He'd been dealing with the biker for years and his client had assured him that he'd find no better speed anywhere, including the SFPD evidence room, Gabriel's other source. Gabriel told Bear he would purchase all he had.

Gabriel carried the shards of speed upstairs cradled on a glossy magazine cover. He walked into the bedroom and found Dustin, naked save for his silk robe, waiting with a pipe in his hand. He handed over the magazine without word and watched Dustin smile and wave him off.

Gabriel glanced once more at Dustin, hunched gargoyle-like with a lighter in one hand and a glass pipe in the other, before quietly closing the bedroom door.

CHAPTER 4

"Dude, you're burning the sheet."

Donny opened his eyes and saw the cigarette he'd been smoking laying on top of the bed. The smell of burning cotton rose with the thin wisp of smoke.

"Shit." Donny brushed his hand at the small oval hole that'd been burning into the top of the linen sheet. "I guess this is only a three hundred and ninety-nine thread count sheet now, huh?"

"Watch what you're doing. We don't wanna rack up a bunch of charges on our golden goose."

"Yeah, yeah, yeah," Donny said as he dropped his butt into an empty soda can. "How long we gonna stay here?"

"Till checkout time, like he said."

"You have enough downtown?"

"Not really. Enough for a small wake up for each of us."

"Did he pay you?"

"Of course he paid me. Fuck, Donny, what do you think I am, his wife?"

"Is it too late to cop?"

"Maybe."

Donny could see Rich thinking about it, working it over in his head, thinking about the time, how many hours till daylight, what they had left. The seed had been planted.

Rich said, "We could try. If not, then we can call Xavier any time after nine."

"What time is it now?"

Big Rich looked at his phone. "Four-thirty a.m. I can try to call Jose, he delivers late."

"Try," said Donny.

Rich tried and then tried again. No response.

"Looks like we're fucked till morning."

"I'll live, I guess."

"You think you'll make it, high as fuck, sitting in a goddamn four hundred dollar a night suite?" Big Rich teased as he went back to what he was doing, whatever it was. He was trying to put the idea of copping out of his mind. He sat at the table going through the contents of his wallet and pockets, searching, organizing, tweaking.

The TV flickered on silently and Donny listened as showers in other rooms started as other guests rose early for flights and business meetings. The muted noise of regular life depressed him.

"Rich?"

"Yeah," said Rich, keeping his head pointed down toward the table.

"You gay?"

"What?"

"You know, are you? It's not like it wouldn't help with this shit we do."

"Fuck no, Donny. I ain't no fag. Shit, I've got a girlfriend and a kid."

Donny was truly astonished to hear it. He had no idea. "Really?"

"Yeah, really. They're up in Oregon; my little girl is two fuckin' years old."

"How come you're not with them?"

"What do you think? Fuckin' drugs, man. I'll be with 'em again. Just gotta get off of this shit."

Donny thought about that for a moment. The comment seemed outrageous. He didn't know anyone who had gotten off of this shit. Rich had never mentioned getting clean before. It was something they never talked about. Donny had thought about it, but it seemed pointless to ever bring up. Not when you're working so hard to stay high, at least. He couldn't imagine Big Rich cleaning up. It was hard enough to imagine himself cleaning up, getting off the street. It was an insurmountable dream. He let the subject drop before it even got started.

About a half an hour ticked by in silence, each of them lost in their own thoughts, Rich still digging through his pockets and Donny still flipping channels on the TV. Then Rich said, "Fuck it, let's do the wakeup now and call Xavier at nine."

Gabriel Thaxton sat in his favorite chair in the living room of his palace, smack dab in the center of his world. The TV was off and the only sound was the muffled scurry of Dustin's chaotic movements in the bedroom above. Gabriel had a fresh scotch in one hand, and in the other a framed photo of his wife and daughter.

The picture was old, when Judy was still viable and pretty, when she still acted as his wife. The photo was taken at his daughter's graduation from law school. He'd taken it himself. Samantha had gone to Stanford and had moved on into environmental work, burying herself in tort cases against big corporations. She had little cause to call on her father for advice. His daughter's absence from his life didn't disturb him much. That is what children did, they left the nest. But what did disturb him were his daughter's willful attempts to keep him from contacting his grandson.

He loved little Jason, but hadn't seen him in over two years. He probably wasn't so little anymore. He felt like the boy could be his prodigy. A natural heir.

The last time he'd seen Jason, the boy was only four years old. It was when he and Judy's marriage had started to break apart. A Christmas dinner, no, maybe it was Thanksgiving. He could recall bringing the boy a gift, but, then again, he always showered the boy with gifts at every opportunity. Christmas, Thanksgiving, Fourth of July, even Arbor Day, if he had the chance. He remembered an argument starting at the dinner table. Insults being thrown shortly before food was. His daughter stood up and had said it was enough, that her son didn't need to see his grandparents fighting like a couple of teenagers. He tried to remember what the argument was about. He couldn't recall.

Gabriel drained the scotch, glanced at the clock, and decided to take a shower. He walked up the stairs slowly, feeling his age. He stood for a minute looking at the oak door of the master bedroom and decided not to use the shower in there. Why disturb Dustin? He continued down the hallway, took two towels from the linen closet, and sequestered himself in the guest bathroom.

He turned on the faucets and undressed while the water got hot. When he could see steam, he opened the glass shower door and climbed in. He stood for a moment, head down, letting the spray of hot water hit the back of his neck, and did his best not to think about Judy and Samantha, about Jason. He tried to think only about the hot water.

He heard the bathroom door open.

"Hello? Dustin?"

The door shut again and he could see Dustin's cloudy form through the shower glass.

The glass door opened. Dustin was naked.

"I'm ready to talk now," he said.

It was nine-thirty in the morning and the boys stood on the corner of O'Farrell and Jones. They were cold and stood hugging the wall where the sunlight heated the brick.

"Fuckin' Xavier. Said he'd be fifteen minutes. What time is it?" said Big Rich.

Donny told him.

"Fuckin' Xavier. I coulda called Jose by now. Fuck."

"Is that him?" said Donny.

"No."

A few more minutes crawled by.

"Is that him?"

"No."

"Shit. What kind of car does he drive again?"

"I told you. It's a white Toyota, a piece of shit."

"That was a white Toyota."

"That was not a Toyota, Donny, you don't know shit. I'm calling him again."

Just as Rich pulled his cell phone from his pocket, a white Toyota pulled up to the curb.

Rich smiled. "It's about time." His tone instantly changed, brightened.

He hopped into the passenger seat and left Donny waiting at the curb. The car pulled away, heading around the block while they did their brief exchange, and returned to the same spot. Rich climbed out, grinning, and the two boys walked briskly down dirty sidewalks toward Rich's hotel.

"We gotta get a phone today," said Rich.

"I have a phone," said Donny.

"No, I mean one that can take video."

"Oh, well, mine is, like, ten years old. It doesn't even take pictures."

"Donny, they didn't even have cell phones ten years ago," said Rich.

Donny was sure that they did, but didn't feel like arguing his point.

"Skye has one. He's got an iPhone," said Donny. Skye was the most tech savvy person that Donny knew. He didn't like the kid, but Skye always seemed to have the latest stuff.

"He ain't lending that shit out," said Rich.

"What's wrong with yours? It's almost new."

"It's fucked up, the video won't work. It always says something about no memory."

"It's like you: no memory."

Rich said, "Fuck you." But he was smiling. They both were. They felt good. The mid-morning sun had warmed up the streets and they had enough dope to last them the day. Maybe enough so that they wouldn't have to work the corner that night.

They decided to get high at Donny's place instead of Rich's, another hobbled hotel in the Tenderloin only a few blocks from Big Rich's and, by Donny's estimation, a little closer to where they were now.

"Besides," said Donny, "they don't hit you up for a fucking guest deposit."

"What are you bitching about? You never pay at my place. A lot of places do it now. They think it keeps out the undesirables."

"I don't think that shit is even legal. They just do it to extort money from the people that're dealing."

"Yeah, well, call the Better Business Bureau."

They reached Donny's run-down excuse for a hotel and buzzed to be let in. This time, there was no one at the front desk and Donny told Rich to stand by the inside gate, the one separating the lobby from the stairs leading to the rest of the hotel. Donny stood in front of the Plexiglass and did his best to block the view of the video camera with his scrawny frame. He hit the buzzer on the desk. They heard it sound somewhere in the office in back. The door behind Big Rich vibrated and the boys ran upstairs before the clerk could see on the monitor who came in. Donny's hotel didn't allow visitors at all.

Once inside the room, the boys restarted the same ritual. Spoons, water, bits of cigarette filter, lighters, then dope. When they were ready, they both crowded under a table lamp near Donny's bed and began to look for a spot to hitup. They rolled up their sleeves and pant legs and pushed, pulled, and flexed. Every day the search for a new place to stick the needle became more difficult. Within minutes both had found a vein and they lit smokes and sat back to enjoy the euphoria.

Big Rich toyed with his cell. "You think that's all I need is a memory thingy?"

"A chip? Yeah, fuckin' Radio Shack, man. It's easy, I'll show you."

"You think this is gonna work?"

"The video? Yeah, we'll test it out first."

"No, the plan, with the old man."

"I dunno. It's your plan. Is it really such a dangerous thing to be outed as a faggot in a city as gay as this?"

"He's got a family. A life. I think he'll pay. *How much* I don't know."

"What're you thinkin', like, ten thousand?"

"Shit, at least. Wait'll you see his house. He drives a Bentley, for fuck's sake. I say ten thousand a piece, then, like maybe, five hundred a week."

"Why would he do that, keep paying us? Seems like it would be cheaper just to tell his wife."

"That he likes young boys? C'mon, since when do any of these freaks that come down to the corner want the world to know that shit. This Gabriel is paranoid, too."

"Maybe he's careful."

"Paranoid."

"When you were in the bathroom at the Nikko, I asked what kind of lawyer he was."

"And?"

"He said criminal."

"So?" said Rich.

"So, what if he knows what to do when someone pulls this kinda shit on him?"

"Trust me. He doesn't know shit. If he had any sense about him, he wouldn't be doing what he's doing."

They sat for a while as their highs subsided and watched the shadows of the day move across the squalid room. Big Rich dropped a cigarette into a half-full soda can and said,

"Donny, I'm out of smokes. Can you do me a favor and run down to the liquor store and grab me some?"

"Shit, your legs broken?"

"I don't wanna sneak back in. Please? I'll buy you a pack."

That tipped the scales. "Okay," said Donny.

"Quicker than givin' 'em to you one at a time."

Donny got up and pulled on his jacket. He looked over his room. Dirty clothes, overflowing ashtrays, syringe caps, and empty bottles.

"Don't worry, I ain't gonna steal nothin'," said Big Rich as he handed him the money for the two packs of smokes.

Donny hit the sidewalk. It was still sunny, but the wind had picked up. It howled through the corridors of the Tenderloin. A homeless man sat huddled near the front door of the hotel, trying hopelessly to light a match for a cigarette butt he'd plucked from the gutter.

"You got a light for this snipe?" The dirty man held up the butt and pantomimed lighting it.

Donny looked at him as if he spoke a different language.

A flat-sounding electric buzzer announced his arrival in the store. The Pakistani man behind the counter got up and eyed him warily. Donny had never stolen from this store, not even a pack of gum, but the asshole behind the counter treated him like an arch criminal every time he entered. Donny grabbed two chocolate bars—Snickers, his favorite, each bar was like a meal—and tossed them up on the counter. He asked the man for two packs of Marlboro Reds. The man rang it up, took the money, and made change without saying a word.

"Could I get some matches, too?"

The counterman gave a pained look and pulled a quarter from Donny's change and tossed down a pack of matches.

"Fuck you," said Donny very quickly.

"What did you say?"

"I said 'Thank you,'" Donny said and repeated it again, "Thank you."

Donny left the store and walked back to his hotel. The wind, at his back now, was not quite as annoying. He flipped the matches to the bum at the doorway and said, "Good luck with that."

The dirty man grunted thanks.

Donny opened the door to his room and saw Big Rich hunched over on the edge of the bed, his back to Donny, phone to his ear.

Donny shut the door quietly.

"I am," Rich said into the phone. "I know, I know...I do, just not yet...I'm working the door at a club, that's how." The voice in the phone buzzed near Rich's ear. "A little, they have me do some barback shit, too. I'm getting my first check on the fifteenth, but I gotta pay the hotel and the corner store guys."

Donny listened to Rich's lies, the life he'd constructed for himself. It didn't seem that bad, the person he was pretending to be. He spoke like a guy who cared about his kid, a guy who was trying his best. He almost wished Rich was that person; he'd be a friend he'd like to have.

"I am, baby, I'm working on it. How's she doing?" he said into the phone. Rich listened for a long time before he said, "Can I talk to her?"

Donny could tell the woman on the other end was not going to let Rich talk to his daughter, the voice droned on and on, berating, nagging, he could tell by Rich's posture. His friend practically wilted.

"Okay, okay," said Rich, "I'll call you then." There was a pause while the other voice said something else before Rich said, "Yes, I will...I'll take care of it, you'll see."

Then Rich hit the end button on his phone and said, "Bitch."

CHAPTER 5

Gabriel Thaxton sat in his office on the twenty-third floor of 655 Montgomery Street facing the wide glass window that stretched from floor to ceiling. The office afforded him a view of most of the financial district. He often sat wondering what went on in the other offices in the high-rises around him. What the people in there did for a living, if it was wholesome busywork they were able to leave in their offices each night, or if the cost of having a window on the world up at Gabriel's altitude had a price tag. Like his did.

Gabriel Thaxton, super-attorney, mega-counsel. He had climbed to the top of the ladder in the law game. He'd done it without looking back at the victims of the crimes from which he'd exonerated his clients. He'd ignored the death threats, he'd ignored the newspaper columns, he'd even ignored his conscience. Especially his conscience. He looked the other way when defending clients his gut told him had to be guilty. He clung to the idea that, no matter how guilty one may seem, one was entitled to the best defense that money could buy. He had to, that's what a criminal defense attorney was. The facts weren't always facts; it was the way one interpreted them.

His meek, young receptionist knocked and opened the office door without waiting for a response. She faced the back of his seat, Gabriel being obscured by the leather back on the tall swivel chair. She noticed his coffee on the desk, cold and untouched.

"Mr. Thaxton, sir. I cancelled your eleven o'clock meeting as you asked. Will there be anything else?"

Gabriel was about to say no, but then paused and, without

turning around, said, "Beatrice, see if you can get a hold of Darrel Mayfield, tell him I'd like to have lunch, I'm buying."

"Bear? Sure thing, Mr. Thaxton." The receptionist liked Bear. He was always friendly when he came into the office, flirting with her in a good-natured way. She knew he was potentially dangerous and had an extensive history with the firm, but he was a likeable character who had an ease about him she found refreshing and in direct contrast from their usual clientele.

Beatrice closed the door gently and returned to her desk. She clicked on the client file on her desktop computer and scrolled down to Bear's number, picked up the phone and dialed.

The phone rang and rang before someone picked up and a gruff voice responded, "Yeah."

"Could I speak to Mr. Mayfield, please?"

"Mr. Mayfield? Who's this?" The voice sounding playful now, coy.

"Mr. Mayfield? This is Gabriel Thaxton's office calling."

"Thaxton? Is that you, Bean? Sweet little brown-eyed Bean? How you doing, girl?"

Beatrice giggled. She loved the nickname he'd given her. She had always hated her first name; it sounded archaic and stuffy.

"Yes, Bear, it is. Mr. Thaxton was wondering if he could maybe meet with you for a late lunch."

"You tell the old man that I'm not in town."

"But," said Beatrice, not sure if she was overstepping her bounds, "I called you at home."

"I know, just walk in there and tell him and see what he says. I'll hold."

She did as she was asked and put Mr. Mayfield on hold and walked back to her boss's office. Gabriel was sitting there in the same position, facing the window.

"Sir, Mr. Mayfield says he's not in town."

"Did you call him at home?"

"Yes," said Beatrice.

"Okay, okay. Tell him I'd still like to see him anyway. Tell him at our usual spot."

Beatrice went back to her desk and took Bear off hold.

"Bear? He says he'd still like to see you."

"Okay, you got it."

"Oh, and he said to tell you, at the usual spot."

"Not in the office? Dang, that means I won't be able to see your sweet brown eyes, Bean."

She giggled again. He told her he'd meet the old man at three o'clock and hung up.

After hanging up the phone, Bear stood in his small kitchen rubbing his belly. When Thaxton called it meant he wanted something. Usually drugs. The man had friends in need and Bear didn't judge or question him about it. He did what he could to fill the old man's requests. This time, Bear let him know that he was out of pocket and the old fucker still wanted to see him. What did that slippery fuck want this time? Bear had no open cases, hadn't been arrested in three years. He owed the old man money, technically, but the firm wasn't hurting so he dismissed that as a reason. No, he wouldn't have called if he didn't need a favor.

Bear opened up his fridge and pulled out a longneck Budweiser, then decided he'd better wait till after lunch. He stood there a moment, thinking maybe he should have set the lunch earlier. It was a forty-five minute drive from his little shack hidden up in the Marin hills; he could easily make it by one. He walked to his bedroom and pulled a black T-shirt from his drawer, nearly identical to the one he was wearing, and changed his shirt. Now he was ready for lunch with the lawyer.

* * *

It was an older taqueria in the Mission and not one of the better ones. It was one of the only places that still had booths and wasn't set up like a cafeteria. The food was average, as were the prices. There were so many taquerias on 24th Street. The competition was stiff and this place just didn't have any fight left. That kept the joint quiet; perfect for indiscreet meets with clients who didn't always feel at home in the expensive tie-only spots in Union Square.

Gabriel sat in a booth near the back. He sipped a strawberry *aqua fresca* and kept his eye on the entrance. At about ten minutes to three, his old friend Bear walked in through the door. Bear was big, bearded, and ugly, but always carried an almost jolly air. Thaxton admired someone who was so comfortable in their own skin. He waved him over to the booth and stayed seated as he shook Bear's meaty hand.

"Gabe, my man."

"How you doing, Bear? Sit down."

"Not till I get a beer first. You want somethin'?"

Gabriel pointed to the *aqua fresca* and shook his head.

"I meant to eat, counselor."

Gabriel told him to order whatever he wanted and to just get some chips and salsa with it. Bear did. He ordered a super *carnitas burrito*, a *carne asada quesadilla*, two longneck Budweisers, and, almost as an afterthought, chips and salsa.

"You on a diet, Bear?" said Gabriel.

"You're kinda long-winded, I want to be prepared."

They made small talk while they waited for the food, Bear draining his first beer. What small talk they could make, anyway. There wasn't much the fifty-year-old biker and the lawyer had in common other than their legal entanglements.

The food arrived and Bear took a pull from his second beer and started eating. He peeled back the tinfoil on the burrito and took huge bites, leaving dabs of sour cream and guacamole in his beard.

Gabriel watched him eat for several minutes before he spoke, "I have a problem."

"Sorry to hear that; I hope I'm not it," Bear said with a mouth full of food.

"No, but I was hoping that you could help me with the solution."

Bear set down the burrito, "I know, or you wouldn't have dragged my old ass down here today."

Donny and Rich's lives ground on in a short cycle of copping, getting high, turning tricks, hiding from the world, then getting sick. Their time was marked by hours, not days. Once the idea of exploiting Gabriel had taken root in their minds, it was hard for them to return to their previous existence.

They didn't hear from Gabriel for nearly a week. Big Rich even tried to call him on the cell number logged in his incoming calls, but there was no answer. Rich assured Donny that he'd be back, the plan was still on. The boys went out and got the memory chip for Rich's cell and waited for the phone to ring.

Time wore on and Donny began to give up on the old lawyer. Maybe he spooked the guy. He told Rich they should start looking for a new mark; there had to be more than a few out there in the endless parade of johns.

"No, Donny, he's the guy, I'm telling you. I feel it. He'll be back. He's an addict and this is his drug," Big Rich said as he grabbed his crotch. "You'll see."

Bear, too, didn't hear from Gabriel Thaxton. After the sick shit the lawyer told him that afternoon at the taqueria, he figured he'd hear from him right away. You call an exterminator, why keep living with bugs? Or, Bear thought, he'd never hear from him again. Maybe the shame kept him from calling. He knew the old guy had some weird habits and unsavory friends—why else would he need all that speed? But he wasn't prepared for the confession he got over lunch that day. This wasn't his thing. He'd done some dirt for his biker buddies, but the kind of thing that Gabriel asked was out of his comfort zone.

Bear tried to forget about it. He went back to doing what he did best: sit around his secluded house, smoke dope, drink beer, and watch satellite TV. He'd tinker with his three Harley's. Two he kept in the garage and one in parts spread across his living room floor. A lifetime on bikes had taught him how to assemble every nut and bolt on the machines.

All three bikes seemed to be apart more than they were together, so he kept his little Toyota running for business. The Harleys drew heat anyway. As much as he loved to ride, he preferred being in a car when he hauled weed back from Mendocino County. Besides, his saddlebags weren't big enough for the sizes of the loads he brought back. He'd made a run up north a few weeks before so he still had cash; no need to worry about making more until he needed to. His expenses were low while he was isolated. He had dope to smoke from the run, beer stockpiled, and he cooked his meals at home.

He was comfortable where he was in life, respected by his peers and left alone by everyone else. His wild days behind him, he could now afford to spend time doing the things he never thought he'd enjoy, like watching golf, getting sucked into soap operas, and not drinking till mid-afternoon. His only social activity was his occasional visit to a bar on the highway near his house. It was the closest thing Marin had to a honky-tonk. There was a waitress who worked the bar. He was trying to get close to her. That was all the action he needed. For now.

It was out of sheer boredom one sunny afternoon that he decided to do a little web-surfing and find out what he could about Gabriel Thaxton's house guest. He sat down at the computer, woke up the monitor, brought up the search engine, and typed in the kid's name. *Dustin Walczak.* He'd scrawled the name on a napkin at the taqueria and made a crack about the kid being a Polack. Gabriel didn't laugh, didn't even try to fake it.

The search brought up a number of results. *Find Dustin Walczak on Facebook! People Finder—sign up to join!* Bear scrolled down till he glimpsed Thaxton's name with an entry. He clicked. It was an article from the *San Francisco Chronicle* dated August 19th, 2004. It showed a picture of a scrawny pockmarked kid, a mug shot. Underneath was the caption: *Derek "Dustin" Walczak at the time of his arrest.* Ugly little fucker, thought Bear. How'd Thaxton let a little shit like this get under his skin?

Bear began to skim through the piece. Dustin, it seemed, had been charged with three murders that occurred down on the peninsula in the summer of 2004. Three separate killings on three separate dates. And Thaxton, of course, was his council. Bear wondered how the little fuck could afford a big league attorney like Thaxton. He read on. The bodies of the victims, all in their thirties, were found in their respective homes. Each had been tortured, then mutilated. This was the only connection among the crimes: the twisted M.O. Bear moved the mouse to a link near the bottom of the page that said, *The Victims.* Photos popped up on his screen of the three men, all square-jawed yuppie-types with jobs and homes in Silicon Valley. The article contained no crime scene photos, only the posed pictures that they always posted for sympathy in these kinds of things. One was a high school graduation picture. Another was from a family portrait where the wife and kids were blurred. Why blur out the family, wondered Bear. The captions gave brief summaries of the victims' lives, their families, and the potential taken from them when the killer wandered into their lives. Bear clicked back to the original article and decided to give it another read.

When he was done, Bear leaned back in his chair and said, "You sick little fucker."

CHAPTER 6

When the phone finally did ring, Rich and Donny were on the corner with some of the other boys. It was a slow night and they were just about to give up till the next day. The ringtone sounded in Rich's pocket. He showed the caller ID to Donny and smiled. "See, what'd I tell ya?"

"I need to see you," Gabriel said.

"Long time, no see," said Big Rich. "Did you get any of my calls?"

"I had to turn my phone off for several days. Trouble with work. I'm sorry, I hope you understand."

"Sure. So, you wanna meet, or what?"

"Yes, I'd like that. Right away, are you...available?"

"For you, Gabriel, I'm always available." He knew the old man would be grinning ear to ear. "But, I'm with Donny. Is that okay? I know he'd like to come along."

"I'll pick you both up and you can cum together."

"Who's the bad boy now, Gabriel?"

"Can you be at Turk and Polk in fifteen minutes?"

"We can be there in ten."

Big Rich pocketed his phone and told Donny, "Let's go. We're on. You still got enough shit on you to last you till the morning?"

"Yeah, but you got some, too, right?"

"We got enough—between us. After we get to wherever we're going, I'm gonna give you my phone and do what we talked about." Rich smiled and looked down Polk Street in the direction they were going to walk and said, "Shit, this is gonna work."

"It's about time," said Donny. "I gotta stop for smokes on the way."

"Stop after we meet. Let the old man pay for 'em"

The boys walked down to the corner of Turk and Polk, their pace quick and energized. They arrived there quicker than Rich had estimated. Across the street was 450 Golden Gate, the federal building. It loomed over them, dark gray, square, and oppressive. Its employee entrance on Turk Street never closed. Lined up in front of it were the usual assortment of police cars and official vehicles. Rich and Donny stood across the street waiting in the wind. Ten minutes went by.

"The fucker is late. He's never late," said Big Rich.

"He could have picked a better place to meet," said Donny.

They waited on in silence, each of them checking the headlights of every approaching car. Rich pulled out his phone every few moments to check the time. He was ready to call Gabriel back when the black Bentley rolled up to the curb. The boys got in.

Gabriel looked tired, his voice hoarse.

"Jesus, Gabriel, is that a bruise on your cheek?" said Rich.

"Yeah, I took a spill in the kitchen the other day. It's okay."

"You need to be more careful," said Rich. He shot a look over his shoulder at Donny in the backseat. He knew the old man was lying.

They stopped at a corner store and Gabriel gave Donny forty dollars to go in and buy cigarettes, beer, soda, whatever they wanted, while he and Rich waited in the car.

"What's the plan, Gabe?"

"I have a room reserved, you know, just a quiet party with the three of us."

Donny came out of the store with a small paper bag in his hand. He got back into the back seat and Gabriel pulled away from the curb. They were heading up the steep incline of

Taylor Street, cresting Nob Hill and making a right onto California when Gabriel's phone began to vibrate inside of his suit jacket. He pulled it out, looked at it, and said, "Shit."

Rich could see from where he sat on the passenger side that the phone's ID read *Home*. He turned and gave Donny a wink.

The phone kept vibrating and Gabriel finally said, "I'm going to have to take this. Excuse me."

The boys stayed quiet as Gabriel pulled into an empty loading zone and answered his phone.

"Yes?" he said. "No. No, I didn't...there should have been enough there.... I can't...I'm working, I can't...yes, you can...yes, I'm in the car, but I'm heading back to the office...can't this wait?" The voice on the other end was shrieking, cursing. Gabriel hit the end button and pulled away from the curb. "I'm sorry, boys, but we're going to have to make a detour."

"That's okay. The wife giving you some trouble, huh?" said Rich.

Gabriel didn't say anything at all. He turned the car around and headed back over the hill toward Pacific Heights. Gabriel hunched over the wheel. He seemed nervous, distracted.

"Everything okay?"

"Everything is fine. I just have to stop by the house for a minute and then we'll be on our way." They reached their destination and Gabriel pulled onto the cobblestone driveway. He turned off the car and said, "I'll be right back."

Rich said, "Take your time."

The boys watched the old man go in through the enormous oak front door. Rich swung around in his seat to face Donny. "See, what'd I tell you. Look at this place. It's a fucking palace."

"Was that his wife on the phone?"

"Who else would it be?"

49

"Sounded like a bitch," said Donny.

"Of course she's a bitch. Only bitches live in houses this nice. What's the address, Donny? Write it down so we know how to get back here."

Donny took out his cell and texted the address to Rich. Big Rich's phone made a beep. He took it out and looked at the message. "Perfect."

They sat waiting in the silent car, watching the huge house for signs of life.

"What do you think he's doing in there?" said Donny.

"Giving the bitch some money to order Chinese. How the fuck do I know?"

"How much you think a place like this costs?"

"Fuck if I know. You figure one of those shitty condos South of Market goes for a million, this place has gotta be, like, fifty million."

Donny said, "It doesn't cost fifty million."

"You know so much, why the fuck you asking?"

"Why you getting so pissy?"

"I'm not. I just wanna get this show on the road. I don't want anything to go wrong. We can do this tonight. You ready?"

"Me, yeah. It's you that's gotta do the work."

"No, Donny, the work ain't it. It's the filming. It's gotta be right. You gotta get his face real clear. You gotta be able to see it's him. That's the only way it'll work."

"Don't worry. I'll get it. Just give me your phone, and, when that fuckin' bib comes out, I'll start rolling."

Gabriel's frail silhouette appeared in the doorway of the house, his back turned, saying something to someone inside. The boys couldn't tell if he was shouting, if he was leaving happy or mad. The old man shut the door behind him and scurried toward the car.

When Gabriel got behind the wheel, he said, "Good news, I've brought a surprise for you boys tonight."

"I don't like surprises," said Big Rich.

"You'll like this one—party favors." Gabriel smiled and started the car. "Now, let's get this show on the road."

Big Rich laughed, "I was just tellin' Donny the same damn thing."

The night went on much like the last one had. They checked in—different hotel this time. They went up to the room, got comfortable, the boys fixing in the bathroom and Gabriel pouring his scotch. Then the old lawyer brought out his party favors to show the boys, about a gram of crystal meth so clean it looked like a bag of crushed-up glass.

"Damn, Donny, check this out. Fucking Gabriel's got the shit. Damn it, Gabriel, you must have one hell of a connect. Where'd you get this shit?"

"It's not polite to ask, Richard. You boys just enjoy. Let's make a party of it. Help yourselves." Gabriel popped open his briefcase and extracted his bottle of blue pills. He shook out two onto the table and swallowed one with his scotch. He waited patiently as the two young men pulled glass pipes from their pockets and began to stick little shards of the drug into each. He admired the boys, looking at their jeans, their crotches. He was free to stare at them as much as he liked. He was already getting hard.

Soon the boys were high, distracted, but not enough to forget about their plan. Rich took off his jeans and underwear and Donny removed his T-shirt. Gabriel got out his lobster bib and took his place on the floor.

Donny, sensing the time was right, moved across the room and took the cell phone out of Big Rich's jean jacket, then he moved behind Gabriel's right shoulder and readied the phone.

Big Rich began his show. They didn't call him Big Rich for nothing. He fondled himself close to the old man's face and got himself hard. He grunted and made faces and said to

Gabriel, "You like that? You want to touch it, lick it? Go ahead? You're a dirty old man. Go ahead, touch it."

Gabriel sat in front of Rich with his pants undone and pulled below his waist. Moaning softly, he began to stroke himself with one hand and grab at Rich's balls with the other. Donny began filming.

Through the lens of the phone, the scene appeared, even to Donny's jaded eyes, decadent and perverse; Rich shaking his hips and stroking his cock, the bibbed old man on his knees begging for the young man to let go on his face. Donny envisioned what someone else would see when they viewed the footage. They would be disgusted.

During the performance, Gabriel turned to Donny, "Donny, what are you doing back there? Why aren't you in front of me? Let me see you. Are you on your phone?"

"I'm only texting someone, just a sec, I'll be right there." But Donny kept on rolling, moving around the room, arm extended, capturing the scene from every angle possible. He waited until Big Rich was finished, and the old man was in the most humiliating position possible, then he turned off the phone. He stood behind Gabriel and grinned at Big Rich, giving him a big thumbs-up.

The tone of their evening immediately changed. The boys began acting less like guests and more like hosts. They did what they liked without asking, they declined a repeat performance and fixed in the main suite instead of the bathroom.

If Gabriel was taken aback by their rudeness, their sudden lack of respect for him, he hid it. He opened his briefcase, took out his tablet and keyboard and began to work as he had last time. Big Rich reminded him that he hadn't paid for their services and Gabriel dutifully dropped two one hundred dollar bills on the table and then added another fifty, saying,

"I'm a little tired, boys. I was wondering if we could call it a night. I'd like to take a nap here in the room before I head back home."

"We don't get to stay here tonight?" said Big Rich.

"If you wouldn't mind, just this one time."

"That's all right. We got shit to do anyway," Donny said. He was anxious to get away from the old man and cop more junk.

"When's next time gonna be?" asked Rich.

"Soon, soon. I'll call you."

The boys gathered their few things: jeans, their jackets, what paraphernalia they'd left lying around. Rich picked up the money, gave Donny one of the hundreds and pocketed the other two bills. When they were ready, they looked at Gabriel who was already laying on one of the beds staring at a blank TV screen.

Rich said, "Hey, Gabe, you want me to turn that thing on?"

"No, that's fine, leave it. I want to thank you boys for another fabulous evening. I'll be in touch."

"Alright, then. Goodnight," said Donny.

"Call us," said Big Rich.

Gabriel stayed quiet. He was either distracted or falling asleep.

In the elevator, the two boys pondered the old man's attitude.

Donny said, "You think he's pissed off? You think he knows we filmed him?"

"Nah, he would have said something. I think he's fucking old, that's what I think. I think we just tuckered the old bastard out." Big Rich was callous. "Hey, lemme have my phone back."

"Wait, let's watch it when we get back to your place. Let's get outta this hotel first."

"It's still my fucking phone, Donny. If you wanna cop, I'm gonna need my phone, shithead."

Donny smiled and pulled the phone from inside his jacket, saying, "Get a couple grams, at least. And let's get some blow this time."

Bear couldn't sleep. It was unusual for him; he normally slept like a rock, without dreams or having to get up to piss. He tossed and turned for a while in the bed before deciding, fuck it. He sat up and reached for his pack of Camels, lit one in the dark and smoked. He'd give it another ten minutes.

After two cigarettes, Bear yawned, scratched his ample belly, and got up to get himself a beer. He stood in his kitchen in a T-shirt and underwear sipping his Bud. He glanced at the clock on the microwave: 4:30 a.m. Goddamn. He sat down at the computer and thought he'd check on used Harley parts. There was nothing new out there in the four hours since he'd been gone to bed. He sat back, wide awake now, wondering what to do with himself. He brought up the search engine and, again, typed in *Derek Walczak*. He scrolled down the page and chose an article, this time from the *San Jose Mercury News*. The same mug shot appeared at the top of the piece. Below it was another picture of Dustin doing the perp walk. Bear started to read. The article contained more details than the first. Dustin grew up in Stockton and had been jailed as a teen for reasons that were suppressed because he was a minor. He went back in at the age of twenty-two: armed robbery and grievous bodily harm. There was no mention of who his mouthpiece was that time. It was alleged that he did some dirt in prison for the Aryan Brotherhood, stabbing some poor bastard in the neck sixteen times, but was ultimately cleared. Nice. He did his full bit that time, five years, and came out at twenty-seven. He was back inside within a year, another robbery charge. When he was thirty-one, he was charged with attempted murder. This time, the article stated, he was represented by "famed San Francisco criminal defense attorney, Gabriel Thaxton." Bear smiled. Fucker should have that embossed on his business cards. It said Thaxton got him acquitted of all charges and later tried to sue the San Mateo County Sherriff's office for false arrest.

The article's editorial slant was that a dangerous criminal had been released and re-released into society only to go on to torture and kill innocent and upstanding citizens. Bear saw it different; he saw a pattern of greed. This kid was robbing people. He figured the reason why the killings were spaced apart was because Walczak was bleeding his victims dry, financially. It was probably the same thing he was doing now to Gabriel Thaxton. What he couldn't figure was why any one of these people would let this piece of shit into their lives in the first place.

Down at the bottom of the page there was a link to related articles. Bear raised his eyebrows when he saw the first one. *Killer Walczak Released, Conviction Overturned.*

Bear skimmed through the article and then went back to the search page. This time he typed in *Gabriel Thaxton.*

CHAPTER 7

"Bear, did you get my messages?"

"Yeah, I did, but I been sleeping in lately. I just got up about an hour ago."

"The situation has gotten worse. I'm going to need you to help with that eviction sooner than later."

"Yeah, about that, I've been doing some homework on your little friend. It seems you didn't quite tell me everything about him." Bear was standing in front of a mirror in the short hallway near his front door, examining the plumes of grey sprouting in his beard.

"But you can still do it, can't you?"

Gabriel's voice sounded thin, metallic, hollow with a slight echo. Bear couldn't quite put his finger on it. Something sounded off. More than just the nervous titter in Gabriel's speech.

"Where are you calling from?" said Bear.

"My house."

"Why does it sound so weird?"

"I don't know. I'm in my house."

"Sounds like you're in a tin can."

"I'm in the bathroom."

Locked in, trapped. Bear pictured the old man scared and whispering in the shower stall, a prisoner in his own home. "Yeah, I'll help you out. When do you think he's gonna be there? For *sure* be there?"

"He's here all the time. He never leaves." Gabriel's voice cracked. He sounded scared. The self-assured attorney was gone; Bear was listening to a terrified child.

"Alright, let me see what I can do. I don't think you should be there. How about tomorrow night, late, like say, eleven o'clock?"

"Thank you, Bear. Thank you."

"Gabriel?"

"Yes?"

"When you go, leave the front door open."

Donny and Big Rich were on the corner with a couple of the other guys, doing their thing, standing against a wall with one leg raised, bent at the knee, trying to look cool, patient. It was nearing nine o'clock and the night was getting colder. Fog was drifting in from the ocean and starting to work its way through the city streets.

Donny pinched a cigarette butt between his fingers and flicked it upward so that it arced out into traffic. "You heard from him?"

"From who?"

"You know who. *Him.* Did he call?"

"Not yet. It's only been one day. Don't sweat it, he'll call."

"You think he knows?"

"Knows what?"

A younger boy named Skye interrupted them. "What're you guys talking about?" Skye was dumb, dumber than most on the corner. His face was scarred with both fresh and ancient acne, and he wore clothes that hung like rags.

"None of your business, Skye. Go stand over there," said Donny.

But Rich said, "Hey, Skye, don't you have a computer in your room?"

"Yeah, so? I'm not printing any checks for you guys. You fucked me over that last time."

"You have an Internet connection?"

"Another guy in the hotel does; it's unlocked, I can use his. I do it all the time."

Donny interrupted Rich before he gave up any more information to this dumbass kid. "I thought we weren't gonna up load it yet? Just let him know what we got."

"We're gonna, tonight. I just want to make sure we can follow through, that's all."

"What are you guys talking about?" Skye repeated.

"Nothing, Skye. Go back over there." Big Rich pointed to a spot on the wall.

"Rich?" Here came the real reason he interrupted. "You holdin' anything?"

"I ain't got shit. Ain't you been out today, yet?"

"Too many fuckin' cops. I haven't been able to stand more than ten minutes without needing to hide. Fuckin' sucks."

Skye was always whining no matter how many tricks he caught. Big Rich hated him. Didn't know why, the kid definitely came in useful sometimes, but Rich couldn't stand his attitude, his voice, his fucking ugly face.

"Why don't you head over to Larkin Street, so you can see 'em coming," said Donny, trying to get rid of him now.

"It's all fuckin' trannies over there, dude. There's no action."

"What're you talking about? Whoever is cruising has to go around the block. You'll have an eye out for the cops and the first look at any johns," said Donny. Reasonable.

"Yeah? You think?" Skye looked up the block toward the next corner, thinking about his options. He took a couple of steps in that direction, then turned and said, "If you guys are gonna cop, let me know. I got to get something together."

"Yeah," said Big Rich, "you'll be the first to know."

Skye's chin moved up and down quickly. He gave a thumbs up to the older boys and started toward Larkin Street.

"Fuckin' dumbass," said Big Rich. "I hate that little shit."

"He's not so bad. He's just out here like the rest of us." Donny searched his pockets for a smoke and pulled an empty pack. "You got a smoke left?"

Rich didn't speak. He only pulled a pack from the breast pocket of his denim jacket and shook one out for Donny.

Donny took it, lit it, and said, "When do you wanna go over there?" He nodded vaguely in the direction of Pacific Heights.

"Shit, I dunno. I was hoping to get some money for a cab first, or maybe even doing a hit. That little shit was right; there ain't been no johns here all day."

"You wanna take a bus?"

Rich wasn't listening. He stared intently at the cars passing the corner. "You got anything left from this morning?"

"Not much. We could split it though. It'll work."

"Let's go down to the Arab's and use his bathroom. I still have clean rigs, just cook it up, whack it in two, and I'll muscle mine on the way to the old man's."

"He won't let us use his bathroom if we don't buy a slice."

"I'll get in line, you slip into the bathroom. Fuck him. You'll be done before the slices are."

"What if the key's not on the counter?"

"Fuck, Donny, you worry too much. If we can't get in, then I'll just grab a glass of water and we'll cook up in an alley. Just don't bother trying to find a vein in there, it takes you too long."

Donny shrugged and stuffed his hands into his pockets.

It was full dark now and the wind whipping up Polk Street stung their faces as they walked down to Alzer's Pizza.

Bear was sitting at his kitchen table staring at his cell phone. He wondered if he should call Thaxton and make sure that he wanted to go forward. He sipped on his second beer of the day and watched the clock on the face of his phone. He didn't want to tip his hand if this Dustin kid was there when the old man answered. On the other hand, he didn't want to walk in and find that Gabriel had changed his mind and was wrapped up in some sick codependent love storm. He thought about the mug shot he'd seen on the Internet. Scrawny, hairless, inbred, white trash piece of shit. Bear had known plenty just like him. No, Gabriel needed this fucker out of his life, no question about it.

He yawned, got up and opened the cupboard beside his fridge. He pulled out a jug-sized bottle of Jim Beam and took a cup from the dirty dishes in his sink. He poured himself a short shot and threw it back.

"Welp," he said to no one, "Might as well get ready." He walked into his bedroom, flipped on the light, and went directly to a small safe bolted to the floor of his closet. He opened the safe and surveyed its contents. In it were three handguns—two semi-automatics and an old Saturday Night Special revolver—six boxes of shells, a stun-gun, some cash rubber-banded in sandwich baggies, and a box of blue surgical gloves. There were a few other things buried in the bottom: some blow he rarely had use for, a little hash he only broke out on special occasions, his passport, and the titles for his Harleys.

Bear picked up one of the two semi-automatics, a Glock, studied it and set it back in the safe. It was too risky to be carrying a gun. He was a convicted felon: semi-automatic time. He'd have the drop on that scrawny fucker anyway. He knew what he was doing when it came to brute force, hand to hand combat. He pictured that pockmarked face again and took out the stun-gun and stuffed it into his back pocket. He then took two pair of the blue gloves and tucked them into his belt, just in case. He pondered the likelihood of punching Dustin and decided to bring along his leather gloves as well.

When he was done, he shut the safe and put the keys back in his pocket, looked at the red digits on the clock radio on the nightstand beside his bed, and decided he had time for one more drink before he needed to head toward the city. Bear walked back to the kitchen, grabbed another longneck from the fridge and poured another short whiskey. When he sat back down at the table, he stared at the time on the phone once again. Maybe he should call and make sure the lawyer was out of the house like he told him to be. *Fuckin' Thaxton, I hope you know what you're doing.*

"What's that?" said Dustin. He could hear the ping pong of Gabriel's cell phone chiming from the kitchen.

Gabriel murmured something, but his mouth was gagged and it was only audible as a groan. He lay face down on the cold tile floor of the upstairs bathroom, his hands roped behind his back and his feet cinched together.

"It's your goddamned phone. That's what it is. Are you expecting any calls? You going to work tonight?" Dustin slipped off the bathroom counter where he sat and gave Gabriel a short, quick kick in the ribs. "Huh?"

Gabriel moaned in pain. He had no idea how long he'd been down there. He heard Dustin's bare feet padding away on the tiled floor. He knew that Dustin was going to get his phone, see who was calling. He hoped it wasn't Bear. Gabriel tried to remember if tonight was the night Bear was coming for Dustin. He couldn't tell. He had lost track of time. He was no longer sure if it was day or night. Time was crawling by.

He heard the bare feet heading back.

"Who the fuck is 742-1837? Is that a friend of yours? One of your boy whores? Don't tell me, it's a client with an important filing he must discuss?"

Gabriel heard the flick of a disposable lighter and could hear Dustin dragging deeply on a cigarette, then blowing off the ash, getting that cherry good and red. He shut his eyes tight; he knew what was coming next.

* * *

"You feel that shit?" asked Big Rich.

"Yeah, I guess, didn't you?"

"I feel better, it just takes a while to come on, I guess. I hate muscling stuff. I can feel the lump on my ass."

"I put in a shitload of water like you said. There was, like, eighty units there," said Donny.

"You think that makes a difference?"

"Of course it does, makes it easier for your body to soak up."

"If I keep having to stick needles in my ass, it's gonna ruin me for this business."

Donny looked up at Rich, trying to gauge his facial expression. He couldn't tell if his friend was trying to be funny or not. He waited a moment before saying, "I don't think the johns care that much."

Rich didn't hear him; he was lost in thought. "Probably be the best thing that ever happened," he said. "Nobody would want ya, you'd *have* to straighten out, find another way."

"Why don't you?" said Donny.

"Why don't I what?"

"Find another way, straighten out. This is a fucked way to get through life, don't ya think?"

"Fuck, Donny, I know. I was out here before you, remember? It's called survival; it's what we gotta do to keep things together. You think I wanna be getting fucked in the ass by some old pervert every night? I told you I wasn't no fag."

For a moment, all they could hear was the sound of their breaths as they hiked up the steep part of Van Ness Avenue. Donny kept his eyes on the sidewalk. He finally said, "You think this shit, this stuff we're doing, is gonna, like, fuck us up?"

"What, the dope? I dunno, maybe. I didn't have too many brain cells to begin with," Big Rich said.

"No. The sex. Like, you know, think it'll turn us? I mean,

not gay, but make it so fucking a girl is all, I dunno, fucked up."

"What'd you mean? Like impotent? Not me. I can still get it going. I ain't worried about that."

"When's the last time you been with a female?"

"When I was with your mother. Fuck you, Donny."

"No, seriously. I been thinking 'bout it. I think this shit is changing me. I don't know what to think anymore. I want to get out, but I gotta stay well. I'm just ... I'm just stuck. I can't stand myself for it."

Big Rich stopped. "Look, we all feel that way eventually. Of course this shit fucks with your head. If it didn't, then you wouldn't need the dope, would you? This is why we're doing what we're doing. This is why we're going to see the old man. So we can stop this shit." Rich paused to pull out his pack of cigarettes. He lit two at once and passed one to Donny. "I didn't tell you this, because I didn't wanna jinx myself, but part of what I'm doing with my share of the dough is getting on methadone. If we're getting steady dough, then I can stay on it for a while, get my shit together. We won't have to work the corner."

Donny nodded his head like he understood, but he didn't. It was always easy to talk when you were a little high. It was when you got sick that things got tough. Logic and goodwill went out the window. He knew plenty of people on methadone and they didn't seem much different, most of them didn't even stop fixing, just doubled their habits. He didn't see what that had to do with getting away from what they'd been doing.

"I'm afraid," said Donny, "that some of these things, these tricks, ain't never gonna leave my head. I'll have a girlfriend, be far away from here, from the city, have a job, all the shit a normal person has, and..."

"And what?"

"And it'll still be there, stuck in my head. The cocks, the

ass-fucking, the faces, the smells, goddamn it." He turned his head away from Rich. "The weird shit."

"You mean, you're afraid you're gonna miss it? Well, don't worry, Donny. You can always come back down here and get off with some of the freaks. They ain't going nowhere."

Rich was trying to be funny, but Donny was serious. He got it, whistle in the dark, sure, but he knew he was scarring his own psyche. He'd never be able to get that normal life. Who was he kidding? You don't come back from this.

Rich interrupted his thoughts, "How far are we?"

They'd reached the top of the hill now. The fog had cleared there and they were above it, standing in the moist air with the crisp black sky above them.

"I dunno, six, eight blocks maybe."

Rich dropped his cigarette butt on the sidewalk and stepped on it. "Well, stop feeling sorry for yourself. You think you're the only one who wants to stop sucking dicks? Fuck, man, I got a kid. I got a girl up in Oregon who still loves me, thinks I'm coming home to her." Big Rich stopped and look down the hill. The lights inside the houses of the comfortably rich residents of the Marina glowed warm, soft, and smudged by the mist. Beyond that, the Bay lie dark and quiet somewhere out there under a blanket of fog. "It's time to toughen up. This is our chance to get off that fucking corner. C'mon."

CHAPTER 8

Bear climbed into the front seat of his Toyota feeling cramped in the little car. He started the engine and turned on the radio, flipping from station to station while the Toyota warmed up. When he found a song he liked, he put the car in drive and pulled away from his house.

The Golden Gate Bridge was wrapped in fog. He couldn't see more than fifty yards ahead. He took it easy, keeping an eye in the rearview for police; they loved to stop speeders on the bridge. Bear paid his six dollar toll and sped up into the city. He wondered if he should try Thaxton again. He wiggled his cell out of the inside of his jacket and scrolled down to Thaxton's name. The phone rang and rang.

He was just hitting the curve onto Lombard Street when he saw the red and blue lights behind him. S.F.P.D.

"Shit."

He found a place to pull over as the cop put on his blinding white searchlight. Bear watched the officer get out of the car slowly and deliberately. The cop was young, white, and all business. Bear hated the dicks who worked the Marina District. They were all assholes.

"Asshole," he said under his breath.

The cop tapped on the window and Bear rolled it down and smiled.

"License and registration, please."

Bear began to fish the registration out of the glove box. It was stuffed like a trash can. Receipts, napkins, and old parking tickets fell onto the floor.

"Let's start with just the license, okay?" The cop acted annoyed and impatient while he waited for Bear to wiggle the wallet out from under his considerable girth. "Take the license out of the wallet, please."

Bear did and handed it to him.

The cop looked at the picture on the license, then at Bear, then back at the license, then again at Bear. "Mr. Mayfield, do you know why I pulled you over this evening?"

"I don't think I could have been speeding."

"Mr. Mayfield, is this your current address?"

"Yes."

"You can't talk on the cell phone while you're behind the wheel."

"Well, I actually wasn't talking."

The cop leaned into the window of the car. "I'd like to settle that. May I see your cell phone, sir?"

"My cell phone? What for?"

"Mr. Mayfield, have you been drinking?"

Bear handed the cell phone over. The cop smiled and hit the phone button.

"Ten-forty-seven. Outgoing call to...Gabriel Thaxton. Mr. Mayfield, it's presently Ten-fifty, are you going to try to..." The cop stopped and wrinkled his nose. "Gabriel Thaxton? *The* Gabriel Thaxton? The attorney?"

Bear hesitated for a moment before answering. He wasn't sure which way this was going to go. "Yeah. The one and only."

"What are you doing calling Gabriel Thaxton at eleven o'clock at night?"

"It was only ten-forty-seven."

"Step out of the car, sir."

Bear did. The cop pointed to the space between the cruiser and Bear's Toyota and said, "Wait right here," and started walking back to the cop car.

Bear said, "Officer?"

The cop turned.

"My phone?"

The cop handed back the cell, kept the driver's license, and turned back toward the car to run Bear for priors. Bear stood and waited. With the white spotlight blinding him, he couldn't even make out if the cop's partner in the passenger seat was a male or a female. Probably couldn't tell if the other cop was right in front of him either, thought Bear.

Bear stood there waiting. He checked the time on his phone. Ten-fifty-nine. He kept waiting. Eleven-oh-six. Taking their sweet time. Bear readied himself for a sobriety test, a vehicle search, and questioning, maybe even an arrest. The cop climbed back out of the cruiser and walked up to Bear. He handed Bear back his license.

"Just for the record," said the cop. "I think your friend is a piece of shit."

The cop spun on his heel and walked back to his car and climbed in. They pulled out into traffic, making a little squeak with their tires, leaving Bear standing behind his car on Lombard Street.

"Thank you, Officer," said Bear to himself.

"You remember which house it is?"

"Fuck, yeah. It's the fucking castle," said Big Rich. "Now, where is it?"

"What street is this? Jackson? It's still a block down. I texted you the address, remember?"

"I don't need it, I remember the place. How could I forget it?"

"You think he's gonna flip out, us showing up like this?"

"Who cares? He should answer his phone."

"What if his wife answers the door?" Donny asked.

"Then we ask for Mr. Thaxton. Way I see it, if she's there, it'll make him that much more anxious to make a deal."

"What if she won't get him, tells us to fuck off?"

"She won't answer the door. She'll probably be on her fat

67

ass watching cooking shows. Probably be like, 'Gabe! Get the goddamn door!'"

"How do you know she's fat, did he tell you?"

"Donny, fuck, what's with all the questions? You scared? You can't look scared. We need to make him believe this shit."

"I just wanna be ready."

"We *are* ready. We got the movie to show him. That's it. That's all we need. Now, c'mon, let's go."

Donny followed his friend down the sidewalk from Jackson to Pacific Street. They both saw the big looming dark stone house ahead of them. Backlit by the light of the city, it was only a shadow.

The boys walked the rest of the block without speaking, each concealing their fear. When they reached the cobblestone drive, Donny walked softly, almost tiptoeing, trying not to make a sound. They walked around the Bentley and up toward the entrance.

"Shit, we're not breakin' in. Stop being such a chickenshit, c'mon."

Big Rich reached the front door first. He looked at the huge iron door-knocker, not sure how to use it.

Donny said, "That's just for show. Ring the bell, there."

"I know, I know," said Rich, reaching out and pressing the small glowing buzzer. A grand chime sounded inside. They waited. Nothing, not a sound.

"You think he's home?" asked Donny.

"His car is right fucking there, of course he's home." Rich pressed the buzzer again and the boys listened to the chime.

The door finally opened. There stood Dustin, shirtless, in jeans, and holding a .45 semi-automatic. A big, black Glock .45. It was pointed at Big Rich's face.

Dustin said, "Who the fuck are you?"

Big Rich was startled, but not too startled to say, "Who the fuck are *you*?" right back.

Dustin reached out with the .45 and poked Rich square in the eye. "Get in here."

CHAPTER 9

Bear circled the block looking for a place to park. He needed somewhere close in case he had to run out of there, or bring Dustin with him. Each time he went past Thaxton's place he checked to see if there were lights on. There were none, but the old man's car was still in the driveway. He hoped that Gabriel wasn't in there. He'd told him in no uncertain terms that he should be gone by eleven o'clock. Why was his car still in the driveway?

On his fourth tour of the block, he found a spot just up the hill toward Jackson Street; a tough little hike for a man of his size and age if he needed to get out of there in a hurry. He loaded up his pockets with the tools he brought. The stungun, the rubber gloves, extra cigarettes. His plan was to go in tough, scare the kid. He decided to leave his leather gloves. It was a bit of overkill since he already had the surgical ones. Besides, they were practically new and he didn't want to ruin them with Dustin's blood. As an afterthought, he climbed out and opened up his trunk and took a sheathed six-inch Buck knife and tucked it into his right boot.

He started down the hill to Gabriel's mansion. He tried to remember the last time he was here. It was for a luncheon, a sort of victory party after an acquittal five—no, maybe seven—years ago. He was pretty well smashed and didn't remember much about the place other than it was too big for the old man and his wife. He remembered he had some friends there, guys from the local club. He recalled doing blow in an upstairs bathroom with some paralegal who Thaxton had since fired. And he seemed to recall being ushered out the door early by Thaxton himself. That was probably the last victory celebration the old man had at home—with his clients anyway.

Bear was on the level sidewalk across the street from the place now, looking, listening, trying to see if there were any signs of life. There were none, not at Thaxton's place, and not at the neighbor's either. The whole block was silent. Bear shook a Camel loose from his pack, lit it, and waited.

"Sit down, both of you, right there." Dustin stood in front of them with the gun still in his hand. Rich and Donny sat down on a long, brown leather couch. The room was dim, the only light spilling over from the kitchen. They sat in silence while Dustin looked them over. It gave them a chance, too, to see who their captor was.

Dustin stood in front of them, bare-chested, his eagle swastika tattoo standing out boldly on his pale skin. He was ugly, his face tight, his upper lip screwed into a sneer that made him appear as though he were sniffing something foul. Thirty more seconds crawled by before he said, "Just answer me one thing. Who are you and what the fuck are you doing here?"

Donny and Rich looked at each other.

"That's two things," said Big Rich.

Dustin's eyes lit up with a glare, "Who the fuck are you?"

"We're here to see Gabriel," said Rich

"*We're here to see Gabriel,*" Dustin repeated in a high sing-song tone. There was another moment of silence before he did it again. "*We're here to see Gabriel. Gabriel. Gabriel.*"

The boys looked at each other again.

"That's not what I asked. The question was, who are you? What're your names?"

The boys didn't say anything.

"Okay, I'm just gonna call you two Dumbfuck and Shithole. How's that, Dumbfuck?" he said to Donny. "You got a wallet? A cell phone?"

Donny shook his head.

Dustin walked over and stuck his gun into Donny's left eye and pushed. Donny felt the steel pressing against his eyeball, beginning to dislodge it. Dustin said, "Get up." Donny got up. Dustin tugged the boy's jacket by the shoulder, spun him around, and took the wallet from the back pocket of his jeans. He dropped it on the coffee table in front of him.

"Now you, Shithole," he said to Big Rich.

Rich pulled his wallet out without getting up and tossed it beside Donny's.

Rich said, "Maybe *we* should be asking who *you* are?"

"Who I am?" Dustin's voice picked up a notch, "*Who I am?* I'm the Grand Emperor of Doom, that's who I am. I'm the goddamn Ambassador of Pain, that's who I am. What the fuck are two little shits like you doing breaking into *my* house?"

Donny spoke up, "We weren't breaking in, we rang the bell."

"No, little man, you were breaking in. And that's how the cops'll see it when they find you dead on the fucking floor." Dustin sneered and showed his teeth. They appeared to be bluish grey, rotting points.

"We rang the bell; we only came to visit our friend."

"Your friend?" Dustin's eyebrows shot up in disbelief. "Your friend, huh? What would an old man like him be doing with *friends* like you?" Dustin stepped close to Donny again, pointing the gun directly in his face. Donny could smell him, his funk. He could see his shiny skin, blotchy and picked over. He stared straight ahead at the swastika on Dustin's chest.

"You guys have all the answers, huh? A couple of..." Dustin searched for the word, "...chatterboxes. That's what you are. Stopping by for a social visit? At eleven o'clock at night?"

Big Rich changed his approach. "We're clients."

"Clients? You're clients of Gabriel Thaxton? What the fuck do you pay him with...bubblegum? Blowjobs? You're fucking liars is what you are. Candy-ass liars." Dustin was working himself up, getting angry. "Where are your cell phones?"

Big Rich didn't want to give up his cell. It was the whole game, and the game wasn't over. "Where is Mr. Thaxton?"

"I told you little shits, this is my house. There is no Gabriel Thaxton here. Now give me your cells." He reached over and poked Rich in the forehead hard with the barrel of the gun. It left a red circle like a third eye. "Now."

Reluctantly, the boys pulled their cell phones from their jackets and placed them on the coffee table with their wallets. Dustin nodded, looking at the cells, wondering what to do next.

"We know he's here, his car's outside," said Big Rich.

"You don't know anything..." Dustin tried to remember what name he called Rich. "...Shithole. If you knew anything you wouldn't be here with my gun in your face. You don't know shit."

"You gonna call the cops?" asked Donny.

"Shut up," was the only response he got. Dustin was thinking.

Rich spoke to Donny, "If he was gonna call the cops, he woulda done it by now."

Dustin ignored the comment and said, "Don't fucking move. Either of you move and I'll shoot you dead. I fucking mean it." He racked the gun and the bullet that was already in the chamber spat out onto the floor. Dustin looked down at the cartridge, "I just wanted you to know that I'm ready for you, peckerwood. Stay right there where you're sitting and don't move a muscle."

Dustin went into the kitchen and started rummaging around for something. The boys could hear him violently pulling out drawers. The drawers fell to the floor and their contents crashed loudly on the marble tiled floor.

Big Rich whispered to Donny, "This guy is fuckin' gacked."

"I know, I can tell," said Donny quietly, keeping his eyes straight ahead on the doorway of the kitchen.

"You think we can take him?"

"Fuck, no. He's a fucking nut."

Rich looked at his cell phone on the table in front of him. He wanted to grab it and run. "You think he's got Gabriel?"

"I don't fucking know," said Donny. He wanted his friend to shut up. He wanted the chance to get out of this house alive.

"Let's break for it," said Rich.

"No way, he'll shoot us. We'll never make it."

Dustin's voice cried out from the kitchen, "Shut the fuck up out there." There was another loud crash of utensils hitting the floor.

"Ready?" said Rich, and without any more warning, he grabbed his wallet and his cell phone and sprinted toward the door. Donny had no choice but to follow suit. He, too, grabbed his stuff from the coffee table and moved as quickly as he could behind his friend, knowing it would be his own back Dustin's gun would be targeting.

Bear was in the driveway now, he was sure that he'd heard something, but the lights were still off. It seemed like there was nobody home at all. Perhaps that noise was a cat on a garbage can in back. He moved toward the huge oak front door as quietly as possible, just in case.

As he reached out to open the door, he heard footsteps rapidly beating toward the entrance. Before he could reach the handle on the door, the thing swung open. The first thing he saw was a young, white face. Bear pulled back his fist and punched.

It would have been a hard blow if the target was stationary, but with it moving toward his fist, the impact was multiplied. The face, and the body attached to it, dropped to the floor. Bear looked down and saw that he didn't recognize the unconscious boy at his feet. He also saw another stranger, stuck motionless, like a child in a game of freeze tag, and beyond that—he saw a gun.

The barrel of the .45 was pointed directly at him. Behind it, grasping the gun with both hands, was Derek "Dustin" Walczak. Bear recognized him instantly, even with his face obscured by the pistol, even with his left eye clamped shut so he could take aim, even shirtless and out of his orange jumpsuit that he wore in the mug shot. It was definitely Dustin. He'd dropped the wrong kid.

Big Rich lay sprawled on the floor, barley conscious. His cell phone and wallet were flung behind him, scattered on the floor. He moaned a little, still not sure what had happened. He felt two thin streams of warm blood trickling from his nostrils down his cheeks and into his ears. He wasn't sure if it was safe to get up. The first thing that crossed his mind was, *is my cell phone broken?* The second was, *shit, I'd like to get high.*

"Who the fuck is this now?" Dustin asked, almost to himself. The boys had no answer and Bear was keeping an eye on the gun. "What is this, a party now? Get in the house. All of you. Get away from that door."

Dustin wasn't lowering the .45, so Bear felt he had no choice. He kicked Rich's legs back into the house and stepped over him. He shut the door behind him.

Dustin bent over carefully, keeping the gun trained on the big bearded intruder, and picked up Rich's wallet and cell.

When he straightened back up, he said, "The three of you, back to the couch."

Big Rich rolled over with a groan, feeling the damage to his face, and slowly got up. Bear waited for the two boys to get to the couch first before he sat down.

"You, big boy, in the middle." Dustin stood in front of the coffee table waiting for the three to settle in. "You, Dumbfuck, put your wallet and cell back on the table where they belong."

Donny complied and the three of them sat in silence, watching their captor, waiting for the next instruction. Dustin only stood there. He lowered the gun. He was thinking. His face tightened and slackened. Three against one was too many, even with the gun.

"Get up," he said.

The three began to rise.

"No, wait, siddown."

They sat back down.

"You, the big one, stand up."

Bear said, "Are you sure this time, Dustin?"

Dustin's eyes lit up, "How do you know my name?"

The boys both looked at the bearded man between them. They had no idea who the freak with the gun was, or this biker who had burst in to foil their escape.

"Oh, I know all about you, Derek. You're practically famous."

Dustin pointed the .45 at Bear with one hand, "Well, keep it to yourself. If you know anything about me, you know not to fuck with me."

Bear was becoming less and less convinced that he would shoot. "Where's the old man?"

"Up your ass," said Dustin, then, realizing how ridiculous that sounded, added, "You know so much, why don't you tell me?"

"Me? I thought he was here. That's why I dropped by. Is

he here? Why don't you let him know? Where's he at, in the shower?"

To the boys, this big biker seemed awfully confident now, not worried about a gun being pointed in his face. Rich said, "I already asked him, he ain't saying shit. He pulled a fucking gun on us. We don't know where Gabriel or his wife are."

Bear turned his head to the left to face Big Rich, acknowledging him for the first time after the punch. "How's your nose?"

"It hurts. I think it's broken."

"Good. Now shut the fuck up before I push what's left of it up into your skull."

"He's hurt," said Donny.

Bear turned to Donny. "How's your nose? You need an adjustment?"

"It's fine." Donny let it drop.

Bear faced Dustin again. He wanted to focus on the threat, the problem. He still had a job to do. "So? Where is he?"

Dustin still looked like he was thinking about it, trying to get a story straight. Finally he said, "Stand up?"

"Who?"

"You," he said, pointing the gun at Bear's face. "Empty your pockets."

Bear stood up and pulled out his wallet, cell, the stun-gun, a fold of cash, a lighter, and a pack of Camels.

"That's it?"

"That's it."

"Turn around."

Bear turned. The blue surgical gloves were still sticking out of his back pocket.

"What are those for?"

"I don't know what kind of god-awful bugs you got." Bear pulled the gloves and tossed them on the table with the rest of his stuff.

"What about this?" said Dustin, pointing to the stun-gun.

"What is that? Some kind of taser?"

"Yeah, I don't need it." Bear still sounding casual, letting Dustin know he planned to kick his ass—.45 or no .45.

"Oh, so you think you're a tough guy, huh?"

Bear smiled and said, "I'm not the guy walking around with a goddamn swastika tattooed on my chest."

Dustin wasn't falling for it. He wasn't going to get pulled in. This guy was playing games with him. He raised his gun and slowly backed into the kitchen. When he came back in, he had a roll of silver duct tape in his hand. "Okay, get up. All three of you, get up. We're going downstairs."

CHAPTER 10

From the shower stall upstairs, Gabriel Thaxton heard the front door open and shut; he thought he heard muffled voices. The bathroom fan drowned out the sound. The steady whir seemed to breathe, pulsate. He wanted to scream out, but when he tried he felt the gag in his mouth. He listened to himself whimper. With his face against the cold, wet base of the shower stall, it sounded like someone else making the sound.

In the delirium of pain, Gabriel had lost track of time completely. Dustin had turned off the bathroom light and he had no way of knowing what time it was. Only that it was night. He lay in a fetal position, feeling the burn of all the torture he'd endured so far: cigarette burns, short and shallow razor cuts, throbbing contusions, and the trauma of having unidentified objects forced into his rectum. And Gabriel felt, on some level, that he deserved it, had brought it on himself.

He heard footsteps now, coming up the stairs toward him. He squeezed his eyes shut when the bathroom light came on and braced for more pain.

"Gabe." He heard Dustin's voice. "Gabriel, are you awake?" He then felt the sharp sting of a kick in his ribs. He grunted and opened his eyes.

"What the hell, Gabriel. Your house is filling up with strangers. I want to know who these people are. What the fuck they're doing here. Gabriel, you listening to me?"

Gabriel grunted. Dustin bent down close to his face, "Did you send for these assholes? Did you have something to do with this?"

Gabriel grunted again before Dustin realized that he

couldn't answer even if he wanted to. He reached down and yanked the gag from his mouth. "Well?"

"Dustin, please. Help me up. Untie me. I'm too old for this, I can't take it. I need help. It's too much, I can't take it."

Dustin hit the old man in the temple with the heel of his hand. "Are you gonna tell me who these fuckers are, or what?"

"I don't know what you're talking about. Please, help me." The old man's voice disintegrated into sobs. Self-pitying sobs.

"They're in *our* house, Gabriel. They both say you sent for them. Were you expecting company? I thought you were going out tonight? Who are these people?"

"I don't know. I don't know what people you're talking about. What people?"

Dustin had bound all three of them before taking them to the basement. The biker first, with his wrists behind his back, then more of the duct tape around his elbows. Then he moved to the bigger of the two boys. When the biker tried to head-butt him while he worked on the first boy, Dustin gave him a shock with his own stun-gun. That seemed to quiet him up. When all three were bound, he forced them to walk, single-file, down into the basement. There was a space down there Gabriel used for a wine cellar that had a locking door. To keep out whom? Dustin didn't know. Gabriel was the only alcoholic in the house.

When the three of them stood in the tiny cellar, complaining about how tight the tape was, Dustin figured he'd better finish securing them. He walked behind the biker and hit him as hard as he could on the back of the head, right at the base of the skull. The big man dropped to his knees, but didn't pass out. Dustin hit him again, just as hard, and the bastard let out a, "Motherfucker." After a third hit, the guy went down—face first. Dustin prodded him with his foot to make sure he wasn't faking. The two boys looked terrified. They were waiting for their turn.

Dustin told them, "Get on the floor, on your bellies, feet up." First, he taped the biker's boots together—tight. Then, the boys. No need to knock them out, the biker was the threat. The boys saw what had happened to the biker and they did exactly what Dustin told them to do.

Dustin checked the room for stuff they might use to break out, tools, utensils, whatever. The place was bare except for the wine. No window, just the one door. Good enough till he knew what to do with them. He thought about killing them, but the idea of dragging their dead bodies back up the stairs didn't seem too appealing. Especially the big one. If he killed them and left them, they wouldn't be found for weeks, months even. That seemed like a better option. He thought about telling them this, threatening them, but decided that it might make them too desperate. Leave 'em with some hope, till you were sure how to kill them, he thought. He locked the door behind him and went up the stairs.

"What the fuck, dude, who is that guy?" said Big Rich.

"I got no idea. You think he's got Gabriel up there?"

"How should I know? Is this guy okay?"

Donny said, "How should I know?"

"Hey, buddy, you okay? You alive?"

Bear was motionless, not making a sound. They could hear creaking on the floor above them, the sound of someone walking around. Back and forth, pacing. They heard the loud thump of things being dropped. Then it was silent again. The boys listened, but the footsteps had ceased.

"Donny, see if you can kick him, nudge him or something. See if he's breathing."

"I can't reach him. I can't even fuckin' move," said Donny. "What do you think that guy's gonna do with us?"

"I got no idea."

They lay there for a few minutes, squirming, wriggling around on the cold cement floor, trying to loosen the tape. Then, they heard a scream. It was a long, baleful howl. It sounded distant, but they knew it was coming from inside the house. They knew it was Gabriel. There was silence, then, another scream.

"You think that's Gabriel?"

"Of course it is," said Big Rich. "He's torturing the poor bastard. We gotta figure out how to get outta here or it's gonna be us that's screaming."

Bear made a noise—half grunt, half snore—as though he were deep in a fitful sleep.

"Well, I guess he's alive," said Donny.

"Can you see his face? Hey, buddy, you alive? Hey. *Yo.* Wake up."

Bear moaned again. Donny rocked back and forth till he tipped over and rolled into Bear.

The old biker moaned, "Motherfucker," as if he were experiencing the worst hangover of his life. He turned his head to get his face off the cement, opened his eyes and let them adjust to the pale light. "What the fuck?"

"We're tied up, taped up," said Donny. "We're in the basement. You remember what happened?"

Bear's voice was full of gravel and pain, "Yeah, I remember. Where is that little shit, Dustin?"

"He's upstairs," said Donny. "We think he's got Gabriel."

"We heard screams," added Big Rich. "Like, torture shit. Lots of screams."

"Who are you guys?"

"We're friends of Gabriel's," said Donny, talking because he was the closest one to the man.

"Oh, I know *what* the fuck you are, don't worry. I'm an actual friend of Thaxton's, so I know exactly what you two are. I mean, what are your names?"

"I'm Donny and that's Big Rich behind me."

Rich said, "Can you move? At all? Can you get us outta here?"

Bear ignored Rich, "How long I been out?"

Donny answered, "Not long, maybe twenty minutes max."

"My fucking head." Bear wiggled around for a few moments and then asked Donny, "Kid, can you move? Even a little? See if you can push your feet against the tape on my ankles. Wedge 'em in there and shove down."

Donny did as he was asked and the two began the process of loosening each other's binds, feet first. After a few minutes, Bear's hunting knife slipped out of the inside of his boot and fell on the cement floor.

He said, "Ah, there she is."

The three worked at getting the tape off. Bear instructing them with such precision, the boys wondered if the man had been in this situation before. They had to get intertwined, lay on top of one another, use their teeth, and hold that big hunting knife with their mouths. Every once in a while they'd hear another scream from upstairs, the unmistakable imprint of pain.

As they worked, the boys tried to find out what they could about their new friend. Bear told them as little as possible. He was a friend of Gabriel's; he was there to evict Dustin from the premises. They asked about Dustin. Bear didn't tell them much, didn't tell them about the murders. No, he didn't know what Dustin was doing there in the first place, and, when they asked about Mrs. Thaxton, Bear scoffed and said, "Long gone."

Bear didn't ask them anything. He figured out as much as he needed to know for the moment. They didn't know him, they didn't know Dustin, and, judging by their question about Mrs. Thaxton, they didn't really know much about Gabriel either. He stayed focused on the task of freeing himself. Soon it became easier, they were on their feet, cutting at each other's tape while they stood back to back. Then when they were free, Bear walked to the door, not surprised to find it locked, and then to the tall wine rack. He took a bottle and said, "Either of you got an opener?"

Dustin had dragged Gabriel from the bathroom into the bedroom. He paced back and forth in front of him, mumbling and trying to make up his mind about what he was going to do. He paused and stood at the dresser, taking a couple of deep hits off the glass pipe. He held it in and blew it out, moaning softly to himself. It sounded like someone had tickled him, just a little. When he was done, he turned to Gabriel and said, "Get up, we're leaving."

Gabriel moaned, "I can't get up. I can't move. I'm still tied up."

Dustin had forgotten the old man was still bound. He looked at him, curled up in the fetal position on the floor, looking pathetic, broken. First, he took another hit from his pipe, then he untied the old man. He was rough and quick and when he was done he jerked Gabriel up by the arms. "Get dressed, fast. We're leaving."

"Where are we going?"

"You know where we're going. Now hurry up. Grab the rest of that speed from your safe, too—and whatever cash you got in there."

Gabriel had no idea where Dustin intended to take him.

Bear was staring at the door.

"Don't bother, it's locked," said Big Rich.

Donny said to Rich, "He knows, he already tried it."

The boys were looking for something to open the wine

with. They figured they'd be here a while. Rich thought, if they could drink a few bottles, it might take the edge off the on-coming sickness. If they had to piss, they could do it in the empty bottles. His mind was already gearing up for an extended stay.

"Hey, you think you could use that big knife of yours for opening one of these," he asked, bottle in hand.

Bear said, "I got a better idea."

The boys watched as Bear went to work on the door with his knife, using its point like a flathead screwdriver. "This thing," said Bear, "was built to keep people out, not in. The goddamn hinges are on the inside."

Bear had the door off in no time. They'd escaped, but as soon as they got upstairs, Bear knew the house was empty. He could feel it. He opened the front door and saw that the Bentley was gone.

"Shit."

Big Rich was in the kitchen, still trying to figure out how to open the wine. Donny was behind Bear at the door. "What is it? Are they gone?"

"Yeah, they're gone."

"You sure? Shouldn't we check?"

"Oh yeah, I'm sure. But we're gonna check anyway, see what we can find. You look around down here. Anything handwritten. Phone numbers, addresses, whatever. I'm gonna look in the bedrooms upstairs. Tell your friend not to steal nothing and don't go anywhere."

Bear walked up the stairs, knife in hand. He opened each door. There was a guest bedroom, untouched. Another bedroom, obviously reserved for the grandchild—kid posters on the wall, a gaming system, toys neatly placed. He moved along down the hallway. He opened the bathroom door. The first thing he noticed was a funk, a musty, sweaty smell. The next thing he saw was the blood on the floor, in the shower stall, on the toilet seat, and streaked out of the bathroom back into the hall.

He followed the streaks of blood to the master bedroom. He opened the door slowly. This room stank worse than the bathroom, cigarettes, sweat, and the odd chemical smell of speed. There were crumpled-up papers all over the floor. Bear picked up one and looked at it. A pencil drawing of a man with his dick cut off. The dick lay at the man's feet and from his groin there were angry streaks representing blood. Bear tossed it on the ground. He picked up another. This one a portrait, a man's head with daggers stuck into each of the eye sockets. More angry blood was scratched in with pencil, streaming down the man's cheeks like tears. The floor was covered in these drawings. Maybe hundreds of them, crumpled up like trash.

He moved to the dresser. There were empty baggies with what looked like speed residue inside of them, an overflowing ashtray—Marlboro Lights—three or four Bic lighters, and a heavy wooden box that, when opened, revealed three dildos in assorted colors and sizes and different kinds of lube. "Fuckin' weirdoes," mumbled Bear. He reached down and pulled open the drawers. Underwear. Pants and T-shirts. Then, there it was, a fat, black, overstuffed address book. The old school kind that people kept before everyone owned computers. There were scraps of paper sticking out of each edge. It was packed so tightly the little leather strap seemed strained with the contents.

Bear went back downstairs.

"You find anything?" asked Donny.

"No," said Bear, "you?"

Big Rich said, "You want some wine?"

"I think there's a liquor cabinet above the fridge. Pour me a glass of whiskey, would ya, kid?"

* * *

Gabriel leaned his head up against the window. Every few moments he let out a quiet moan. The night was black and fog filled the streets. He paid no attention to what direction Dustin drove.

"Where are we?" he asked.

"Where the fuck do you think we are? In the middle of San Francisco."

"Where are we going?"

"We're going to finish up the work we started. We have some unfinished business, you and me."

"Dustin, I told you, I can't do as you asked. It's impossible. The courts will never ratify it. It's not even legal."

"Of course it is, all you have to do is make it legal. And you know what'll happen if you don't."

Gabriel looked out the window and said, "I know, I know."

They were rolling downhill now and Gabriel knew that they were heading to the Mission District. Soon the streets leveled out and they were in the flat underbelly of the city. The fog had thinned to a mist and the sky began to lighten to a shade of dark blue. Dustin pulled into an all-night gas station. He rolled the Bentley up toward a set of payphones near the back of the lot by the air and water pumps. The shiny black car magnetized the few homeless guys who were waiting around to pump gas for strangers.

Dustin stayed in the driver's seat staring at the phones he took from the intruders. There was a gentle knock at the window. Dustin rolled it down.

"Hey, buddy, nice car. You want me to do the windows?" An unshaven bum with only a few teeth left in his head stood there holding a bucket and squeegee.

"Get the fuck away from the car before I cut you, scumbag," Dustin hissed.

The man frowned and backed away. To the next bum walking up to the vehicle, he said, "Don't bother. Guy's an asshole."

Inside the car, Gabriel asked, "What are we doing here?"

"I gotta make a phone call."

Gabriel waited for a moment before asking, "Why don't you make it?"

Dustin looked at him, blaming him. "Because I left my fucking phone book at the house." He got out of the car and paced between it and the phone booth, hoping to conjure the number he wanted to call. Gabriel watched him. When the conjuring didn't work, Dustin climbed back into the driver's seat.

"Where are we going now?" asked Gabriel.

"Somewhere else."

Gabriel said, "I'm thirsty."

"You still haven't told me who those bastards were tonight."

"I've told you, again and again, I don't know. I didn't even see them. I don't know who they are."

"You know," said Dustin. "You know something."

Gabriel swallowed. His throat was dry. He didn't mention it again. He just stared out the window.

"Fucker took our phones."

The three sat at Gabriel Thaxton's kitchen table. The two boys with sodas in front of them and Bear with his whiskey and the contents of Dustin's black address book spread out in front of him, separated into piles—neat piles, trying to make sense of something that made no sense to him.

"So what? Buy new ones," said Bear.

"No, I have to have that one; it's got pictures of my kid when she was just a baby. Tons of 'em. It can't be replaced. I have to have that one."

Donny stared at the Coke can in front of him, not listening.

"Pictures of your kid, huh?" There was clear doubt in Bear's voice. "You fellas never told me what exactly you were doing here tonight."

Big Rich wasn't listening. "I have to get my phone back."

"You think it's more important than Thaxton's life?"

"I'm just saying I gotta get that phone back. Doesn't mean I don't care about the old man." Rich took a sip of his soda. "I do. I do care about the old man. If we can get him, we should. We should save him from that ugly fucker."

"We, huh?" said Bear.

That breezed right past Rich, too. "Yeah, and when we do, I want my phone back."

Bear went back to puzzling through the scraps of paper before him. The book itself turned out to have very little written in it. Mostly, it was made up of the scraps of paper. A chaotic product of a chaotic mind. He had no idea what he was looking for.

Rich asked, "Find anything good in there?"

"Good?"

"Yeah, you know, like, useful."

"No," said Bear. He went back to his work, fanning out the slips in front of him. One slip of paper stood out. It had a name and phone number that had been circled several times with different ink. The name was Gilly. Below it, in pencil, was one word: Marin.

Donny, who hadn't spoken since they'd sat down said, "Rich, I think I'm gonna be sick."

Bear interrupted, "If you're gonna puke, do it in the toilet. That way."

"No," said Donny, still speaking to Rich. "I think I'm gonna be *sick* sick."

"You'll be fine; you can hang on a little longer. It only seems like it's been a long time, but you're still well. We gotta hang on to what we have, just in case. Go check the medicine cabinet upstairs. Find something to hold you over."

Donny got up slowly from the table and ambled toward the stairs. Rich called after him, "If you find somethin' bring it back down here, don't hold out. I ain't feeling the best myself."

Bear raised his eyes from the scraps of paper. "Sick, huh? You gave up your precious phone with your baby's pictures, but you managed to hang on to some dope? Nice to see you got your priorities straight."

Big Rich wanted to say, *Fuck you*, but decided that they were gonna need their new friend to help him find his phone and Gabriel. One without the other just wouldn't do. He told himself that he had the big picture still forefront in his mind. The plan might still work. In Rich's mind the phone equaled money.

Bear said, "That's what I thought." And Big Rich still didn't say anything.

Bear sat weeding through the scraps, remembering that he had his own wallet taken. There were numbers in there that would come in handy right now. There was one number, though, he had memorized.

"Hey, kid, you see a phone around here?"

"You can stop calling me kid," said Rich, pointing to the counter behind Bear.

Bear got up and began to dial.

Big Rich asked, "Hey, why do they call you Bear, anyway?"

"Because I can run thirty-five miles an hour and I'm great at climbing trees."

Rich sneered at his sarcasm and watched him make his phone call.

"Hey, Roberta, it's Bear. Is Sheila workin'? I know you're closed, but is she still there?" Bear waited, listening to the sounds of the Roadhouse. It always sounded louder on the phone than it really was—more rowdy, more fun. Now, all he heard was the clang of silverware, the hum of vacuums. There was no music, no laughter. It still seemed like a place he'd rather be. It took a while before Sheila got on the line.

"Sheila, honey, it's me Bear...Yeah, I do, baby, I'd really love to." To Bear, the sound of Sheila's voice was always warm and inviting. She had a flirty rasp in her voice even now after work, counting her tips. "...Well, you never know...I know, I'm glad I caught you, I need you to do me a favor...no, it can't wait, not really...okay, I will, I promise...You know, Johnny Watson, right? Silver-haired guy, they call him the Doctor?...Yeah, that's him. Sheila, listen, I need you to get his phone number for me...I know it's late, but it's important...You know who might have it? Davey or Victor...Yeah, I know he's a dick, but he'll pick up the phone. Can you do this for me? I can't do it, I've lost all my numbers and my phone...It's a long story, I'll say that much...Thank you, sweetheart. When you get the number, I want you to call me back here at this one. You got a pen?"

Big Rich watched Bear speak into the phone and thought about his own girlfriend, up in Oregon, how her voice would sound on the phone. Shit, he could never ask her for a favor in the middle of the night. She'd hang up on him. Women were bitches.

Donny came down the stairs with two pill bottles, one in each hand. "Pay dirt," he said. "Two bottles of Vicodin, fives and seven and a halves. This will hold us over."

Big Rich immediately forgot about Bear's phone call. "I dunno, those things never did shit for me."

"You gotta eat a few of 'em, but they'll work." He tossed one of the bottles over to Rich, the fives. Rich missed the catch and pulled them off the floor. "What else you find up there?"

Donny reached in the pocket of his jean jacket and pulled out two glass pipes, both blackened and thick with residue.

"Check these out; I'm guessing these were Dustin's."

"Nice," said Big Rich. "I guess we'll make it through the night after all."

Bear hung up the phone and looked at the two boys dividing up their finds. "Don't smoke that shit in here. We're not through. There's still a pretty good chance the cops're gonna show."

"Why? Don't you think if they were gonna show, they would've by now?" Big Rich stared into the bowl of the pipe, admiring the crystals, guessing how much was in there, marveling at how much had been smoked through the thing.

"Just hold off, alright?"

"What are we doing? Did you find out where they went?"

"We're waiting," said Bear with a sound of finality.

"Then wait, we shall," said Rich, touching a lighter to the bottom of the glass bulb.

They sat waiting for the phone to ring, Bear with his whiskey and the boys alternately chasing their painkillers with Coke and hitting the speed pipes. The two discussed how the effect of the two drugs were cancelling each other out, how they couldn't really feel either one, but Bear could tell that they were both getting higher and higher. And more annoying. He settled in with his drink, got himself a Coke chaser, and listened to the boys yammer.

He wasn't following all their drug talk. He didn't care. These were conversations he'd listened to a thousand times. His mind was on Thaxton, where that freak might have taken him. He tried to recall some of the stuff from the articles he'd read. The only things that came to mind were the grisly details of the murders.

The phone rang. It startled both of the boys. Bear picked it up by the second ring.

He spoke for a brief moment, hung up, and dialed again.

"Doctor Watson," he said. "How you doing?" He listened to the voice on the phone and watched the boys, disinterested by the answer. When the voice finally stopped, he said, "I got a problem. I need to find somebody, somebody you know. Gilly...Yeah, that Gilly. Does he still live up there? I think he may know a guy I'm looking for...No? Where'd he go?...Where in the city?" Bear went on, pressing the Doctor for answers but getting none.

The boys stopped talking when Bear mentioned Gilly's name. Rich kicked Donny under the table.

When Bear was done, he sat back down at the table and said, "Hey, you know, considering all that screaming we heard earlier, your *friend*," he made little quotation marks with his fingers, "is gonna probably need them pain pills when he gets back home."

Big Rich thought he was kidding and ignored the comment. He asked, "So, Bear, right? What's the plan?"

"What do you mean, what's the plan? The plan is: I'm gonna go and rescue my friend from that piece of shit and you're gonna go back to Polk Street and suck dicks. The plan is that I won't ever have to be in the same room with you two dope fiends again. How's that sound?"

Donny asked, "You know where he took him?"

"That's what I'm gonna find out."

"How am I gonna get my phone back?" said Rich.

"What's with you and that phone anyway?"

"I told you..."

"I know, I know, it's got pictures of your kid, your wife, your real life. The one you lead when you're not sucking dicks for dope money."

Donny interrupted, "He's got all our phones, and all our wallets."

"You'll live," said Bear.

"We can help you," said Big Rich.

"How?" The whiskey was starting to affect Bear, he was ready to laugh in the kid's face.

"We know Gilly."

CHAPTER 11

The three of them crowded into the Toyota, Bear and Rich in the front with Donny in the back. They started out toward the Mission District to see if the Gilly in the notebook was the same one that Rich and Donny knew. Bear thought it was pretty likely; how many Gillys could there be in San Francisco? He'd taken a chance calling Watson; he'd found his number, too, in Dustin's address book. Watson was a scumbag, a tweaker, but at least it was a name he recognized. Maybe, Bear thought, Watson knew this Gilly character. It was worth a shot. All these fucking tweakers seemed to know each other. Maybe they had clandestine union meetings at some dumpster in an alley somewhere.

Big Rich described Gilly as a wayward soul from Texas, spun in the City. He was a methhead who dabbled in computer scams, identity theft, stolen property, and, of course, drugs. Rich had said the guy lived in a flat on Treat Street at 22nd in the Mission District. He also said that he had a lot of roommates; Big Rich was pretty sure that someone would be up. Big surprise.

"How do you know this guy?" asked Bear.

"Oh, he's a good guy. I used to trade him computer stuff for speed. And for a while I was cashing checks for him."

"He's got money?"

"Nah, he ain't got shit. He was printin' 'em up on the computer. He's good with that stuff. He can do ID's and everything."

"Sounds like a real class act," said Bear.

They drove down Gough Street with Big Rich monopolizing the conversation. He went on about how Gilly was a great fence, and, then, paperhanger. How he'd employ tweakers to root through garbage cans and dumpsters looking for discarded checks and other information. He'd take the checks and print them up on his own, using special ink and printers, then, he'd forge ID's for people to take into the bank, California driver licenses with the same name that was on the check. The banks eventually got wise and technology got better. Rich got popped a few times. They took his fake ID and he spent a few nights sick in County lockup. Gilly had to find a better scam. That's when Gilly moved into selling speed, and then manufacturing it, too. Right there in his flat, said Rich. The whole placed smelled like paint thinner.

Donny stayed quiet in back while Rich rambled on about his criminal accomplishments. It took a while to sink in, but Bear's comments about sucking dicks had stuck with him. The man was obviously disgusted by their company. In truth, Donny couldn't blame him. They were dope fiends: the lowest kind of criminal. He was already thinking about getting high. Even now, he was wondering if he could find a way for them to cop, wondering if he could just get out of the car and go fix at his hotel and forget all about tonight. Donny tuned out completely from the conversation in the front. A fragment of a pop song he hated played over and over in his head.

He snapped out of his daydream when he heard Big Rich ask Bear, "If you're a biker, how come you're not on a bike?"

"'Cause all three of us couldn't fit on a bike."

Rich nodded like this seemed to make sense to him.

"Okay, Twenty-Second and Treat," said Bear, "Where's this guy's place at?"

Rich told Bear to take a right onto Treat Street and they crawled up the block. Rich pointed the place out, a decrepit-looking two story in need of a paint job. Bear kept going.

"What are you doing? Looking for a place to park?"

"I'm looking for the old man's car, the Bentley. See if it's near here."

They tooled around the surrounding blocks. Each time they passed the flat where Rich had said Gilly lived Bear would slow and look up the marble stairs, hoping to see some kind of activity. Nothing. Bear kept going, and, after not finding the Bentley, looked for a parking spot of his own.

They found a spot about a block away and walked back to the house. As they walked up the steps toward the door, Bear could hear music, voices. Rich rang the bell. No response. Rich knocked on the door. They waited until they heard footsteps.

The door cracked open and a prematurely aged woman stuck her head out. Bear could tell she would have been a looker in her youth, but the speed had obviously taken its toll. Her teeth were gray and she had that sickly pallor that all drug fiends get when the years stack up against them.

"Kathy," said Big Rich. "Is Gilly up? I need to see him."

Kathy said, "Tommy?"

"No, Gilly."

"No, I mean, are you Tommy?"

"No, I'm Rich. Remember me?"

"Not really. Who did you want to see?"

"Gilly."

"Hang on," she said and shut the door. They heard her footsteps pounding up the inside stairs, and, after a few moments, heard them coming back down. The door opened, "What was your name again?"

"Rich, Big Rich. Tell Gilly it's important. He knows who I am."

She shut the door again and went back upstairs to give Gilly the message. Rich said, "Fucking cunt. I stood next to her every day at the methadone clinic for six months and she don't even 'member who I am."

"Yeah," said Bear. "Drugs fuck people up."

Big Rich missed the joke entirely, but Donny smiled. Bear caught him and shot Donny a wink. The door opened again, wide this time, and another person stood there, fat and greasy, face full of acne framed by glasses so thick they made his eyes look like they were being squeezed out of his head. He wore a dirty white T-shirt that clung to his humid body and a pair of dark blue sweats that were peppered with burn holes. He said, "Hey, Rich. Gilly says c'mon up." The man didn't inquire as to whom Rich's guests were, so they all followed him up the stairs single file. When they reached the top, the fat man turned and said, "Just wait in the kitchen for a minute, okay? Gilly's finishing up some business."

The fat man walked away to a bedroom down the hall, so the three followed the source of the most noise and found the kitchen. They crowded into the tiny space that was already occupied by five others. Three of those five sat around a red Formica table looking over heated in their interchangeable white T-shirts that were spotted and speckled with what looked like dried blood. The other two nodded solemnly while they stood and smoked near the doorless pantry that was stocked with not food but well-used appliances. They let their cigarette ashes drop to the floor and seemed to communicate only with quiet grunts.

The first thing Bear noticed was the sink. There was no other place to stand, so he was forced to be closest to the pile of abandoned dishes that filled the sink. They were piled above the level of the counter, balancing high and leaning on one another like a filthy house of cards that may come crashing down at any moment. The basin was bone dry, but the dishes still managed to grow a spectrum of molds. The stink was sour and he couldn't understand why no one else was wincing because of it.

He fought back a gag and turned to see the table. On it were two scales—one electric, one weighted—empty baggies of every size imaginable, glass pipes, burned spoons coated inside with brown goo, overflowing ashtrays, needles—some new, some filled with dried blood—an empty bag of cat food, which immediately made Bear notice the ammonia smell of cat piss mixing in with the decomposing food. He reached into his coat for a Camel to combat the stink.

The moment Bear shook out a smoke, one of the fiends at the table turned to him and said, "Hey, buddy, mind if I get one of those?"

Bear said, "Sorry, last one," and slipped the pack back into his pocket. The guy at the table turned his attention back to his drugs, shaking some white powder into a dirty spoon.

Donny didn't bother lighting up. He wasn't sure how many smokes he had left and he didn't want to give any up. The action at the table made him jones a little. He wanted to ask if he could get in on some, whatever they were doing. He knew Rich would be feeling the same way. He watched them work, drawing up the shit in their rigs, arguing about who got more, who was going to pound the cottons. He looked over at Rich and saw him staring wide-eyed, mouth open, lost in his own desires.

One of the guys at the table said, "Don't put coke in mine, I gotta muscle it."

The one on the end said, "I already did, I thought you wanted it. Have Kathy hit you in the armpit. She's good at it."

The one in the middle said, "At least she's good for something."

Then the first one, "I can't hit my armpits, they're blown out."

"You can't blow out your armpits, you're just missing. I been getting a spot in there for months. You just have to know how to do it."

The wise-ass in the middle said, "Try your neck, that's easy. I hit mine almost every day."

Sure enough, Bear noticed, there was a dark blue bruise crowned with tiny scabs running up the man's jugular.

Big Rich interrupted, "I can hit you in the neck, or in the

armpit. Just give me the wash and I'll do it."

The guy on the end turned to Rich, seemed to be considering it, but then the first guy said. "You can't give him the wash; it's not yours to give. I promised Sarah the rinse. She's sitting back there in the room sick."

The guy with the needle decided he was going to muscle it anyway.

The one in the middle, who seemed to know everything, told him, "You can't muscle coke, you'll get an abscess."

"Sure you can, I do it all the time. Just no rush, that's all." He stuck the needle into his shoulder and pressed the plunger. Bear watched a lump form under his skin. Bear was disgusted. He flicked his ashes in the debris behind him and wondered how much longer it would be until he could question this Gilly character.

"Rich?" a voice sounded from down hallway, "Big Rich? C'mere."

Bear was relieved. He couldn't take another minute in the kitchen. He followed the two boys out into a dark hallway. The three followed the voice.

At the end of the hall, standing in a doorway, was a young, spindly man. He had dirty blond hair and wisps of a beard, more peach fuzz than whiskers. He was grinning and showing a gap where one of his front teeth had rotted out—or been knocked out. He wore camouflage pants that bore the same burn holes as the fat man who'd answered the door. He wore no shirt to cover his skinny frame and his skin was covered in a film of greasy sweat.

"Gilly," said Rich, "long time, no see."

"How're you doin'? Come in, come in." He ushered them into a cramped space that was lit with colored bulbs. The room was sealed off to outside light; it would be impossible to tell from inside if it was day or night. Bear let his eyes adjust and looked around. The walls were stacked with computer equipment, most of which looked like it had been pulled from a dumpster. The floor was knotted with wires and cords tethering some of the pieces together. A large, old TV was playing without any sound, but music came from somewhere, a fast heavy metal song that playing so low it sounded like violent static.

"Move that shit," said Gilly, pointing to a couch that was covered with cardboard boxes and papers. Donny scooped up enough of the debris to make room for the three of them and they sat down, in the same arrangement as when they'd sat on the couch at Thaxton's

When they had settled, Gilly introduced himself. He was friendly, polite, and laying on that thick Texas accent.

"So," said Gilly to Rich, a serious tone creeping into his voice. "What brings you around? You haven't been seen since all that bullshit went down."

"I been broke, haven't had anything together lately. You know how it is."

Gilly nodded thoughtfully. His mind was already far away from the conversation. Then he said, "You guys want a hit, see what's new in pharmaceutical science?"

Rich grinned and said sure and Donny quickly nodded. Bear sat still. He was still assessing, thinking about when to break in with his line of questioning. Gilly took a loaded glass pipe from the top of a monitor and held a lighter under it. He inhaled deeply and passed it to Rich while he kept the smoke in his lungs. He watched Rich re-light the pipe and suck in the smoke before he asked, "So, who are your friends?"

"This is Donny, I think you know Donny. He's been over here before. And that there is Bear."

"You lookin' to buy something?" Gilly said to Bear, "I got this shit, and some cheaper stuff, all you need. The glass you can fuckin' see through and the raw, it's cheap, but it's got a real...*ka-bang*."

Big Rich passed the pipe to Donny and it went right under Bear's nose. It stank just like any other speed he'd smelled and he pulled back his head a bit so as to not breathe any more of the fumes than he had to. "No, not me. I'm looking for a friend of mine. He's a friend of yours too. His name is Dustin."

Gilly made a face, a thoughtful frown, and said, "Dustin? Nope, I don't know any Dustin."

"Think harder," was all Bear said. He knew this punk was lying and he wanted to give him a chance to answer without losing face.

Gilly looked over at Rich with a look of concern, thinking maybe Rich had brought an undercover cop into his home. Rich said, "It's pretty important."

Gilly was still shaking his head. "Sorry, don't know him."

"Yeah, you do," said Bear. "Your name is all over his phonebook, and I know, for a fact, that you two have done business together. So cut the shit. I need to talk to this motherfucker right away." Bear stood up from the couch, his size now very apparent to the scrawny Gilly.

"What the fuck, Rich? Who you bringing in here to my home? I don't know this guy." Then, to Bear, "Rich brings you here to buy," he stuttered, "used computer stuff, and you got no manners. Now, I don't know who you think you are, but..."

Bear pushed his face a little closer, "You think I'm a cop? Is that it? You fuckin' wish I was a cop, you dumbfuck, 'cause I'm gonna fuck you up in a minute. I'm gonna give you the kinda pain a cop never could. Now, where is Dustin?"

Gilly stepped back, bumping into a monitor. A few empty beer bottles filled with cigarette butts fell to the floor. "Dustin? Dustin? Oh, shit, I thought you said Justin." Talking fast now, selling it, "Yeah, yeah, I know a Dustin. But I ain't seen him, I swear. Not for a long time. I think that dude's in prison or something. I used to know him. I don't anymore, he and I don't see straight. If I see him I'll tell him you're trying to find him, but I won't see him. I barely even know him."

Bear reached forward and wrapped his fingers around Gilly's throat and squeezed. Gilly's face turned red. "Bullshit," said Bear.

The bedroom door opened. No knock, no warning. Bear let go. There was Kathy, the girl that had let them into the house.

"What's going on," she said. "What was all that noise?"

Gilly couldn't answer; his throat was still closed up. Bear glared at her, his face still red with anger.

So Donny said, "We're looking for Dustin."

"Oh, you just missed him," Kathy said, smiling, thinking she was being helpful. She was. "He was here with some creepy old guy, like, an hour ago. He slinked outta here without sayin' nothin', as usual. If you see him, tell him from me..."

Bear cut her off, "Excuse us." He kicked the door shut. She pulled back her face in time to avoid getting it caught in the slamming door. With one quick motion, Bear grabbed Gilly's elbow and smacked him, mid-biceps, with the palm of his hand. There was a loud crack and Gilly's face turned white with the shock, the pain.

Gilly dropped to his knees, crying, "You broke my arm, you broke my arm."

There was knocking. Kathy's voice. "Hey, what's going on in there? Hello? What was that? Gilly?"

Bear turned to Rich. "The door."

Rich moved fast and pushed up against it with one hand holding the knob. Donny began to move through the room, digging, stuffing things into his pockets.

"What did I tell you?" Bear said to Gilly who only cried out, "My arm, my arm."

Bear hadn't let go of the elbow, he held Gilly down by squeezing it with one hand and reached into his boot with the other hand and pulled out the big hunting knife. He pushed it against Gilly's throat. "Where the fuck did they go?"

There were more voices at the door now, more knocking and pounding. The whole diseased herd of junkies were trying to push their way in. Bear twisted Gilly's arm some more; he could see the broken bone pushing against the skin. "Where are they?" He was growling now, trying not to push the knife too hard against his throat.

"I don't know, I don't know." Gilly was whimpering. "Maybe Terrence's, or Gavin's. He said something about seeing his lawyer."

"What did he come here for?"

"To get some speed and use the computer. That's it, that's all I swear."

Bear let go of his elbow and smacked him in the face with the butt of his knife. Gilly curled up in a ball on the dirty carpet.

"Okay," Bear said to the boys, "I'm ready to go."

Donny said, "What about the computer? We can check the history, see what he was doing."

Big Rich said, "I can't hold these fuckers. They're gonna break down the door."

Bear moved behind Big Rich who was barely holding the door closed and said, "Open it."

Rich stepped back and let the door swing open. When the junkies saw the big biker with a buck knife in his hand, they stood still. They weren't sure if they wanted to fight this battle for Gilly.

"Get the fuck out!" one of them shouted.

"Gladly," said Bear and, knife still in his hand, punched one of them hard in the nose. The blood flowed and the junkie went down. The rest of them stepped aside, still trying to look menacing.

Bear, Rich, and Donny moved as fast as they could through the hallway and down the stairs to the front door.

They heard more shouts behind them: "I'll remember you"

"Get the fuck out"

"That's fucked up."

And Kathy's voice screaming, "I'm calling the cops."

But no one there was calling the cops.

They hit the street and moved as quick as they could to the parked car. Rich was practically skipping.

"Did you see that shit? Holy fuck, that was some wicked-ass U.S. Marine-type shit you pulled on that dude. Man, Donny, did you see that shit?"

Donny was speed walking with his hands stuffed into his jacket pockets. "I saw, I saw. I was there, remember?" He checked over his shoulder to see if anyone had come out of the house to follow—or shoot at—them.

They reached the car and piled in, all three out of breath. Rich, still excited, hit Bear in the arm, saying, "Dude, you are a fucking badass."

Bear was still wheezing. He started the car and looked over at Big Rich. "I'm not as young as I used to be."

They drove through the Mission for several blocks, waiting for the adrenalin to subside, before Big Rich said the obvious thing. "Where're we going?"

"Looks like we're back to square one. That's a lot of excitement that didn't yield much information. I don't know either of those fuckers he mentioned, do you?"

"I didn't even hear what he said; it was too crazy in there."

Then, in a quiet voice, from the back seat, Donny said, "I got his gun."

"What?" said Bear. "You got that son of a bitch's gun?" He laughed. "I wish you hadda said somethin', we could have used it to get outta there."

"What kind is it?" said Big Rich, excited.

"I dunno, but it's heavy." Donny pulled the piece out of

the inside pocket of his jacket and held it pointed toward the floorboards.

"Whoa," said Bear. "Put that thing away. That's the last thing I need is for one of you dumbfucks to shoot himself in the foot."

"We're just taking a look," said Rich.

"I've had bad luck with other people's guns, that's all. Just put it away, we don't need it now, not yet," Bear said, adding, "Smart move, kid. Volatile situation like that, better us have it than him. Although, I doubt he was gonna be using it."

"Way to go, Donny. Good lookin' out," Rich chimed in, proud of his friend.

"I got his phone, too."

Bear looked at Donny in the rearview mirror. "Nice," he said. "You're smarter than you look, kid. We just may be able to do something with that thing."

Donny smiled. It was half an insult, but it still made him feel good.

CHAPTER 12

Gabriel woke with his head bouncing off of the Bentley window. The sunlight pierced his eyes and he felt nauseated and in pain. He had no idea where they were, winding on a country road with Dustin taking the sharp curves way too fast. He lifted his head up and could smell tobacco and the ocean.

"Well, look who decided to join us," Dustin said.

"Us?" said Gabriel, almost to himself. He looked in the back seat and saw no one. The car veered left around a hairpin turn and Gabriel began to get his bearings. He knew this country. They were in Marin, driving near the coast. He could tell by the hue of the light that it was still barely morning and he could feel, by intuition, that they were driving north, away from San Francisco. Where to, he had no idea.

Dustin turned on the radio and began immediately punching buttons when he heard Thaxton's classical station. He settled on a pop station that promised, *More Hits, Less Commercials,* and he tapped his hands on the steering wheel cheerfully. Gabriel wasn't used to seeing Dustin out in natural sunlight and noticed how awful his skin looked. The red blotches on his hands had been freshly picked over and looked irritated and infected. Except for the blemishes, his pale skin was nearly translucent. He had a cigarette dangling from the corner of his mouth and the ashes fell from the cherry onto his lap.

"Where are we going?" asked Gabriel.

"To see a friend of mine, to finish our business. We'll get you some lunch, you'll feel better."

"Where?" Gabriel noticed his own voice sounding weak,

raspy. He fought the urge to ask to see a doctor. He knew that would be pointless. There would be no doctors where they were going.

"Just up the street here. You'll see," said Dustin, then he added in a strange sing-song voice high in pitch, "*You'll see when you get there!*"

Gabriel put his head back against the window and let it bounce lifelessly against the glass. He tried to shut his eyes. He wasn't sure whether it was the tobacco smoke or the winding road that was making him more nauseated. He settled in and kept the rest of his thoughts to himself.

Even at the high speed Dustin drove, the road unfolded slowly. Twisting back and forth, first toward the water, then toward the hills, they slowly wound down to sea level. Gabriel recognized the town as Stinson Beach. He hoped they'd be stopping, but Dustin drove straight through and the small town disappeared behind them. Dustin paid little attention to traffic laws or posted speeds. Where were the police, thought Gabriel, where were the CHP when you needed them?

Soon they were driving away from the coastline again, up into the hills. The road grew narrower and eventually turned to gravel. Dustin pulled into a long driveway that was lined with trees and turned off the radio.

"Be polite when you meet my friend, okay? He's gonna help us out with our problem."

Gabriel looked up and saw a huge house. The front consisted of almost all pane glass facing the direction of the ocean. The sun was high enough now to reflect off of the house and the result was blinding. You almost couldn't look at it, like some real world version of the Emerald City; it shimmered and burned like the sun itself.

Dustin pulled the Bentley between two other cars in the gravel drive—a Jaguar on the left and a Volvo on the right—and put the car in park. The Jag looked like it hadn't been moved for months. They both sat for a minute squinting at the great glass house, waiting for something to happen. Dustin laid on the horn.

"Dusty," a voice cried out. Neither Gabriel nor Dustin could tell where the voice was coming from until a shadowy figure appeared at the right of the place. The man was older, looked a bit like a cowboy, Gabriel thought, and seemed to have that bow-legged gait one got from too many years on a horse. He wore a dirty white cowboy hat, too; that helped. His white hair stuck out from under the hat like straw, uncombed and unclean. Gabriel got the impression that they'd just interrupted him from some kind of yard work. He was tanned and leathery from the sun, or maybe just from being in front of that house.

The cowboy walked in front of the car where Gabriel could get a better look at him.

"Dusty, my boy. How're you doin'? I see you brought your friend." The cowboy didn't acknowledge Gabriel; instead he strolled over to the driver's side and shook Dustin's hand as he got out of the car.

"How ya doin', Terrence? Yeah, I got him. He ain't doing so well right now, had a rough night. He'll feel better after a shower and some lunch." Dustin turned his head back toward the car, smiling a fake little smile that looked like it didn't belong on his face. "Won't cha, Gabe?"

Gabriel felt more exhausted than he had the whole ride. He was too tired to guess what Dustin's game was, why he'd brought him here. He let his head fall back against the seat and was painfully reminded of the cigarette burns up and down his back. He leaned against the headrest and let his mind drift. He fell back asleep.

Gabriel dreamed he was far away from the car, outside somewhere on a sunny day. It was a wheat field, deep in the country, but there was a baseball diamond etched into the flowing grass. He was there with his grandson, Jason, alone under a stretching blue sky. He sensed his daughter's presence, but she was nowhere to be seen. Perhaps she was hiding among the stalks of wheat. Gabriel and the boy played catch. Then, it formalized into a game. Jason was wearing a little league uniform. He pitched the ball while the boy was at bat. He wasn't sure who was catching, maybe it was him. He wasn't even sure if it was baseball, but it felt like it. He wound up and threw, feeling youthful and energized. He could feel the warmth of the sun on his back, and when his grandson got a hit, he was forced to squint into the daylight as the ball arced above his head.

The next thing he was aware of was the slamming of the trunk; the noise and action shaking the car and jarring him from his sleep. He had no idea how long he'd been out. The sun still shone but had moved off the front windows of the house. He was covered in a film of sweat. He limbs felt heavy and stiff. He tried to sit up and was reminded of how much pain he was in.

In the rearview mirror, he saw Dustin walking from the back of the car with a large briefcase in his hand, one of the old-style leather ones with the brass clasps. He wondered for a moment if it was his own. The briefcase looked heavy and his mind drifted off to his younger days as a lawyer, lugging such a piece back and forth to the courthouse. He envisioned his younger self; the eager attorney he thought was so naïve. He knew better now, he longed to once again be so full of optimism.

Then he saw the cowboy, standing in front of the car with his hands on his hips. It startled him, the cowboy standing there grinning, not moving or saying anything, but staring right at him.

After an uncomfortable few moments, Dustin reappeared beside the car and opened the passenger door.

"C'mon, sleepyhead. Get outta there. I want you to meet somebody." Dustin pulled at Gabriel's elbow before realizing that the seatbelt was still strapped across the old man's body. Dustin reached in and unbuckled it.

Gabriel sat, unable to move. He could smell Dustin's chemical sweat, the methamphetamine oozing out his pores. It repulsed him.

"Gabriel," Dustin said, trying carefully to help the old man from the car, "this is Terrence Halford. He's a friend of mine. We're gonna be his guests for a few days"

Terrence Halford? Gabriel knew that name. In his fog, he couldn't recall where, but there was a feeling of *déjà vu* in hearing the name. He squinted in the sunlight to try and place the face.

"Gabriel Thaxton," the cowboy said, "The man, the legend. I've heard so much about you—for years. It's a real pleasure to finally meet you." The man stepped forward and stuck out his hand.

Gabriel eased himself out of the passenger seat. His shirt peeled away from the seat where the puss had soaked through and stuck to it. He straightened out stiffly and shook the man's hand. Getting closer to the cowboy didn't help him place where he knew that name. The man stood smiling, not letting go of Gabriel's hand, his grip tight and calloused.

The cowboy said, "C'mon in, have a little lunch, get yourself cleaned up. We're having tacos."

The boys sat in a booth with Bear. The boys on one side, Bear on the other. Jimmy's on Mission Street was a landmark, Bear told them. To the boys, the cracked, red vinyl booths and grease-spotted menus made it seem like any other shitty diner they'd been in. It was noisy in there even though there were only a few patrons. One Mexican cook toiled over a grill while three waitresses shouted orders at him in Korean or Vietnamese, Bear was never sure. He just knew it wasn't Chinese; he could recognize Chinese. The place was a seventies diner that had not updated its décor since it was originally put up. Oranges and reds that had faded over the years now looked as pale and tired as Bear himself.

When their food arrived—three cheeseburgers and three orders of fries—Rich and Donny's assumptions were confirmed, it *was* just another shitty diner. Bear took a huge bite out of his burger and made a deep growling sound to let the boys know how good it was. Rich and Donny each picked up a French fry and took an unenthusiastic bite.

"What we have to do," said Bear, speaking with his mouth full of burger, "is to figure out how to," he searched for the word, "analyze the information in Gilly's phone. Figure out who's in there that Dustin might know, if he's called anyone. Then figure out what to do with the information. You know, detective work."

"Sounds like kind of a kind of a long shot," said Donny.

"You got any better ideas? That's the best thing we got right now." Bear took another bite. "Shit, you were happy about it when you took the damn thing. You musta thought it'd be worth something."

Big Rich squirted some ketchup onto his plate. The plastic squeeze bottle made a farting noise. He stirred the red blotch with another fry. "We need to check them names," he said, "quick, before Gilly shuts off that phone. What were they again?"

"I don't think it's gonna get shut off quick. I think your friend is probably still at the hospital gettin' a cast on that fucked up arm of his. And I kinda doubt he stopped to look for his phone before he left, or his gun, for that matter."

"He's not a friend of mine, just some guy I know. That's all."

"Don't get defensive there, son. Eat your burger."

The three ate on in silence, the boys barely touching their burgers. Bear finished his and asked for the rest of the boys' burgers. Not much of a question, he reached over and picked up the scraps.

After eating both of their burgers with quick determination, Bear said, "You gonna finish those fries, or what?"

Donny pushed his plate across the table toward Bear. He took the phone from his pocket and looked at it. "We'll probably lose the charge long before it gets shut off."

Bear spoke to Big Rich, but pointed to Donny and said, "The brains of the operation." Bear waved to the waitress, his favorite, an Asian woman named May whose accent was so thick little of what she said was understood, other than "Mr. Bear." She greeted him as though he was their best and oldest customer.

"A chocolate shake, please, May. You boys want anything?" They both shook their heads and May retreated from the table. Bear picked up Dustin's black address book from the seat beside him, opened it, and began to sort through the slips of paper. He asked Donny for the phone, turned it on, and started the long process of cross referencing numbers.

The boys sat and watched Bear work. He scrolled through the phone, through the made calls, the missed calls, the contacts. Most of them were first names only. He found a Terrence, also a Terry—both in the 415 area code. He wrote them down. He also found a Gavin. And, although he didn't refer to himself as a friend of Gilly's, he also found Big Rich's number.

He took the piece of paper he'd written down the numbers on and began comparing it to the notes from the address book.

Donny and Rich sipped at their waters and fidgeted. They shot quick, knowing glances back and forth at one another. It was getting close to copping time. They still had a little cash from the tricks they turned the night before last and it was burning a hole in their pockets. Both of them still hung onto the bottles of Vicodin they'd stolen from Gabriel's house, but neither wanted to use them; partially because they would, for the most part, be ineffective for the oncoming sickness, and partially because they were saving them as a last resort. Big Rich still had a half gram of Mexican tar crammed into the pocket of his jeans, but he didn't want to remind Donny for fear he'd have to share. He'd slip upstairs and use the bathroom at the restaurant, but he had no needles with him.

Donny whispered to him, "You still got that thing?"

Big Rich might lie to his mother, but he wouldn't lie to his friend. "Yeah."

"Don't sound so happy about it."

"There ain't much is all. You got a rig?"

"Yeah, I got two." Donny always kept a coupled stashed in the inside lining of his jacket.

Donny took a spoon from the table and slipped it to Big Rich along with the rigs. Bear pretended not to notice.

Rich waited all of ten seconds before announcing, "I gotta shit."

Bear waited until Rich had gone through the door at the back of the place that led up to the bathroom, then he said to Donny, "I don't know what to make of this shit. Yeah, I got some numbers, but I don't know what I'm supposed to do with 'em. I mean, call 'em, ask for Dustin? I don't know."

Donny shrugged and put his arms on the table. His mind was on how long it would take Rich to get out of the bathroom.

Bear looked up, "You fuckers got no shame, you know that?"

"It's a..." Donny was stuck. He felt shame, more than he had in quite some time. He wanted the biker's approval. "It's a necessity."

Bear went right on, "But then again, look what you guys do for a living, you definitely got no shame. It's in the fucking job description."

Donny was hurt, torn, half of him wanting to deny what he did, what he was, half of him yearning to be up in that bathroom right now, needle in his vein.

"You two ought to think about making some big changes in your lives. I mean, I'm not one to judge anybody, believe me, but, what you two got going, you got some bad karma coming. It ain't right. It ain't right, right on down the line. This is no way to live your life. You know this." Bear paused to see if he was getting through. He could tell he was, the kid looked like he was on the verge of tears. "You guys still haven't told me what the hell you were doing at Thaxton's last night in the first place. I gotta assume it wasn't the usual funny business—whatever it was that brought you all together in the first place."

Donny felt like he was being admonished by his junior high school principal. He slunk down in his seat, unable to drudge up anything to say. Bear was right—about all of it—he was right. The door leading to the bathroom opened behind them.

"It's in the usual spot," said Rich and he stood waiting for Donny to slide across the bench in the booth.

Big Rich sat down across from Bear. He wore a loose smile; his facial muscles were relaxed, almost drooping.

Bear said, "Feel better?"

Rich nodded his head, but didn't say anything. He wasn't big on secrets or subtlety. "You got any of that shake left?"

The house smelled like spiced beef and onions, a warm hospitable smell that reminded Thaxton he hadn't eaten since yesterday. Dustin led Gabriel past a modern kitchen, high ceilings, lots of light. Gabriel saw a young Latino man stirring something at the stove. Taco meat. He looked up from his huge frying pan and smiled as Gabriel moved past. Gabriel wasn't sure if he'd smiled back.

He felt Dustin's hand pinch him above the elbow. He was being hurried along. Dustin led him up a carpeted set of stairs and down a long hallway. It was painted white and all the doors were closed but one on the left. Dustin gave him a shove in through the open door and they stood in a bright bathroom. A skylight kept the space warm and bright. The towels were yellow and matched the rug, the sink, the toilet paper, everything. He wondered if he were being held prisoner or if he'd been taken on vacation. The thought made him smile.

"What the fuck are you grinning at?" Dustin's voice hissed; he was trying to keep it low.

"I just...it's nice, that all."

"Yeah, that's all. That's all." Dustin shut the bathroom door. "I want you to clean yourself up. Take a shower; wash some of that blood off. There's a robe right there. When you're done, come downstairs and eat."

Gabriel nodded obediently. Dustin opened the door and started to leave. Gabriel said, "Dustin?"

"What? What is it?" he responded, his tone impatient, as though he were dealing with a child.

"What day is it?"

"Saturday. Saturday morning. Now hurry up. Don't take too long up here and make me come and get you." He closed the door and left Gabriel alone.

Gabriel gazed at himself in the mirror. He had a bruised cheek and a small cut on his forehead. The sunlight warming the bathroom did him no favors. He looked old, drawn, and tired and he wanted desperately not to recognize himself, but he did. He had great difficulty pulling off his shirt, his back was sticky with the wounds he'd suffered and he could tell without turning and looking that it was mostly black and blue. He dropped his pants and saw the belt marks on his pale thighs. A body this aged shouldn't be made to endure such abuse, he thought. He turned on the shower and stepped in.

* * *

"What I need is a computer, something that'll tell me the locations of these numbers." Bear was behind the wheel and the two boys were in the same seats they occupied before. They were moving through the Mission in a zigzag pattern with no destination.

"Like one of those reverse number programs." Donny said, confident and high now, eager to be of help. "I know what you're talking about. You can put almost any number into a computer and it'll kick back where it's coming from."

"You think he's using our phones?" said Rich. "We could call the phone company maybe and ask."

Bear was scanning the storefronts, "Don't they have those Internet cafes anymore?"

"We know a guy with a computer. In the 'Loin. He'd let us come use it," Rich said

"Everybody on planet earth has a computer, kid. I need one right *now*." Bear wasn't ready to go on another adventure with these two fools quite yet. "It's been a long night. I think I need to head home and use mine there."

"Great," said Rich. "Where do you live?"

"No offense or nothin', but my place is off limits. I think it's time I drop you guys off and continue this quest on my own."

"But how am I gonna get my phone back?" said Big Rich. "I gotta have my phone. Donny needs his too, don't cha, Donny?"

Donny voiced a response from the back seat, but Rich was talking right over him. "And what about the old man? We wanna know he's okay, too."

"*Sure* you do. Tell you what, let me know how to reach you, and I'll call and tell you how things turn out."

"He's got our fuckin' phones, you can't call us. That's what I'm sayin'."

There was no way Bear was bringing these two mutts home with him. He had a rule in his house about guests. The rule was: No Guests. Especially not two heroin-addicted, speed-freak, boy whores.

Donny leaned in from the back seat and said, "We wanna help." And, in case it didn't sound sincere enough, he added, "We wanna help save him."

Bear looked in the rearview at Donny. He felt bad; he was beginning to like this kid. Too bad he was so full of shit. "Look, tell me where to drop you, I'll go home, do some recon shit, tomorrow I'll pick you up at the same spot. I'll share what I know and we'll go find this fucker who's got our friend."

Rich flopped against the back of his seat like a spoiled child, but before he could begin to whine, Donny said, "Okay, I trust you."

"Donny, what're you talkin' about? He ain't coming back. How am I gonna get my phone?"

"He'll come back," Donny's voice was calm and even. "I trust him."

"I promise you," Bear said, "I'll come back. If I make you a promise, I'm gonna keep it."

"Shit," said Big Rich. "Take us to the Tenderloin."

Bear pointed the car in the direction of downtown and they went on silently. He cracked the window and lit a smoke. He was exhausted from a night of no sleep and his eyes burned in the daylight. The boys were nullified by their drugs. No one reached for the radio, all of them lost in their thoughts.

By the time they reached Turk and Taylor, Donny had fallen into a nod, freeing his mind from the problems in front of him. But Rich was still twisting in the front seat, not wanting to let go of the pursuit of his phone, of Gabriel, of their score. Rich believed with every fiber of his being the video on his phone was his only ticket off the streets.

Bear broke the silence, "Where do you want me to drop you?"

"Next corner is good. Donny? Donny, wakeup, we're here."

Donny was awake, he wasn't asleep, not real sleep. He was only in a nod, a half dream.

As Bear pulled into a bus stop, Big Rich pressed him, "So, here, tomorrow. Right here, at the bus stop, in front of this liquor store. What time did you say again? Noon?"

"Let's make it one," said Bear. "It takes me a while to get into the city."

"One it is," said Donny from the back seat, his throat raspy from the dope.

"How do we know that you're gonna show up?"

"Shit, what your friend said, you're gonna have to trust me. Believe me, I don't wanna come here and cart you two buffoons around, but I said I would, so I will. Goddamn it, have a little faith." Bear reached across Rich's lap and opened his door for him. "Go on, I'll see you tomorrow."

Reluctantly, Rich got out of the car. Donny had already climbed out of the back and was trying to light a smoke in the wind. They watched Bear's Toyota pull away and move up Taylor Street.

"Oh shit," said Rich.

"What?" said Donny.

"He's still got the gun. The piece you took from Gilly, it's still in his car."

"He'll still have it tomorrow. What, were you planning on shootin' somebody tonight with it? C'mon, let's go get well."

"Fuck, Donny. Why'd you have to agree with that fucker? You know he's never coming back right? We're fucked. The phone is gone; we'll probably never see Gabriel again. The plan is fucked."

Donny looked down at the dirty sidewalk beneath his feet. "It's not fucked."

"It's fucked all right. Now what do we do? You got any money to get us through tonight? You wanna go back to that fucking corner?"

"I got a little left."

"A little. That's what I got too. Fuck, we're gonna have to go down to the corner and work for it now."

"Not now," said Donny. "Not yet. Let's go upstairs and do a hit first."

On this point there was no discussion. They'd finish what they had, call the man, do some more, then hit the corner. They were back on the wheel, in the groove, in the rut.

CHAPTER 13

Gabriel Thaxton stood in the shower, waiting to drip dry. He'd tried the towel, but it was too painful on his back, so he stood waiting. He noticed the water snaking into the drain was light pink. Christ, he thought, what have I done to deserve this?

The sunlight in the bathroom hadn't shifted, but he knew he'd been in there a long time. He was surprised that Dustin hadn't come upstairs and hurried him along. He heard muffled voices coming from the direction of downstairs, the way he'd come in, so he knew he wasn't alone. More voices than just Dustin's and the man he'd introduced him to. Then he remembered the cook, if that's what he was, and thought maybe his was the other voice. To Gabriel though, it sounded like a party. There was the soft thump of music, too, just the beat; no way to tell what kind of music. It blended with the voices and the sound made Gabriel feel like he'd just as soon stay in the bathroom forever.

He began to chill so he stepped out of the stall and started to put on his dirty clothes. The white robe was too pristine to wear, not with his cuts and sores; it would be ruined. He picked up his dress shirt, one of his favorites. It was crusted along the inside and dried puss scraped his shower-softened wounds as he put it on. He slowly finished dressing, underwear, pants, socks, shoes. When he was done, he sat on the toilet seat with his head in his hands.

The music stopped, only for a minute. Then he heard footsteps coming up the stairs, down the hall, toward him. The door flew open.

"What the fuck are you doing up here? What the fuck is

121

taking you so long? Why are you sitting there like a scared little baby?"

Gabriel couldn't answer. He looked up at Dustin's face; it was knotted and snarling. Gabriel felt a whole new wave of exhaustion pass over him.

"We're guests here, Gabe. You're being rude. You get the fuck downstairs and be nice. You got five minutes to get down there or I'm coming up here and sticking that hairbrush straight up your ass." Dustin pointed to a rather large antique silver hairbrush.

Gabriel looked at the hairbrush and nodded.

The music got louder as he walked down the stairs. At first he thought it was disco, but now could hear it was some sort of Latin hybrid, something you'd hear at a nightclub when you knew it was time to go. He moved toward the voices and music that were coming from the kitchen.

"Well, look who decided to join us," the cowboy said. The hat was off now, but he still looked like a cowboy.

"Hello," said Gabriel. He hated hearing the meekness in his own voice.

"Hungry? I think the meat is still warm. Raphael?" he said, turning his attention to the young Latino helper, "See if that meat is still hot. Get Mr. Thaxton a plate."

Gabriel looked at the counter where they were sitting, a high marble island with tall stools lined around it. There were three plates of food already set out. They looked like they had barely been touched. Three beers sat in tall, thin glasses and, beyond that, a square silver piece of mirror with several lines of white powder cut into neat little rows.

The man, his host, noticed Gabriel eyeing the drugs and said, "You want some blow?"

Gabriel thought for a moment about the numbing anesthetic effect of cocaine and wished he could pour it over the burns on his back. "No," he said.

"You like a taco? You want avocado? Let me make one for you. You like cilantro? Maybe just a little bit? Give me one minute, I fix you a plate," said Raphael. The young man was full of life, energy, and, now Gabriel was noticing, very good looking.

"Sit down, sit down, Gabriel," the cowboy was saying, "Let me pour you a nice cold beer."

"I'm sorry, I don't mean to be rude, but I've forgotten your name already."

The man was pulling a beer from the fridge and popping off the cap. He turned to Gabriel and said, "I'm sorry, we rushed you in here, we didn't get a chance to say anything but hello. I'm Terrence Halford. You can call me Terry. This is my place, my palace. Make yourself at home." Then to Raphael, "*Me casa, su casa*, eh, Raphael?"

"That's right," Raphael sang back to him, gyrating his hips to the beat while he fussed over Gabriel's taco plate.

Halford, thought Gabriel, I know that name. He watched the man pick up a straw and bend over the mirror to inhale a stout line of the blow.

"I know who you are," said Gabriel, the fog clearing. "You're an attorney."

Terrence straightened up, his face tight from the coke, and smiled. "Used to be. Not anymore."

Gabriel saw in his grin that his teeth were perfect and white. They were false.

Bear had come home, didn't bother to lock the front door, and splayed himself out on the couch. He slept for five fitful hours until he was woken up by his phone. He reached for his pocket before remembering that his cell was gone. It was the home phone that was ringing. He let it ring. After about three more minutes, it started ringing again. This time Bear got up to answer.

"Hello," he said, although he wasn't sure if his voice made any noise.

"Hello?" said the voice on the other end. "Hello?"

He tried again. "Yeah, hello."

"Bear? I'm so sorry to bother you at home. It sounds like I woke you up."

He recognized the voice immediately. It was Thaxton's secretary, Beatrice.

"Bean, that you? You didn't wake me; I was just, uh, napping. What's up?"

"Bear, I didn't want to call you, but I don't know what else to do. You were Mr. Thaxton's last appointment on Friday. I haven't seen him since. He hasn't been answering his calls. I just don't know what to do."

"Appointment? That was last Friday—a week ago. He hasn't been into the office since then?"

"No. He's called on the phone a few times, but he hasn't made any of his meetings. He had me cancel everything. I know sometimes he keeps a funny schedule, but Mr. Spreckle is quite concerned and I'm starting to worry now, too. Have you heard from him?"

She was trying to sound composed, but Bear could hear the shaking in her larynx; she was scared. He wondered if she'd had a few drinks to get up the courage to call.

"Only once," he said.

"Is he okay? Is he sick?"

"Bean, why don't you give me a day to try to reach him. Let me poke around and see what I can find, then I'll give you a call."

"Thank you, Bear. I really would appreciate anything you can do. Let me give you my cell number. If you find out anything, please, call me right away. Even if it's late, please call."

She recited the number and Bear scratched it down on a piece of paper stuck under a magnet on the fridge.

"Bean?"

"Yes, Bear."

"When you finally gave me your number, I was hoping it'd be under different circumstances."

She didn't appreciate the flirt, but her voice softened just a little. Bear felt stupid the moment the comment left his lips.

"Seriously," she said, "if you find out anything, call."

They said goodbye and hung up. He was awake now; time to get to work. He pulled the most prominent numbers he'd collected from Dustin's notebook and sat down in front of his computer. He started to pump the phone numbers from the top of his list into the search engine. He then focused on the numbers that were cross referenced with the ones from Gilly's phone. The calls made and received. The sites weren't being very helpful. The information they gave was barebones. Once the number was fed in, it spat back an inaccurate blip on a map of San Francisco—and they were all San Francisco numbers. That was about it, all it would tell him. He could have figured that out on his own. Bear stopped and lit a Camel. He sat back in his chair and tried to think back on exactly what Gilly had said. Two names: Terrence and Gavin. Something about an attorney. The bitch at the door mentioned an old guy, but he assumed that meant Thaxton. Christ, he couldn't imagine Thaxton being dragged through that shooting gallery. If it was him, the old fucker had to be under duress to even sit down in that shit hole. Bear checked the numbers taken from the phone. No Gavin, one Terrence, one Terry. Terry L. He typed in Terrence's number. No result. Then he put in Terry L's number into the computer. It had a 415 area code, but it came back as a Marin location. Southern Marin. He knew these things didn't pinpoint exactly where a private number came from, but he knew from experience it was roughly accurate. Marin. His neck of the woods.

Who was this Terry L? He had to be a scumbag; otherwise his number wouldn't be sitting in this punk's phone and Dustin's little black book. Bear smoked and wondered who would know such a person in Marin. He decided the best place for him to find out would be the Roadhouse. If there was any information to be had, he could get it there. If there wasn't, well, then he'd spend a little time with Sheila, have a few beers, and forget about this shit for a minute or two.

Big Rich and Donny had gone back to Rich's hotel room. The boys first did their hits—what was left in Rich's pockets—and smoked a bit of the raw, soapy speed that Rich seemed to have an endless supply of, and then decided to call Jose to cop. Jose was the best deal for what cash they had left. They wandered the nearby Tenderloin streets trying to find a payphone, cursing Dustin the whole way for stealing their cells. By the time they were done, it was nearly eight o'clock. They were good and high, but out of money and out of drugs, save for the few Vicodins they'd lifted from Gabriel's house.

"We better start thinking about what we're gonna do," said Donny.

"What'd ya mean, what're we gonna do?"

"I'm out, you're out, right? We gotta have it together tomorrow when Bear is picking us up. We got to make sure we're well. What if we end up on some wild goose chase? I don't wanna be gettin' sick half-way through."

"What the fuck else we gonna do, Donny? We gotta go down to the corner to find some money."

"One last time."

"Right, one last time." Rich's tone was thick with sarcasm.

"I been thinking. What'll that old man give us for saving his ass? We rescue him from that freak, gotta be worth something."

"That's what that biker is thinking, too."

"I know, I know," said Donny, "but there's enough to go around. He gives us a sweet reward; we wait a few weeks, then hit him with the video."

"*If* I get my phone back. No phone, no video: no point."

Donny looked at Rich, wondering why he was being so snide. His tone had changed; he kept shooting down everything Donny said. Rich seemed, for the first time, resigned to giving up on their plan.

"You don't think Bear's gonna show tomorrow, do you?"

"I'm just sayin', don't be surprised if he don't. I mean, why would he?"

"Because he said he would."

"Jesus, Donny, maybe you should see if that biker's got any dough. You can go suck his dick tonight, let him be your Daddy."

Donny let the comment hang in the air. He wasn't sure how to respond. He hated Rich for his cynicism, for his instinctual inability to trust anyone. He didn't want to end up that way, with that black hole for a heart. He looked around the room—the dirty spoon, the dirty floor—at anything but Big Rich. He lit a cigarette, got up, and went to the window. It looked cold outside, windy. Scraps of garbage were blowing down Eddy Street.

Big Rich softened his tone, "C'mon," he said. "The sooner we get down there, the sooner we get back. We'll cop, get higher'n fuck. Everything'll be alright."

"One last time," said Donny. It didn't even sound like *he* believed it now.

CHAPTER 14

"It's fuckin' freezing out here. I can't even light a goddamn smoke," said Donny. They both were bent forward, pointing themselves into the wind. "I don't think anybody's gonna be out here. It's too cold."

"What do ya mean? It's warm in their cars. Rain, wind, fucking earthquakes, there'll always be someone out there buying it or selling it. It's the way of the world. People have needs. It's like when stock people sell the stuff that people need, you know, what do they call that stuff, that people have to have?"

"I dunno," said Donny, still trying to light his cigarette and walk at the same time.

"Yeah, you do. You know, like orange juice and coffee and shit."

"Oh, you mean commodities."

"Yeah, sex is like a commodity. People are gonna buy and sell it till the end of time."

"Shit, if that was the case, we shoulda bought stock."

Rich laughed. Despite the weather, the situation with their phones, the lack of money or drugs in their pockets, they both felt pretty good. Being good and high probably had something to do with it.

"Fuck, Donny, how do you know all this shit? You know about stock shit and school shit. Maybe Skye was right; you're too smart to be out here doing this stuff."

"Skye said that?"

"Yeah, that's what he told me. You're smarter than you act. Maybe you grew up rich or somethin'."

"Fuckin' Skye is the one that thinks he's too smart to be out here."

"True," said Big Rich, "but he'd be wrong 'bout that. He ain't even smart *enough*. And that's sayin' something."

They both laughed about that.

Rich decided he wanted a cigarette too, so they both stepped into a doorjamb to light up. When they were sheltered from the wind, Rich said, "Hey, I been thinkin', maybe we should check out that name the biker told us. Dustin whatever it was. Maybe look him up on the Internet like he did and find out what we're dealing with."

Donny took it as an apology for doubting him earlier. An acceptance of the fact they were going to show up for the meet and wait for Bear no matter what happened. They both wanted to push forward with the plan. They were a team now, a team with a goal: to get the hell off that corner.

"Good idea," said Donny, "Knowledge is power. We can ask Skye if he's up there tonight. Maybe we can go by later and use his computer. Smoke a little crank with the poor fucker. It'd make him feel good, like he had friends."

"He'd have more friends if he was the one paying for the drugs he always smoked."

"He's alright. He's just a weird little kid. He's like a nerd or somethin', but instead of being in the math club, he's out here on the street with the rest of us. You know they say there're book smarts and street smarts? Well, Skye's got book smarts, and he ain't equipped to deal with the world, you know?"

"Whatever, I doubt he's got any smarts, I think he might be part retarded."

Donny decided to let it drop. "He might be that, too."

They reached the corner and, sure enough, there were johns cruising and boys hustling. It was business as usual. "Fucking God, please, let this be the last time," said Donny to himself. He didn't have the will tonight. He was high, but maybe not numb enough.

They were out there about ten minutes, leaning against the wall with one leg up, trying to look both casual and bored while the wind whipped around them, when they saw a familiar face coming up the block. It was Jerry, one of kids that came to the corner around the same time as Donny started showing up. His name was Jerry, but everyone out there called him Cherry because his story was he'd never turned tricks before. That's what he told his johns. He figured that's what they wanted to hear, just an innocent boy who needed some money and, no, he'd never let a man do this and that to him before. Rich and Donny joked that the ruse wouldn't last, he'd be too worn out to sell it, but Cherry kept at it, a virgin re-born every night.

Cherry was out of breath, "Hey, you guys hear about Skye?"

Rich said, "We were just talking about that little dumbass. You seen him tonight? I wanna talk to him about somethin'."

"No, dude, I won't see him either. You really didn't hear?"

"Hear what?" said Donny.

"He's dead."

"Bullshit," said Big Rich, instinctively not believing any kind of story that originated with Skye, especially if it was coming out of Cherry's mouth.

Donny thought different. The first thing that came to his mind was, yes, of course he was dead. Because we were just talking about him, like their thoughts had the ability to curse anything and everything. Then he thought, damn it, he's been murdered. Struck down by one of these sick-assed motherfuckers who are cruising the corner right now, some psycho serial killer preying on young men. He'd always known it was possible—even probable—with the kind of lives they were leading. Hell, in some ways, he thought they were taunting death, temping killers to do them in. What did they expect?

"How?" said Donny, wishing he hadn't as soon as he'd asked.

"He OD'ed," said Cherry. "They found him in his hotel room the night before last, sitting in front of the computer, you know, like he does. Didn't even take the needle out of his arm."

Donny didn't know why it surprised him. It made more sense than murder. He wondered if he actually sighed with relief, if it was audible. He felt bad for Skye and could imagine him sitting right there in the chair he'd dragged off the street, his skin grey, staring at the blue computer screen. He was a statistic now, not so much a victim. He now felt a kinship with Skye that he never could have felt when the boy was alive.

"Poor fuckin' kid," he said.

Big Rich's reaction was different. He said, "Poor? At least he could afford enough dope to off himself." Rich was callous, but it struck Donny as bravado. Donny could tell Rich was processing the news, trying to think what it meant to him, if Skye owed him anything or if there was something in Skye's hotel room that Rich could use. Big Rich finally said, "I wonder where he got his dope from. Musta been good shit."

After recognizing Terrence, Gabriel pieced together some of the cowboy's story in his mind. Terrence had been a defense attorney, just like Gabriel, but he was disbarred under a dark cloud in the late nineties. Gabriel recalled that Terrence Halford was somewhat of a rising star, but didn't know the exact nature of his downfall. It happened at the same time Gabriel was having his own troubles, having invested a good portion of the firm's profits in some dot-com

startups that failed miserably. Embarrassed by his misjudge-
ment, Thaxton had insulated himself from the news and
gossip that floated around the legal scene, the insulated gaggle
of high priced lawyers that fed on bad news. Gabriel did,
however, remember rumors of drugs, of money laundering,
but couldn't recall what the details were.

"You had a practice in San Francisco, no?" asked Gabriel
after he finally accepted a cocktail, a margarita expertly
blended by Raphael.

"I had more than that," said Terrence leaning into the
mirror for another line of blow. "I had a whole career, a
future."

"What happened?" said Gabriel.

"I got fucked, that's what happened." Terrence sucked in
one of the white lines through a short straw. "The State Bar
had it in for me, didn't like some of the friends I was
making." He pinched his nose, then sniffed hard again. "They
didn't like the money I was making. But, shit, that was a
million years ago. I'm over it, moved on."

Gabriel took that to mean the subject was closed. He
sipped his margarita and tried to act as though all of this were
normal. A nice, late luncheon with his captors. Perfectly
normal.

The lunch turned into dinner, and, then, a kind of dinner
party. The mood was deliberately light. It barely masked the
underlying conspiracy. Terrence and Dustin had plans for
Gabriel, but they weren't discussing them. Something, Gabriel
surmised, was keeping them from moving forward. Dustin
kept quiet, drinking his beer and accepting a line of coke
whenever it was offered. Coke wasn't really Dustin's thing,
but he wasn't one to turn down free drugs, especially of the
stimulant variety.

The afternoon wore on to early evening. The drinks kept
flowing and Gabriel started to catch a buzz. Over and over,
Terrence would offer him a line of cocaine, but Gabriel

refused. "I'm too old for that stuff now," he said, acting almost flattered. "Maybe there was a time, but it's gone past."

Raphael said, "See, Terry, we should have asked him sooner."

"He doesn't mean today, silly boy. He means earlier in...he means he's too old, that's all."

Raphael said in that same sing song voice, "You're only as young as you feel." And he, too, bent over for another hit from the mirror. He moved around the kitchen, light on his feet, playing host and making sure everyone's plates were filled. No one, however, was doing much eating. The only thing being devoured was the pile of cocaine on the mirror and Terrence saw to it that it was replenished every hour or so.

Gabriel tried to take on some nourishment to regain his strength, but his teeth and jaw were sore from one of the many smacks that Dustin had given him the night before. The blended ice drinks, on the other hand, felt nice and soothing in his mouth. He sipped at his drink and tried to relax, knowing that the pleasantries weren't going to last forever. Every once in a while, Dustin would give Terrence a blank, expectant look and Terrence would shrug his shoulders before carrying on with whatever he was doing. They were waiting for something.

It was dusk now and the weather had cooled. Raphael suggested they go outside to smoke their cigarettes and have more cocktails. Without waiting for an answer, he opened up the glass doors leading out to a large wooden deck and turned up the music so it could be heard outside. All four of them grabbed their drinks and headed outside to the patio.

It was still warm and the house sheltered the deck from the wind blowing up from the direction of the ocean. With the drinks, the music, the cheerful company, Gabriel felt again that it was almost like a vacation; except for the pain from the torturous night before and the unavoidable truth that he was being held hostage.

Raphael was going on about his margaritas. "No salt. Real margarita is no salt; that is for the tourists. And you have to make it from scratch, no mixers." He poked a finger toward his mouth and feigned vomiting. "That stuff makes you sick. In fact, it is best when there is no blenders either, just ice cubes. That is the way God would want his margarita." He paused to sip. "Dustin, you are so quiet, you like me to make you a margarita? I can make it real strong, some kick, you know."

Dustin shook his head and got up from the lounge chair. "No, I'm gonna piss and grab another beer."

He ambled through the sliding glass door into the house. Raphael waited till he was inside. "I think he no like the cocaine. It make him nervous."

Gabriel noted that with every margarita that Raphael drank, his accent became thicker and his manner more effeminate. Clearly, he had a good buzz on now; he talked and talked and talked. "Maybe I go help him. See if he wants something stronger." Raphael followed Dustin into the house to flirt with him.

"How's your cocktail, Gabriel?" Terrence asked. He was leaning on the wood rail with his elbows, beer in hand. Still keeping up that cowboy pose, thought Gabriel.

"Fine, fine. Delicious."

"Did you get enough to eat?"

"Yes, I'm fine."

"Good. That Raphael is one helluva cook when he wants to be, but when he's had a few, his mind...wanders. I don't want you to go hungry, a victim of a poor host."

Terrence laughed, but it wasn't a funny joke. An awkward silence fell upon them. The music inside thumped away and Gabriel looked in to see Dustin and Raphael hovering over the mirror on the counter, doing more lines.

"No, you have a beautiful home. It's been a great evening," said Gabriel. "I'm just wondering..." Gabriel's voice trailed off.

Terrence smiled with his too perfect white teeth. "What you're doing here? What the plan is?"

"Yes," said Gabriel, still keeping an eye on Dustin, hoping he wouldn't come back outside before he got his answer.

"Tonight, you're my guest. Enjoy yourself. Try to relax. I know that hanging out with Dustin can be a, well, a *trying* experience. Try to unwind here, get some rest. I've got plenty of room upstairs, don't worry about anything."

"And tomorrow?"

"Tomorrow we have a bit of business to attend to. Dustin wanted me to help him navigate a few things. Don't trouble yourself about it. Have another drink."

There were still diners at the tables when Bear walked into the Roadhouse. The nighttime crowd—the drinking crowd—had yet to filter in. He only nodded to the hostess, mostly because he'd forgotten her name, and walked straight up to the bar. He loved that bar; dark antique carved mahogany, a mirrored back with recessed lighting, a brass rail, it made Bear think of the old time saloons he saw in the movies. He'd logged in enough time there to know the polished-over scratches and scrapes intimately. He'd even made a few of them himself.

He didn't even find a stool before the bartender, Richie, spotted him and said, "Hey, Bear, what's it been, like, a week? Sheila will be glad you showed up. She's been wonderin' where you been." Roadhouse Richie was a veteran bartender and worked the daytime and dinner shift. When he was done, the night crew came on, usually Sheila and Donna trading off duties behind the bar and working the tables. Without being asked, Richie the bartender pulled a long-neck

Budweiser from the cooler, popped the top, and set it on a cocktail napkin in front of Bear.

"Ah, just what the Doctor ordered." Bear took a long satisfying pull.

"What kind of doctor is giving those orders? That's what I'd like to know."

"Shit, Doctor Zhivago? Doctor Seuss, maybe?"

"I wouldn't be takin' medical advice from anyone who prescribes green eggs and ham, if I were you."

Bear said, "Speaking of doctors, you seen old Watson around lately?"

"Not tonight. Not yet. But it's still early; he'll probably be in a little later on. You want anything else, Bear? A shot maybe?"

"You know, that's a prescription I'm gonna take. Sneak me some of the good stuff, will ya?"

The bartender smiled and spun a shot glass in front of Bear and filled it to the brim with Jameson and knocked on the bar before walking away. Bear took a small sip and let it burn his tongue for a moment. Nothing tastes better than a free drink, thought Bear, and he tossed down a fiver for a tip.

He turned and surveyed the place. The white tablecloths would soon be removed from the booths as each group of diners finished. You could still order food, but the dinner service was over. Busboys clanked away silverware and plates and the piped-in music was replaced with the sound of the jukebox. Regular patrons trickled in and took their stools at the bar. For Marin County, it was a rough crowd. In a place that was known for left-leaning affluent yuppies, this was as rough as it got. This was the old guard, a throwback to the earlier days—or at least they thought so. Bear recognized most of them and nodded hello to a few. He was one of them, in a way. He fit in well with the aging hippies, the old ex-whatevers—drug addicts, bikers, rock stars, stock traders. Everybody used to be something; everybody had a story to tell. One thing for sure, they were all survivors. In Marin, you had to have come out of your tribulations okay, otherwise the county wouldn't have you; it'd spit you out like stale tobacco.

Bear was well-liked because his story had some resonance. Getting close to Bear made them feel like their own exaggerated tales had some authenticity. Bear was the real deal and respected for it.

A country and western song came on the jukebox. It was new country, the kind Bear hated, but it still made him feel like drinking. He waved over Roadhouse Richie and ordered another round. Richie complied, poured the shot, and, like a good bartender, waved the charge. Bear threw down another five and lifted the Jameson to his lips.

Roadhouse Richie pulled the bar towel from his belt and told Bear, "I'm about done with this shit; I'm ready for one myself. Your girl shoulda been here by now, I need some relief."

"She's not my girl; she's what you call 'her own woman.'" Bear tipped back the rest of his shot. "What time is it, anyway?"

On the corner, Big Rich had found a trick almost immediately. A cherry-red Lexus pulled up, waved him over, and he was gone. From the passenger seat he signaled to Donny that he'd be back in half an hour. Donny nodded and settled into a doorjamb to hide from the wind.

It was crowded out there for a Saturday night. All the boys were working. So much competition made the prospects of making money slow down. There was Cherry, Omar, Little Darren, Orlando, Stevie, Tyrell—all of them. Donny lit a cigarette and settled in to let the herd thin. He was tired, fried from speed, and didn't feel much like being there in the first place. If he could wait it out, sit in that doorway till Big Rich came back, maybe he wouldn't have to turn a trick. If Rich came back with enough money for the both of them, he'd be spared this one last time.

Donny watched a new kid, a boy he really didn't know, Travis or Tavis or something like that, climb into a white GMC van. It was an older model with no windows. It reminded Donny a bit of the kind the city used to pick up dead bodies when the police were done. The meat wagons, Rich called them. The kid got in without even negotiating. Donny would never have done that—too risky. These new kids were dumb.

Cherry saw Donny smoking and asked him for a cigarette. "I'm still trippin' on what happened to Skye."

Donny didn't say anything; he only reached for his pack of Marlboros and shook one out.

"I mean," Cherry said, "he didn't deserve that."

"Deserve what?"

"To go out that way. Shit, Donny, I thought you were his friend."

"I am...I was. But the guy overdosed. He didn't get murdered, for fuck's sake. Nobody did that to him. He did it himself." Donny heard how harsh his words sounded as soon as they left his lips, felt like an asshole for saying them. Cherry was getting on his nerves, just like Skye had. "What do you expect? What we do, the drugs we're doing. This is what happens, dude. People die."

Cherry looked hurt. He took the cigarette and tried to light it a couple of times before Donny rolled his eyes and cupped his hands over his own lighter so Cherry could get the thing lit. Cherry stood there smoking, looking out at the street, not knowing what to say.

Finally, Donny said, "I'm sorry, man. I'm just, like, messed up. I'm bummed he's gone, too."

Cherry nodded and took a long thoughtful drag from the smoke and said, "We all deal with our grief in our own ways." It was something he'd heard somewhere else and memorized.

"Yeah," said Donny.

A large truck pulled up. Not quite a semi, but a moving or delivery truck. Cherry waved to the driver and climbed up the step on the passenger side. After a few moments of barter, he climbed into the cab and was gone. That left Donny alone again. He wondered about the time. He wished again he had his cell phone to know what time it actually was. He tried to guess by the light, but it was dark now and the low clouds and fog had left the sky flat and black.

At the bar, Bear repositioned himself so he could watch the door. When Sheila finally came through the doors, he smiled at her, getting a big, red lipstick grin right back.

"You're here a little early," she said.

She was a beauty. A big girl by other people's standards, but what Bear considered just right for himself. He liked his women strong, purposeful, with some flesh on their bones. Wispy, frail girls who constantly fretted over their calorie intake were never his thing. Meaty is how he referred to Sheila when she was out of earshot, but to her face he only called her sexy—'cause that's what she was. She was over forty, divorced, and well past playing the games of love. She was perfect for him.

"I got here early to see you. I missed you, baby."

"Bullshit," said Sheila, "looks like you were just thirsty."

"You didn't know? They sell this stuff in stores now. I could drink this shit at home, but without," he looked her up and down, "the scenery."

She pinched his cheek. "Well, look while you can, it's probably all you're gonna be able to do. I'm late and I gotta get behind the bar." She wiggled away with a walk she only walked when she knew Bear was watching.

Bear turned back to his drink. "Get to it, I need a refill." He waited until she was around the bar and had looped a towel into her belt before signaling for another drink. She popped another longneck and brought along the Jameson.

"Sorry about that latenight call last night."

"No problem," said Sheila, leaning in. "We're a full service operation. You ever find him?"

"Yeah, I found him, but I need to find him again. I thought he might be in tonight."

"Like every night. He'll be in—till closing. You only missed him by about an hour last night. We usually have to kick his ass out of here." Someone was waving Sheila over from the other end of the bar. Before she moved she said, "Scenery, huh? Bear, you're such a bullshitter."

He watched her move down the bar. He loved to watch her work. She'd spin her own homegrown Mae West act on these Marin County types and they'd eat it up and throw the tips down. Hell, it's what pulled him into the Roadhouse for their overpriced drinks in the first place. Watching her, for a brief moment, he'd forgotten all about the reason he was here. Buzzed from the shots, tired from last night, nothing seemed more appealing than sitting on the same barstool till closing time and following Sheila home like a puppy and passing out in her bed.

Then he heard the voice. That high cackle that always sounded like it was trying too hard to have fun. Doctor Johnny Watson. Bear turned on his stool to see Watson and a younger man coming in together through the glass door at the front of the bar, Watson with his trademark silver cane in his right hand. Bear was never sure whether he needed that cane, or if he just used it as an affectation, some sort of symbol of sophistication, like he had a past worth knowing about. It was silver, like his hair, and looked ornate, antique. Bear figured it was a garage sale find. Watson nodded to Sheila, but missed Bear's presence entirely. He worked his way through the bar, saying quick hellos to those that knew him, and plopped himself down in his favorite booth, ready to hold court. Bear waited until he'd sent his young friend to the bar for drinks before he got himself up and walked over to the table.

"Doctor Watson, how's tricks?"

Watson looked up and saw Bear looming over him and smiled. He had a pencil-thin mustache that was as silver as his cane and the hair on his head. "It's still early, most of 'em are still up my sleeve."

Bear slid into the booth across from him and forced a smile to greet Watson's.

"You ever find that fella you were asking me about last night?"

"Sure, sure," Bear nodded. "I'm wondering if you could maybe help me out with another favor."

"Another? Bear, my good man, I won't discuss favors without a drink in my hand." Watson was acting regal, pompous, very over the top for a guy who'd lived on a houseboat in Sausalito for the past decade. Bear figured that he was high and overconfident, being on his own turf, enjoying the accolades from the other patrons that bought into his whole mysterious stranger bit. Bear knew him well enough to know there was no mystery. It was annoying as hell. Bear sat back and waited for Watson's friend to return with the drinks. When the guy came back, Bear realized he'd recognized him, a wormy little guy that did petty crimes, mostly drug rip offs, in and around Southern Marin. The guy was a scumbag, but then again, so was Watson. The Doctor was just a scumbag in sheep's clothing.

"Bear, this is Rivas. Rivas, meet Bear. He's an old friend of mine from the good ol' days, my heydays. Yours, too, huh, Bear?"

"I dunno," said Bear, ignoring Rivas's outstretched hand, "I like to think that my best days are ahead of me."

CHAPTER 15

The half hour came and went. No sign of Big Rich. The other boys had gone and come back. Donny was starting to think he was going be stranded for the night with no junk. He pulled himself off the wall and stood a little closer to the curb.

He hadn't even finished his cigarette when a sleek Mazda pulled up. Maybe it was one of those new Hyundais, or an Acura, he didn't know. Donny was never that good at telling those Japanese imports apart. The driver rolled down the passenger window and Donny smelled the faint odor of marijuana. Not his favorite drug, but it meant the guy probably wasn't a cop.

"How ya doin'?" said Donny.

"I'm awesome. How 'bout you, sweetie."

"I'm alright. You lookin' to party?"

"Party? Yeah, I'm lookin' to party. Hop in."

"Two hundred."

"Two hundred? For what?"

"For everything," Donny said.

The guy looked at his steering wheel and drummed his fingers for a moment, "How about one-fifty?"

Donny opened the door and climbed in.

"You got a place?" the guy asked.

"I know a place," said Donny. "But it'll cost you extra. They rent rooms same as anybody else."

The guy shrugged and said, "I got a place. The place where I'm staying at. We'll go there, no problem."

When he spoke, Donny could smell the alcohol on his breath. Alcohol mixed with mints. The guy wasn't much older than Donny, it seemed. They pulled away from the curb and the guy turned up the volume on his radio. Some club music filled the car with its noxious beat. Under his breath, Donny said, *one last time.*

"I'm at the Travel Lodge on Market," the guy said.

"The one on Polk is closer," said Donny.

"Yeah, but I already have a room at the one on Market. I got some drinks and stuff there, we can relax."

"What kind of stuff?" asked Donny, hoping for party favors.

The guy did his best to give him a flirtatious look, "You'll just have to wait and see, won't you?"

Donny cracked the window so some fresh air would dilute the smell of weed and booze. Somewhere in the car the guy must have had one of those pine tree deodorizers, too, because the smell was making Donny feel sick.

They drove down Polk Street, the beat to that song never ending, the guy nodding his head in time, trying to look cool. He looked out the window for other hustlers and then would look Donny over.

"You mind if I smoke?" said Donny.

"Go ahead. It's a party."

Donny wondered how much cash this asshole had on him.

They got to the motel before the song ended. Donny figured that song was never going to end. The Travel Lodge was a big open-faced building, three stories tall, with the motel doors all facing the parking lot. The guy climbed out first and pointed to an orange door on the second floor. "Two-thirty-seven, the stairs are over there, c'mon."

Donny knew where the stairs were; he'd been at this motel dozens of times. It was a partying place. Not just for sex workers, but for teenagers, cheaters, drug fiends—anybody that could afford a room. The guy walked ahead of Donny. Donny watched him still nodding his head to the rhythm of the song from the car. He looked at his clothes, his shoes, for signs of wealth. New, but not expensive. Nothing special, just another john.

The room was dark and musty. The guy flicked on a light and then the TV. He picked up a roach from the ashtray and lit it. "You want some?"

Donny shrugged and waited for the guy to finish his hit, then took the roach and took a deep pull. It was good green weed, but not what Donny had in mind.

"You got anything stronger?"

"Look at you, mister anxious." The guy giggled as he took back the roach. "I got some drinks, some vodka and OJ?"

"I meant to smoke."

"Maybe we should get started first."

"Yeah, okay," said Donny. "You got the one-fifty?"

The guy smiled, took out his wallet, and laid three fifty dollar bills on the dresser.

"How's that? There you go. I don't even know your name."

"Donny."

"I'm John," he said with that same stupid grin pasted on his face. Donny wasn't sure if the name was supposed to be a joke, or what. The guy kept on grinning at him. Donny wanted to move things along.

"What d'you, you know, what d'you like?"

"I like *you*, Donny. I like cock. I like sex. I like to party, have a good time. Don't you?"

"Yeah, sure." Donny wasn't sure what this guy's game was, but something wasn't right. He looked over at the cash on the dresser. "Lemme just grab this and we can get started."

The guy grinned that same creepy grin and watched Donny move across the room to the dresser. He massaged his cock through his jeans.

Donny took the bills and stuffed them into his pocket.

"You smoke rock?" the guy said, left hand still at his crotch, the right holding the joint.

"No, no so much. Not anymore. Speed is more my thing."

"I don't have any of that shit. I got rock, you want some?"

Donny sighed. "Sure."

"Sit down, take your jacket off. Relax, get comfortable. I'll get my stem."

Donny took off his denim jacket and sat down on the edge of the bed while the guy disappeared into the bathroom. He stared at his hands. Smoking crack was going to make him feel worse. He knew it was a mistake every time he smoked it, yet whenever he got another chance, he'd make the mistake again. He wondered why he was unable to say no. He felt weak, stupid for being there in the first place. The guy was still in the bathroom, probably taking that first hit himself. He thought about running out the door.

The next thing he felt was something around his neck. Tight, pulling, strangling. He was pulled backward onto the bed by the cord, or rope, or whatever it was. He could see the guy above him now, upside down, his eyes were lit up, but he was still grinning. He was holding Donny down with whatever he had around his neck.

He heard the guy say, *Hold still you fucking faggot*, before he got hit. White pain right from the top of his head. The guy must have kneed him. He couldn't get any air. The guy was now holding him down by the throat with one hand and punching him in the temple with the other. Donny wondered for a second if he was going to die, then he saw a glint of light—silver light. It was a huge carving knife. The guy held it before his eyes before Donny felt it poking under his chin.

"Roll over, or I'll stick this fucking knife into your skull."

Donny felt weak, dizzy from the lack of oxygen and the blows to his head. He felt a small trickle of warm blood dribble down from his chin to his neck. He rolled over.

The guy grabbed Donny's right arm and twisted it behind his back, the way the police do. Donny felt both of the guy's knees pressing down on the middle of his back.

"Gimme your other hand, fucker," the guy said.

Donny felt the blade poking right underneath his shoulder blade. He couldn't tell if it had punctured his skin or not. His hands were now pinned by the knees that pushed down on him. Donny felt his wrists being wrapped together with something, then being cinched tight. Donny moaned, "What are you doing?" and was answered with two more blows to the back of his head.

Roped tight and face down on the bed, Donny wished he would lose consciousness. He felt his pants being pulled off. Then, he felt the same material binding his ankles before he felt the man's knees in his back again.

"Do you know what this is, motherfucker?" The guy pulled Donny's head up by the hair. "You see this?"

It was a gun. A black semi-automatic, inches from Donny's nose. Donny couldn't tell what kind, what caliber. It looked shiny, wet. He could make out the words *Beretta U.S.A. Corp* along the barrel. He could smell the metal, but something else, too. *Lube.* The end of the barrel was covered in lube. Donny squeezed his eyes shut.

"Don't you fuckin' move. You move and I'll cap your ass. I'll fuckin' shoot you like it was nothing."

"Please..."

"Shut the fuck up."

He felt the guy's weight move off of him. Donny hoped it was over, hoped that maybe the guy was only robbing him. Except Donny had nothing to steal.

"You move, or scream, or anything, this gun is going off. All I gotta do is pull the trigger, no one's gonna hear shit, 'cause you're the silencer, you understand?"

Donny didn't understand, but he moved his head anyway, nodding his chin into the bedspread. Next, he felt the guy's hands pulling at his ass. Then, the gun. The awkward barrel shoved right into his rectum. Blunt and cold. Donny moaned in pain.

"You like this shit, don't you, you little bitch." The guy was pushing the barrel of the gun in hard, pulling it back a little, then pushing it back in. "I got my finger on the trigger, faggot, don't fuckin' move or it's going off."

The pain was incredible. He felt the front sight on the barrel, the small metal wedge, tearing the inside of his anus. He wanted to cry out, but instead bit onto his lip and pushed his face into the bed.

Then, the gun stopped moving. The barrel was still inserted but the guy had let go. Donny could hear motion, soft grunting. The freak was jerking off. He was kneeling behind Donny, watching that gun stuck in his ass and jerking off.

"Yeah, you piece of shit, yeah." The bed was shaking some now.

Donny held still, waiting. Waiting for what, he didn't know. The motion stopped. He could tell the guy finished. The gun was ripped violently from his ass, the front sight no doubt tearing out more of his insides. Searing pain. Warm blood. Then he lay there, face down, waiting to see if the guy was going to kill him or not.

The room was quiet. Donny could hear muffled sounds from the other rooms. TVs, laughter, hip-hop beats. He heard the traffic from the street, Saturday night traffic. He tried to visualize it, being out there in the cool air, headlights, noise—freedom.

"Don't you fuckin' move," the guy said again as he walked back into the bathroom and shut the door. Donny was alone.

This was his chance, maybe his last. Donny twisted himself and rolled over onto his back, onto his bound wrists, and struggled off the bed. He looked down at his tied ankles and saw they were roped with nylon. Fucking nylon stockings.

He turned to the right so he could see his back in the mirror. His hands were bound with the same material. Nylon, stretchy nylon. He pulled with all he had left. He could see his hands in the mirror, the material giving just enough. He could do this, he thought. He hooked a thumb over the knot, pushed his wrist through, and the stocking fell to the floor. He sat back on the bed and quickly pulled the ties from his ankles and looked for his pants.

There on the floor beside his jeans was the gun. The freak had left it there. It froze Donny. He wanted to grab it, kick open that bathroom door and shoot the rapist while he was sucking in another hit of crack, stick that filthy barrel into his mouth. He wouldn't do it. He couldn't do it. Another thought flashed. Open the door and show him the gun, then beat him with it till he was close to dead. Donny looked at the gun still shiny with lubricant and blood and decided to listen to his instincts. His instincts said, grab your pants and run.

That's just what he did. Without bothering to put them on, Donny took his jeans and ran out of that room. He bolted down the stairs; he could put his pants on around the corner. He ran, his stocking feet pounding the cold pavement. One block, two blocks. The cold night air filled his lungs. He didn't care who saw him, who was honking at him, pointing, laughing. He only ran.

Gabriel was getting good and drunk. The pain from the wounds on his back and the contusions on his head had receded with every margarita. The conversation had rolled through vacation spots, restaurants, movies, politics; he was starting to feel like an actual guest instead of a prisoner. The night had grown cool and the air felt good on his skin. He could smell the salt on the ocean breeze drifting in.

Dustin was keeping quiet, not able to contribute much to the conversation. It was clear he felt out of place in this environment. He hadn't taken a vacation ever; he rarely ate, didn't watch movies, and couldn't care less about politics. The cocaine wasn't helping either. He sat, legs crossed, arms folded, gulping his beer and waiting for Terrence or Raphael to go inside for another line. Whenever either got up to go to the kitchen, Dustin would follow them in hoping for another hit. When they weren't lining them up often enough, he went upstairs and smoked some speed in the bathroom.

When Dustin was gone, Gabriel felt even more relaxed. He sensed Terrence didn't want to talk about anything related to his profession, so he avoided it. As the alcohol calmed him, he began to piece more memories together with Terrence's face. He recalled the man was involved in some sort of scandal. That he was eventually disbarred, maybe even prosecuted. He was pretty certain of the money laundering, but there was something else, something more ominous. Terrence, he recalled, was the focus of much gossip, but Gabriel still couldn't remember what exactly for. Gabriel tried to push it to the back of his mind.

"I don't want to rude, but it's about time for me to turn in," said Gabriel with a yawn.

"No, no, no. You're my guest. Please, if you're tired, then go ahead upstairs. I believe Dustin showed you where you'll be sleeping."

"Thank you. It's just that, well, it's been a rough day for me."

"I hope," said Terrence, standing now, "that we've made it a little less rough for you. If you need anything, please ask Raphael or myself. Tomorrow, we'll get the business out of the way and then maybe we can have a nice dinner before you go."

Gabriel nodded and smiled, hoping it wouldn't appear as false as his host sounded. He went in through the sliding glass doors and found his way upstairs. The room they'd set aside for him was decorated like any guest room, an ugly floral comforter on the bed, matching curtains, a framed landscape print hung on the wall over a dresser full of empty drawers. The only thing missing was Gideon's Bible. There was no bathroom attached, Gabriel would have to use the one he'd showered in down the hall.

Gabriel sat down on the bed and realized he hadn't even considered an escape. Their plan of making him relax had worked. He was tired, full, and a little drunk. He realized he had no toothbrush, none of his personal items. He didn't want to make the walk back downstairs to ask if they had any extras. The margaritas would put him out anyway. His drink, however, was downstairs, too.

With a sigh and then a grunt of effort, Gabriel lifted himself off the bed and made his way back down the stairs to their makeshift party. The music was still playing, but the kitchen was empty. He heard Terrence and Dustin's voices on the patio. The tone had shifted, they seemed to arguing. Gabriel froze and listened.

"Fuckin' bullshit, Terry. You said she'd be here today. Now you say tomorrow. But come tomorrow, what're you gonna say? Have you even talked to her today?"

"Yes, I talked to her; I told you I talked to her. Why would I say I spoke to her if I hadn't?"

"Because, Terry, you're a fucking liar. It's what you do. It's how you make your goddamned living."

"Look, Dustin, I said I'd help you with this deal for a reason. It's not going to make or break me if I back out. In fact, you can probably do it on your own. I'd just as soon not be a party to the litany of felonies you dragged into this house anyway." Terrence's index finger was pointed toward Dustin's face. Dustin looked like he wanted to break it off.

"Fuck you, Terry. You're gonna help me. You're in this far, you can fuckin' well see it through. Don't act like you're doing me any favors. We both know you need the money."

"I said she'll be here tomorrow and she'll be here. She had some sort of personal problems. I can't control that shit, you know that."

"Why do we even need that cunt anyway?"

"Because, Dustin, my boy, we have to keep this legal. It's going to be contested most likely, and you don't want any chinks in your armor."

Gabriel felt an icy hand at his shoulder. Fear gripped his stomach; he could taste it in his mouth.

"You need something, Mr. Gabriel?"

It was Raphael, his hand still cool from mixing yet another margarita.

Gabriel said, "I wanted to ask about a tooth...you know, just a nightcap, I thought I'd take a drink to bed, help me sleep."

"It's no problem, you can have this one. I go make another. You want to say goo-night to the boys?"

"No, thank you, this'll be fine. You have a good night, Raphael."

"Goo-night, Mr. Gabriel. Don't let the bed bugs bite."

Bear was getting drunker by the minute. He, Rivas, and Watson had been sitting in the booth for almost an hour now. Every fifteen minutes, Watson would tell Rivas to go to the bar and get them another round. Jameson for Bear, Jagermeister for Watson, and tequila for Rivas. Rivas was paying for the drinks.

"Watson, I really need to talk to you about this shit."

"All business. Jesus H. Christ, Bear, can't you just have a good time for a change. It's always shop talk with you."

"It's not that I don't enjoy the company of you and your *compadre*, here..."

"Or the drinks," interrupted Watson. "Don't forget the drinks."

"Yeah, them too. But I ain't got all night, I got some folks waitin' on me and I was wondering..."

"You feel like a smoke, Bear? I feel like I haven't had a cigarette in days."

"We just had one about twenty minutes ago," said Bear.

"C'mon," said Watson. "Let's go outside and have a smoke. Rivas, you coming?"

Rivas nodded like a good dog and followed Watson and Bear to the door.

Sheila made eye contact with Bear on the way out. He knew he was wearing that certain look on his face and knew she was concerned. Her eyes asked, *Is everything okay?* That's what he thought anyway. It may have been one of those *Please, don't cause any trouble at my work* looks, too. He wasn't sure; he got both looks from Sheila so often when he'd tipped a few down at the Roadhouse.

Once outside, Bear shook out a Camel from his pack and wasn't surprised to find Rivas holding open his box of Marlboros for Doctor Watson. Watson took one without saying thank you and waited for a light. Rivas quickly produced a Bic and cupped his hand for Watson to light his, then Bear's.

When Rivas didn't light one of his own, Bear said to him, "That's handy, the Doc smokes 'em for you, too."

Rivas curled his lip at Bear the way a child sneers across the dinner table at a sibling.

"So what's got you so fired up you gotta call me at four in the morning, then track my ass down here on a Saturday night?"

"Wasn't much trackin', Watson. You're here every Saturday night." Bear took a pull from his Camel and continued, "You know that kid I asked you about last night?"

"Don't even bring him up, Bear." Watson came close to pointing his finger at the big man, but then thought better of it and only used his knuckle, like a politician. "What you did to that boy was atrocious. He called me today from the hospital, wanting to know if I knew you. He said he was robbed and beaten, arm broken in two places. I don't even want to know why you'd do such a thing."

"That's convenient then, 'cause I wasn't gonna tell you. I'm looking for someone else. Somebody named Terrence, or Terry. He's a lawyer, I think."

"Shit, Bear. There're a couple million lawyers out there. I heard once that there's one lawyer for every three people in the state of California." Watson leaned on his cane. "That's a hell of a statistic. You think that's true?"

"I don't give a shit is what I think. This guy, the guy I'm looking for is most likely local, here in Marin."

"You in some kind of trouble, Bear. You need represent-tation?" Watson raised his eyebrows, teasing Bear now.

"I'm not gonna stand here all night being polite, Watson."

"You're real nosy," Rivas interrupted. "You know that?"

He hadn't even spoken for the last half hour. Bear thought Rivas had gotten so drunk he'd forgotten how. Bear ignored him. "What about it, Watson, you know this fuckin' Terry, or what?"

"You don't have to get rude, okay? He's thinking about it," said Rivas.

Bear turned toward Rivas. "Look, you little fuck, I want to hear you squeak, I'll step on your toe. Stay outta my line of questioning, so you won't get any more confused than God has already left you."

"Fuck you," said Rivas.

"Nice response. You got that written down somewhere?"

"No, fuck *you*, man. You come around here asking my friends about my friends and you acting all like some kinda cop. Maybe you *are* some kinda cop."

Bear let the cop slight pass. "Your friend? Did I hear you say, your friend?"

Watson rolled his eyes and looked around the parking lot. This was going to get ugly.

"C'mon, Rivas, Mr. Badguy of the underworld, tell me about your friend." Bear stepped closer to Rivas. Rivas stepped back.

153

"Johnny here is my friend. I'm just sayin', you asking a lot of questions. Any friend of Johnny's, you know, is a friend of mine."

"No, shitbag, you said, *your* friend. I heard you. Now you're saying he's a friend of Watson's, too."

Watson cut in, "I don't think that's quite what he was saying, Bear."

Bear held up a palm to Watson's face to quiet him. "Rivas, you know who this fucker is, you got about five seconds to tell me."

"Or what?" Rivas sounded like he was back at the dinner table taunting his siblings again.

Bear said, "My watch runs fast."

"Your what?" said Rivas.

As quick as he could, Bear counted down, "Fi-fo-tree-two..." and punched Rivas hard in the cheek, right below the left eye. Rivas stumbled back, but didn't go down. Bear stepped forward and hit him again, on the chin this time. Rivas flew back and landed flat on the gravel. He lay there, arms and legs splayed out wide, like he was making dirt angels.

Doctor Watson hadn't moved; he looked horrified. "Bear, Bear, Bear. There's no need for that. Shit, c'mon, Bear. We've all had a few, let's go back inside and talk about this."

"Fuck that," said Bear. "I been listening to your bullshit for hours now. I want you to tell me what you know about this Terry cocksucker, or I'm gonna kick the shit out of both of you. Right here, right now." To show Watson that he was serious, he wound up and kicked Rivas hard in the balls. Rivas moaned and curled up into the fetal position.

"Bear, please, there's no need for that."

"Gimme your phone."

"What?"

"You heard me, gimme your phone, Watson."

"My phone? What for?"

Bear didn't hesitate. He reached out and grabbed Watson's shirt collar and pulled the man toward him. He twisted his hand in the material to tighten his grip, and then felt inside Watson's jacket pockets for a cell phone. When he'd found it, he pushed Watson back hard enough to make him fall on his ass. He crashed backward as his cane flew into the darkness to his left.

"Thank you. You're so fucking helpful," said Bear, slightly out of breath. Bear turned on the phone and found Watson's contacts, scrolled down to the T's. There it was—415-626-47—*the same number.* "You shitbag, I ought to fuck you up just for giving me the goddamn runaround."

Watson was getting up off the ground, dusting himself off. "Oh, that Terry, I thought you said, Terrence. This gentleman I know by Terry."

"He's a lawyer?"

"I believe so. At least he used to be a lawyer. I think he might be in real estate now."

"Real estate, huh? Let me ask you this, you know where he lives?"

"Bear, you know, some of these people. They've got their fingers in so many pies."

"I'm gonna ask you once more, Doctor. If you don't tell me, *you're* going to need a doctor—a real doctor. You get me, bright boy?"

"Shit." Watson looked at the gravel at his feet. He glanced around for his cane. He seemed to be weighing his options. He seemed utterly deflated; he dropped his pompous tone. He voice sounded dry and quiet. "He has a house up by Stinson Beach. A huge place, it's up in the hills though, past Stinson a ways."

"Where exactly?"

"I don't know exactly. I've only been there once and I was fucked up, okay? Just one or two roads past the town. You take a right; turn up McKenzie or McKenna, something like that. It's up a few miles of turns. You can't miss it, the place is huge. Faces the ocean. The entire front is glass, plate glass, looks like a giant mirror."

Bear stepped again toward Watson.

"Bear, please, I'm serious. That's all I know. That's all I got."

Bear scowled, "If you're bullshittin' me, Watson, I swear, I'm coming back and I'm gonna sink that piece of shit boat you live in, in the middle of the night, when you're dead asleep."

"Awe, c'mon, Bear. We've been friends a long time."

"No, I'd say we were more like acquaintances."

Bear turned and kicked Rivas one more time in the stomach. Not too hard, he just didn't like the son of a bitch. Then he walked back into the bar to have Sheila pour him a double. Watson didn't follow; he was done with the Roadhouse for tonight.

CHAPTER 16

As soon as Donny pulled on his jeans, he knew the pockets had been emptied. The three fifties, his hotel key, even his disposable lighter—all of it: gone. That sick fucker had robbed him. He slumped down onto somebody's stoop. He was far from home. It'd be a long walk in his condition. The pain in his rectum flared as soon as he'd stopped running. The adrenaline had worn off, so, too, had anything else in his system. He felt exhausted, abused, and, to add to the misery, he was getting dope-sick.

He hadn't bothered to grab his jacket when he ran out of there so he had no cigarettes either. Pathetic. He sat on the stoop and pulled his knees as close to his chest as he could. No money, no smokes, no drugs, far from home without even a jacket. And no shoes, he ran out of there without his goddamn shoes. He felt like crying. His eyes were already watering from the withdrawals. He felt the familiar gurgle in his stomach that could only be quelled by junk. He hated his life. He hated himself.

If he could get into his hotel room, he could pound some cottons and maybe beat out enough dope to get well, but it was too late to wake his hotel manager and get a replacement key. The prick would want ten bucks for it anyway. He could head back to the corner and see if one of the guys could lend him twenty bucks to cop, but even then, he had no works, no spoon, and no way to call his dealer. His phone was probably long gone with that Dustin character. He tried to recall the number for Jose in his head, but came up blank. He wished he could sit where he was forever. Let the sun rise and warm him, wait for the sickness to pass. But it wouldn't pass, not for days and days and days.

He had no choice but to hoist himself up off the stoop and begin making his way back to the Tenderloin and hope that he didn't start puking before he got there.

He realized he was in Stevenson Alley, only a few blocks from the Travel Lodge. As he shuffled in the direction of his neighborhood, he was forced to pass the motel monstrosity once again. He looked up at the place—the wall of identical orange doors layered up three stories—and spied room 237. It was closed and quiet and looked like any other door up there. No signs of life. He wondered if that sick fuck was still in the bathroom smoking crack. Donny lost it and began puking right there on the sidewalk. He heaved and heaved until there was nothing but bile left.

The retching left him gasping for air. He slumped back against a parking meter and sucked in what oxygen he could. He noticed the sky over the roof of the Travel Lodge Motel was turning from black to gray. Soon it would be blue. A light, hopeful blue, morning was coming. How long had he sat there? He had to get up, keep moving. One way or another, he'd get well soon.

Donny got up and pointed himself toward home. Either his hotel or Rich's. He didn't know exactly what time it was, but it was only a matter of counting down the hours until he was supposed to meet Bear. He walked as fast as his stocking feet would carry him. He was in pain from being violated, but his entire body was now aching. His nervous system was put on high-alert from the lack of junk. His pain receptors were ratcheted way up. He was in full withdrawal now. Every step, every movement, rocketed pain throughout his body. His skin began to hurt. The goosebumps from his chills, his fever, prickled and annoyed him. Even his hair hurt.

He kept his eyes on the sidewalk, hoping to spy a healthy enough cigarette butt to pick up. There were none. Even if—

when—he reminded himself, he did spot a decent smoke, he didn't have anything to light it with. He felt his stomach seize. His intestines rumbled. He stumbled forward. Lunging, grunting, whimpering. People on the sidewalk pulled back from him. Whether they did it out of repulsion or caution, Donny didn't care. He was an animal now, moving ahead on raw instinct.

Bear woke up thirsty. It took him a moment to figure out where he was. There was a ceiling fan spinning directly over his head making him nauseous. Sheila's fan. Sheila's apartment. He was on Sheila's couch. Not a good sign if he didn't make it into her bed. Sheila must be pissed. Before he tried to piece together the end of the evening, he needed water.

He pulled himself up from the couch and stumbled into the kitchen, the hardwood floor lurching beneath his feet as though he were on a ship. It was still dark outside, but Bear could see the sky had begun to lighten. He made it to the sink and hit the cold faucet. He leaned in and gulped and gulped like a dying man in the desert. When he was done, he stood up straight, felt the water sloshing in his stomach, then leaned in and drank some more.

"Well, well, well, look who's alive."

Sheila's voice startled him. He turned to find her leaning against a door jamb, arms folded across her chest. Dressed only in a T-shirt, she looked as though he'd woken her up.

"Oh, hey, baby, what's up?" His voice was so full of gravel, even Bear hardly understood what he'd said.

"Don't baby me, Bear. Do you have any idea what you did last night?"

He groaned involuntarily and leaned back against the sink.

"I'll tell you what you did. You beat the shit out of two regulars *at my work*. Two guys who come in almost every night. Then, you come into the bar—*my job*—and start demanding free drinks. I don't mind slipping you free drinks, Bear, but to stand there and demand liquor saying we have to 'pay the exterminator' was not cool."

"I'm sorry, baby."

"Oh, I'm not done. It didn't end there. When I told you that you'd had enough, that the police may show up and haul your drunk ass to jail, you tell me to go fuck myself and climb over the bar and grab yourself a bottle. This is my fucking work, Bear. Do you even get that? Tony the manager was there last night, Raul, Percy, everybody there was a regular."

"I said I'm sorry. I had a few too many." His head was pounding; his mouth had already dried up again.

"You already said you were sorry, I heard you. It doesn't undo what happened last night."

"It's been a tough couple of days." It sounded feeble as soon as it came out of his mouth.

"I know about your tough couple of days, and, thanks to your loud mouth, so does half of Marin County. Just what I need, a boyfriend who spends his spare time running around San Francisco with a couple of gay hustlers. Do you know how sick that shit sounded? These are my customers, Bear. I have to see them every night."

"Look," said Bear, finally growing tired of what was becoming a lecture. "I'm gonna lay back down on that couch for a couple more hours. You do what you like. When I wake up, we can have a little breakfast, talk this over. If you don't want to talk, then that's okay, too." Bear stumbled back to the couch and flopped down with a loud moan. He heard Sheila mumble something about never cooking him breakfast again, but he couldn't quite make it out. He covered his eyes with his forearm and waited for her bedroom door to slam.

"Good morning, Sunshine."

Raphael's voice was as piercing as the sunlight streaming

through the window. The yellows and whites of the guest room were even more abrasive on the eyes than they were the night before. Gabriel lifted his head, looked at the bright, beaming face of Raphael, and laid his head back onto the pillow.

"Come on, Mr. Gabriel. This is the big day. Terry says to wake you up and make sure you get downstairs. You have to get up and have a good breakfast, then you feel better. I'm making a frittata. Maybe you like a bloody Mary first, maybe a mimosa?"

The idea of alcohol brought forth a wave of nausea. Gabriel lay still under the covers and blinked open his eyes. "What do you mean it's the big day?"

"You and your friend have the business with the lady that's coming. Then we have a little party afterward. Come on, get up. I'll help you."

Gabriel felt Raphael's weight press onto the bed. The young man was lying next to him. Gabriel turned his head and there was Raphael, beside him with his white robe open, exposing his smooth, youthful brown skin.

"You need some extra help? Maybe a little massage, a morning release?" Raphael reached over and lightly touched Gabriel's thigh through the comforter. "I was told you like younger men. Is this true, Mr. Gabriel?"

Gabriel didn't know what to say. He felt like he'd been in a car wreck. A sexual encounter was the last thing on his mind. "No, no thank you, Raphael."

"What's a matter? You no like Latino boys?" Raphael move his hand a little further up Gabriel's thigh. "We are very passionate."

"Thank you, really, but no. I'll be able to get up. Tell Terrence that I'll be down in a few minutes."

Unperturbed by the rejection, Raphael hopped up off the bed and asked, "So, what would you like, mimosa or coffee?"

"Just coffee, please. I'll take it downstairs." Gabriel tried to sit up and realized just how sore he was. He moaned out loud as he swung his legs over the side of the bed to find a pair of new slippers waiting for him. On the back of the bedroom door was a white robe identical to the one Raphael was wearing. His hosts were making a great effort to make him feel pampered. He decided he liked it, but promised himself he wouldn't let his guard down.

He got up, joints popping and muscles straining, feeling every bruise that Dustin laid on him, donned the slippers, the robe, and made his way downstairs.

The aroma of coffee and baking frittata filled the lower level. It smelled warm and comfortable. He looked into the kitchen and saw Raphael hard at work at the stove, a pint glass mimosa in front of him. Terrence was at the kitchen counter, perched on a stool, with a steaming cup of coffee and a sheaf of legal documents spread out before him. He wore reading glasses and looked deep in concentration. Gabriel stood there a moment wondering if they would notice him. The scene was almost idyllic. Almost.

Gabriel looked around for Dustin and then noticed him out on the deck sitting and smoking, his white skin repelling the sunlight, refusing to tan. He looked uncomfortable in the sunlight, twisted up like a pretzel, his arms folded, legs folded, his body language a tight knot. Gabriel knew he'd probably been up all night. It reminded Gabriel that he was no guest at all. It made him wonder when the hospitality would end.

Donny felt he had no choice but to curl up and wait. He'd lost track of the time and stopped caring. He plunked himself down on the sidewalk on Eddy Street in front of his hotel. He'd found a space between a hopeless drunk and sleeping baglady. He stayed curled up in the fetal position for a while, until the drunk wet himself and the puddle crept out onto the sidewalk. Donny saw the urine creeping outward and straightened himself up and shoved a little closer to the crazy lady, who was only feigning sleep. She sat with her head in her hands, breathing loudly. Every once in a while she'd say something that sounded like "Sunny Beach." Donny wondered if, in her delusion, she thought they were basking in the sun at some tropical locale, but, after she'd said it three or four times, he realized she was calling him a son of a bitch.

The sun was slow to warm the sidewalk and the concrete felt like the marble slab at a mortician's. Donny did his best to hold still, but muscle spasms and the chills made it almost impossible. He couldn't remember the last time he was this dope-sick. He swore to himself that he was going to make changes, that this would no longer be his life. He was done with hustling, done with the street, all he had to do was get well and then, only then, could he figure out what to do.

He felt a sharp kick in his shin.

"Hey, dude, what's up? I fuckin' knew I'd find you here. You waiting on your biker boyfriend?"

Big Rich was towering over him, blocking the sunlight. Donny grunted. He wanted to say something, but was holding back another stream of bile.

Rich bent down on his haunches. "What the fuck, Donny? You look awful. Where the fuck you been all night? I went back to the corner to look for you, but you disappeared. Where's your jacket? Where're your fuckin' shoes?"

Donny tried to speak again, but couldn't. He managed a high whimper and that was it.

"You sick, bro?" It was a stupid question. Big Rich reached into his pocket and pulled out his fist. Under Donny's runny nose, he opened up his hand and in his palm were seven small multi-colored balloons. They looked like some strange candy. Salvation: his prayers had been answered. Donny wanted to cry.

"C'mon, dude. Let's go get you well."

Donny felt Big Rich's hands pull him up on his feet. He felt his rubbery legs moving under him. Rich was guiding him toward the hotel's front gate. "No...can't. No key," Donny managed to say.

"No key? What happened to your key?" Rich didn't wait for Donny to answer; he understood the gravity of the situation. "No problem, we'll go to my place." He took Donny by the elbow and steered him toward his hotel, telling Donny it'd be all right, that he had plenty of junk. "Xavier's got the best shit right now, we'll get you well. Hang in there."

Rich threw a crumpled ten dollar bill under the opening at the bottom of the Plexiglass before the manager could protest that he was bringing someone so sick and decrepit into the hotel. Like sick and decrepit weren't on the regular menu here at this shit hole.

The manager called after them as Rich dragged Donny up the stairs. "What is wrong with your friend? No calling ambulance, take him out of here. No dying upstairs. Take him out to the street."

Donny sat slumped on the bed and watched Rich perform the familiar ritual. As soon as the water in the spoon hit a boil, the acrid, vinegar aroma made Donny lurch toward the sink and gag. He was already drained of bile. All there was left to do was dry heave.

Rich giggled. "Holy shit, you are sick. Hang on a minute, Don, it's almost ready." Big Rich rolled up a piece of cigarette filter between his fingers and dropped it into the spoon. He took a new rig from a fresh bag and pulled the cap off with his teeth. He drew it up as Donny's dry heaves began to subside.

"You wanna tie off and I'll hit you?" asked Rich.

Donny answered by grabbing the rig, still warm from the spoon, and plunging it straight through his jeans into his thigh. He pushed the plunger down as fast as it would go and then flopped backward on the bed to wait for some sort of relief.

After about a minute he asked Rich for a cigarette.

After the cigarette, Rich asked, "Feel any better?"

Donny said, "Little bit. Let's cook up a bit more so I can hit it in the vein."

"Now you're talkin'. That's m'boy, you must feel better."

They repeated the whole procedure again, this time taking several minutes to find veins and, after a couple of tries, successfully got the dope into their bloodstreams. They both fell back onto pillows and lit new cigarettes.

After drifting off into a nod for a few minutes, Rich asked Donny, "So what happened to you last night? Where's your shit?"

Donny related the whole story: the car, the motel, the crack, the gun, everything. Big Rich sat with his mouth hanging open, his facial muscles slackened by the heroin, occasionally saying, "Shit," or "Fuck." When he was done, Donny hung his head down and said, "I'm done with this shit."

"With what shit?"

"With the corner, with junk, speed—all of it. I can barely fuckin' walk. That fucker was gonna kill me, I know it."

Big Rich sighed, "I know, man, I know. But if you want off the corner, it's gonna take some cash. What're you gonna do until you can figure out how to kick? You gotta pay the hotel, you gotta pay for methadone, you gotta eat."

Donny knew where this was going.

"If we can get those phones back, my phone, we can get enough dough to get out. Really get out. We won't have to be out there again. Shit, you can probably pay for one of those rehabs that the movie stars go to." Rich's voice was serious now, selling it. "It's about ten-thirty right now. We're supposed to meet the biker at one o'clock. We can still go, get the phone, get Gabriel, show him the video and collect."

"I dunno, man. I dunno."

"Sure you do. C'mon, Donny, what else you gonna do? Sit

around here and wait to get sick again? Let's stick with the plan. I got some extra shoes—Chuck Taylors—a jacket, too. In fact, I got that jacket you left here about a month ago. Let's get ready. We'll meet the biker, go get what's ours, and then you can decide what to do."

Rich's comment hung on the smoky air for a moment. Then he said, "At least with some money, you got options."

Donny reached for Rich's cigarettes on the dresser, took one out and lit it.

"I dunno, man," he repeated. "You got any idea what I been through?"

"Yeah," said Big Rich. "Of course I do. We all been through..." he paused, searching for the right word, "...unspeakable shit out there. It doesn't matter what you been doing or what's been done to you. What matters is what you're gonna do." Rich seemed quite pleased with himself for sounding this philosophical and waited for his words to sink in.

"You know what I wanna do, Donny?"

Donny, only half listening, lifted his head and said, "What?"

"I wanna go back to Oregon. I wanna be with my daughter. I wanna get off this shit, too. Get off the street and go up there and show her bitch of a mother that she was wrong about me. Show her that I can be a good father. You know, provide and all that shit. I can do that. I *want* to do that, Donny."

Donny saw that Rich's eyes were beginning to water. They were glassy and pinned, but there were definitely some kind of tears forming there. He'd never heard his friend talk this way. Not about quitting.

"Okay," said Donny.

"Okay, what?'

"Okay, we'll go meet Bear at one. We'll go get our phones back. We'll see if we can get some money out of this old

166

fucker, but, Rich, promise me one thing."

"Yeah, of course, what?"

"No more of this, 'one last time' shit. If we're gonna do this, let's do it for real. I mean it; I don't want to be out on that fucking corner ever again."

Rich smiled and said, "That's m'boy."

Bear hit the road after a hurried breakfast. Not because he was late to pick up the boys, but because he didn't want to go over last night with Sheila again. When he woke back up on the couch to the smell of frying bacon, he knew her mood had lightened. Bacon was definitely a peace offering. She was quiet while she fixed him a plate of scrambled eggs, toast, and bacon. He was grateful and didn't say much while he shoveled it down. They managed to make a little small talk before he told her he had to run an errand.

"An errand?" she said, her voice full of doubt. "I hope it's nothing to do with those little faggots you were telling everyone about last night."

Bear only said it was something he had to do. He didn't want to get into the whole story of Thaxton and Dustin and Terrence. For all he knew, Sheila might know who this Terrence was, and although he could have used another opinion, something told him Sheila's wasn't going to be so helpful. He got up from the table, told her he'd call her later, and gave her a kiss. Her lips were cold and unresponsive.

Before heading to the city he slipped back up north to his place to pack the trunk. This time he decided he'd bring a gun. Definitely not the piece that Donny had picked up from Gilly. Who knew where that thing had been? He would hide that one deep in his cottage and bring something of his own. He owned a Walther PK .380 and a snub-nosed .38. He held one in each hand, trying to decide which was better suited for the occasion. Then he put them both in the trunk. Under a moving blanket in the well of the spare tire he placed the guns, extra ammo and clips, his trusty hunting knife, and a half pint of Jim Beam.

He got back into the driver's seat and headed out for the city. He drove with the radio off. He wanted to clear his head and think about what the hell he was going to do once he got to Terrence's.

While he crossed the Golden Gate Bridge, blue sky peeked out over his head. The fog was receding and it was turning out to be a nice day. As he reached into his pocket for the bridge toll, he wondered why he was going to the city at all, why he was going out of his way to bring those two fuck ups back into this mess. He doubted that saving Thaxton was their reason for wanting to be included so badly. Getting their phones back didn't really seem like a good enough reason to risk their lives either. There had to be something else they wanted.

Bear reminded himself he gave his word. If there was one thing he tried to cling to in life, after all the bullshit he'd been through, it was his word. Being a man of your word meant that you were a real man. It was the only thing that had real value. Maybe he shouldn't have given it, but he did.

It took a few minutes and a few miles for Bear to admit to himself, though, that he needed them along. If Thaxton was being held at Terrence's by Dustin, that meant he was at least outnumbered by a crooked mouthpiece and a psychopath. Bear had no idea who else, or what else, was at that house. The last place he looked for Dustin and Gabriel was crawling with junkies. He'd be foolish going it alone. It was too late to drag any of his biker buddies along to help. Besides, the story was too ridiculous. They'd wonder why he was putting his ass on the line to save the old pervert anyway.

Bear lit a Camel and wished he'd thought to have a beer at home before he started out on this journey. His head was killing him.

* * *

Gabriel finished his coffee in the kitchen and decided to have a mimosa after all. It couldn't hurt, he figured. In fact, it may help ease the pain. He sat at the counter, while Raphael worked at the frittata, and watched Terrence and Dustin argue on the sundeck. They were trying to keep their voices down, but Dustin was having trouble remaining calm.

From what Gabriel could gather, the two were still waiting for someone. Terrence had promised Dustin that the person in question would be here Saturday and it was now Sunday and Dustin didn't seem to think this person was going to show at all. It must be the lady that Raphael had mentioned, most likely. This missing person seemed to be integral to their plan.

Their plan. What plan? Dustin had spouted off so many ideas over the last several months. Gabriel thought most of them were grandiose delusions. It was the speed talking. He was afraid of Dustin and what he knew about his personal life, but he had no clue as to how this maniac would piece together a plan to emancipate himself from him. He felt that he and Dustin were tethered somehow. Tethered by needs. Dustin, he felt, lacked the wherewithal to go out on his own. The boy had been institutionalized and needed looking after.

That's why he had called Bear, because Gabriel felt there needed to be an outside force separating them, untangling them. He hoped, on some level, that Dustin still cared for him.

Gabriel felt an uncontrollable wave of emotion pass over him. Watching the frail and pale Dustin out on the deck, he was reminded of his grandson whom he may never see again. There was a sadness that he was not able connect to this life, to couple this bizarre circumstance with the wholesome reality of real life. He'd let things get too far out of hand. He knew, in his heart, there was no going back. His wife, his daughter, his grandson would never be able to resume a normal healthy relationship with him. He'd crossed a line.

He lifted his mimosa and took another sip, then set it down, wondering if the champagne was feeding this melancholy. He needed to keep a clear head, perhaps look for an escape. He didn't like reminding himself that he was a prisoner here, a hostage, but it was true. If he could spot an opening, an opening that an old man like him could fit through, he'd have to take it.

His thoughts were broken by the chime of the doorbell. The sliding glass door to the deck area slid open and Terrence came in first, followed by Dustin.

"I'm glad to see you decided to enjoy yourself this morning. Relax and have Raphael serve you some of his world famous frittata. It's excellent." As Terrence spoke he moved past Gabriel toward the entranceway of the house, saying, "At last, she's arrived."

Dustin stayed behind in the kitchen. He thrust a boney finger out at Gabriel and said, "Watch your fuckin' manners, you old fuck. I'm keepin' an eye on you."

CHAPTER 17

It was ten minutes after one when Bear pulled up to the same spot where he'd dropped the boys. He saw them sitting on the sidewalk, backs against the building, with cigarettes in their mouths. At first he thought they were sun tanning, sucking up what little sun San Francisco had to offer. Then he realized they were on the nod, eyes closed, slack-jawed, near unconsciousness. He honked the horn; when that failed, he rolled down the passenger window and shouted, "Hey, you assholes, you can't sleep here."

That got a little rise from them. Donny opened his eyes and nudged Rich with his elbow. They both struggled up off the sidewalk and moved toward Bear's open passenger window. Big Rich leaned in and said, "Shit, we thought you weren't coming. We been waitin' out here for a while."

"Bullshit," said Bear. "Climb in."

The boys resumed the same positions as the day before, Big Rich in the front seat and Donny in the back. Bear asked if they were ready, and, without waiting for an answer, said, "Let's go."

They were already heading out of the Tenderloin on Geary Street before Donny thought to ask, "Where are we going anyway?"

"To Marin, just past Stinson Beach. I don't know exactly where, but we'll know it when we get there."

"What the fuck is up there?" asked Rich.

"Dustin's lawyer. Or at least who Dustin thinks is his lawyer. I don't know for sure that he's hiding out there, but chances are he is. And, if he's there, then I figure he's got Thaxton with him."

171

"The old man?" said Rich, feeling confused.

"Gabriel," corrected Donny.

Bear said, "Right."

Donny leaned in from the backseat and said, "What do we do?"

Bear kept his eyes on Geary Street and admitted, "I don't know. We take a look-see at the place, I guess, then we go in and get him."

"Get who?" asked Rich.

"The old man, who do you think?" Bear was realizing that this kid was pretty fucked up.

After another block, Rich added, "And our phones."

"Yes, your goddamn phones. What the hell is so important 'bout those phones, anyway?"

"I already told you," Rich said.

"I know, I know, I know. You got your baby's pictures on there. What else?"

When Rich didn't answer, Bear looked into the rearview at Donny. He wasn't talking either. "I'm just sayin', it seems like a lot of trouble you guys are going to trying to get back a couple of phones."

"We got our reasons," Rich said with a defensive tone.

"What about Thaxton, aren't you guys worried about him? When I met you at his house Friday, you said you were his friends."

Donny said, "We are. We want to know that he's okay." Donny waited a moment for Rich to chime in, when Rich didn't, he punched the back of his seat, "Don't we?"

"Yeah, yeah, of course we do," Rich croaked. "We wanna know if the old fucker is okay. He's been very good to me, to us."

Bear let that one go. After a few more blocks of silence he hit the radio and turned it up. They rode along the streets of the city, out Geary, up Franklin, and toward the Golden Gate

Bridge. They each lit a cigarette and Bear cracked the windows for air.

Big Rich seemed to be deep in thought, nodding off, or already asleep when he suddenly asked Bear, "How come you're going to all this trouble? Seems, like, if that guy is your lawyer, you already have to pay him. What's he to you? Why are you puttin' *your* ass on the line?"

The question was tinged with challenge. They were getting off on the wrong foot. Bear was thinking they needed to at least feel like they were on the same side. Besides, it was a long, winding drive up there; he may as well pass the time with a story. He reached out and turned the radio back down.

"Gabriel Thaxton helped me out a long time ago. He's been lawyerin' for me and my buddies for years, seen us through a lot of scrapes, but there was one time he really pulled my ass out of the fire. I kinda feel like I owe him."

"What happened?" asked Donny from the back.

"Years ago, I was at a party. Well, wasn't really a party, just some guys gettin' together to do some business, but we were partyin'. Doing blow, drinkin', you know. This was up north, real isolated spot. I was into some shady shit in those days and it was like a safe house situation." Bear paused and shook his head at his own memory. "Anyway, I used to run with some ruffian types."

"You? Nah," said Big Rich.

Unfazed by the sarcasm, Bear said, "I know, hard to believe, huh? Like I said, this place we were at was way out in the boondocks. I had a chemist friend of mine cooking a little go-fast in the shack in back."

"Nice," said Rich, his interest perking up.

"This was the real deal, too. Not that ephedrine shit you guys are gettin' nowadays. The old school biker meth made with the red phosphorous. Anyway, this guy Ramirez was up there for another reason, supposedly. We had a little weed crop out back and he was there gettin' a sample for his old lady. She was in that business. So," Bear paused to flick his cigarette out the window, "we were there most of the day, drinkin', doing lines and shit, and this guy Ramirez is gettin' kinda snakey. Everybody else is good and relaxed, enjoying the day, and this fucker's gettin' shifty, going into rooms he ain't invited into. Snoopy, y'know?"

The boys, both paying attention now, nodded.

"So it gets to be dark, I'm fuckin' tore up. Drunk from the whiskey and beers and numb from the coke, I'm not noticing this guy is sneaking around, digging through stuff and casing the place. Finally, it's getting late, me and a few of the boys are sittin' out by the fire and I notice this guy, Ramirez, is trying to get into the shed in back."

"The lab," said Rich.

"Right," said Bear, "where we been cooking this shit. The guy is trying to rob me right under my nose. I see the guy rootin' around in there and I get up to say, *What the fuck*? None of my so-called brothers seem to be backin' me up. So I go to this Ramirez and I tell him what's what, that I want him gone, I don't want him coming 'round no more and so on. He don't wanna hear what I have to say. We end up in a square off and this fucker swings at me. At *me*, at my own place. So we tussle, man-style. We're rolling around and trading blows and, still, nobody's jumping in. After a minute or two of this shit the guy breaks free from me, gets up and pulls a fucking piece on me. Now, nobody's steppin' in for sure. The guy's got a goddamn pistol pointed right at my chest and you know what he says?

"He says, 'We're here for the shit, Bear. We're takin' it with or without your permission.' *My permission*? You know what that means, right? Give us your stash or we're gonna shoot you. Well, I know what kinda guys these are, and, more importantly, they know what kinda guy *I* am. They know that if they take my shit, I'm coming after them hot, so I know that I'm as good as fucked. They're gonna bury me no matter what I say."

"So what'd you do?" asked Donny.

"I'll tell you what I did; I reached out and grabbed this fucker's gun. Right by the goddamn barrel. I twisted it to one side and yanked it out of his hand and punched that piece of shit in the face. He went down, but not out. He got off the ground and came running at me. So, I shot him. Right in the fuckin' chest. One shot. Dead."

The boys were quiet, listening to the old biker recount the tale.

"Self-defense, right? Open and shut. Guy brings a gun onto my property and tries to kill me. Then, I look down in my hand and, holy shit, the fuckin' pistol is mine. Fucker stole my gun when he was in the house. I just shot the guy with my own damn gun."

"It's still self-defense, though, right?" asked Donny.

"You'd think so. But it would have been cleaner if the gun was the other guy's. Now it gets a little more complicated. I think I got witnesses to back up my story; they, one by one, turn and run. Turns out this Ramirez is more connected to the big club than I realize. He's got a brother who's flyin' the colors of the big club, you know who I mean. And he's also got some other connections that come to light.

"To make matters worse, the cops get there, they see all the other shit, the lab, the weed, another firearm or two, they book me for all kinds of shit. The prosecutor says it's murder during the commission of a felony and, bam, that's it, fucking capital case. One minute, I'm having beers and warming my toes in front of the fire, the next I'm on my way to San Quentin, death row."

"Shit, that's so fucked," said Big Rich. "What happened?"

"I'll tell you what happened. Gabriel Thaxton of Thaxton, Spreckle, and White, that's what happened. I'd dealt with him once before and the guy did me right. It wasn't cheap, but he did good work. So, I got a hold of him and he came right down and seen me. Right away, he believed me. I was still cuffed in the holding cell, looking guilty as hell. I know that all lawyers are supposed to believe their clients, that's their job, I get that. But this Thaxton, I could tell, really had my back, right from the start. He's got good instincts, that's why he is who he is. There was no talk of pleadin' out, taking any kind of deal, giving up nothin'. You gotta understand the cards were stacked against me, really stacked. I thought I didn't have a chance in hell to beat this shit, and ol' Gabriel, he just kept sayin' 'Don't worry, I believe you' and 'we're going to get you out of here. Free and clear.' He meant it and he did it." Bear took his eyes off the road and looked at his passengers before adding, "I guess, in a way, you could say I owe him my life."

Donny sat back in his seat and thought about this. What it must mean to have a friend like that. Someone who you could count on. Someone to save you. Donny knew that Big Rich was his friend, his good friend, but he also knew it was the drugs that drove Rich. He knew that, if shit got bad enough, Rich would abandon him. He knew he had no one in his life that would save him. Donny was alone. He looked at the back of Bear's head while the biker drove and felt a terrible sensation of sadness overcome him. It swept over his pain from the previous night, it swept over the drugs he'd saturated himself with to quell that pain.

Gabriel was still in the kitchen when the front door opened. He could hear Terrence making the same welcome pleasantries as when he had arrived at the house. Dustin's back blocked Gabriel's view of the entrance. He stood facing the doorway, as curious as Gabriel.

They heard the heavy front door shut and a moment later a short, squat woman entered the kitchen with a large box under one arm, and a fabric briefcase under the other. The case looked worn. It had a faded floral design and the zipper was broken along the top. The woman flopped it onto the kitchen counter and said, "Sorry I'm late."

She had muddy, dark red hair with a few strands of grey woven in. There were sparse, thin dreadlocks in between the natural curls. She looked tired and, for whatever reason, Gabriel thought, she looked like a heavy smoker. Perhaps it was only because she was feigning being out of breath.

"Late?" said Dustin. "That's an understatement. It's fuckin' Sunday."

The woman ignored Dustin and pushed the big box from under her arm up onto the counter beside the floral briefcase. To Terrence she said, "Terry, honey, do you know how hard it is to find a VCR in Marin County these days? I had to drive all the way over to the East Bay and find a Walmart to get one. When's the last time you were on the Richmond/San Rafael Bridge? That thing terrifies me. What the hell do we need this thing for?"

Terrence, still playing host, said, "Thank you so much. Diligent effort, indeed." He moved beside her and took her elbow lightly. "Miranda, I don't believe you've met my associates. Miranda, this is Dustin. He's one of the interested parties here today, and behind him there is the famous Mr. Gabriel Thaxton."

The woman merely nodded at Dustin, but at hearing Gabriel's name lit up and put out a hand to shake his. "Mr. Gabriel, well, I've certainly heard of *you*. Quite a big shot 'round these parts. It's a pleasure to meet you in person. I've been a great admirer of your work."

Gabriel took the hand and noticed each finger was outfitted with a large gaudy ring. Turquoise, jade, big fake rubies. The rings pinched and hurt his own fingers when they shook hands.

"And, of course, you know Raphael," said Terrence.

She smiled at Raphael like they had an inside joke and said, "Of course. Raff, sweetie, could you fix me a cup up tea? Anything herbal, I do not need any caffeine, not after the day I've had."

Raphael smiled and sang, "*Si*, Senorita."

Gabriel could smell her perfumed funk from where he stood. It was a stale blend of flowers and must. Her hair was clumped and uncombed and the dark clothes that hung loosely on her tiny frame were covered with cat hair.

"And, if you could, put in a dollop of that organic honey. I read an article last week about the store bought stuff, and I swear, I'm never going to use it again. I'm thinking of getting my own hive. Y'know, do my thing for the pollinators of this world. They're in decline, y'know. It's all over the Internet. They need all the help they can get."

Dustin stood behind the short woman, feeling ignored, rolling his eyes. "Can we get this thing started?"

Terrence said, "Dustin, there's a TV in the second guest bedroom upstairs. Why don't you go set up the VCR and I'll help Miranda get settled in. Gabriel, would you like a cup of tea?"

Gabriel shook his head while he watched Dustin grab the box with the VCR and run up the stairs two at a time.

"Mimosa, coffee, water, anything?"

"No, thank you," Gabriel said, but Raphael poured him a coffee anyway. He looked again at the woman. He wondered if this was indeed the person they had been waiting on, what role she could possibly play in whatever they had planned. She was almost a caricature. An aging hippie, right down to her overpriced Birkenstocks. A thought flashed through Gabriel's mind that she might be a witch, one of those Wiccan, earth-goddess types, but the papers peeking out from that floral valise were not spells. They looked like files, legal papers stuffed into manila folders.

"Raphael, is that one of your frittatas I smell?" She smiled and Gabriel saw that her teeth were yellow and stained.

"Still warm," said Raphael, proud that she noticed, "You like me to fix you a plate?"

"What kind of eggs? I hope not those cruel little Safeway ones. I will not eat those little tortured orbs. I can't stand to think where they came from."

"Organic, free-range, of course. We only buy organic," Raphael lied. "Parmesan, fresh spinach, ham, a little parsley..."

"Ham? Oh no, I couldn't. You know I don't eat meat. Good Lord, neither should you two. Don't you know that meat ages you? Your body works so hard to break it down that it deprives itself of other vital needs. It has to absorb all those antibiotics and hormones. It sits in your stomach for weeks, months even. It's an abuse to the human body. Not to mention what the poor pig went through. I gave up pork when I was still a teen. I think one slice of bacon might kill me now."

"Okay, suit yourself," said Raphael, trying not to sound as disappointed as he looked. The frittata sat unsliced on the kitchen counter.

"Now," said Miranda, "before we get started, I just want to do a little clarification about what forms we're going to be using and which ones need to get recorded."

Terrence interrupted her. "Miranda, please, you just got here. Let's have our tea, relax a few minutes before we get started."

"Relax? I thought you said I was late. Your little friend there is acting like he's about to miss the last bus to happy town. I thought you all were in a hurry to get this thing done."

Before Gabriel could inquire as to what that thing was, Terrence said with his rich and silvery tone, "Please, you're here now. That's all that matters. Let us just enjoy the morning and then we'll get down to business."

Gabriel looked at the clock. It was well past one o'clock. They'd slept through the morning and he was beginning to wish he'd stayed in bed.

They arranged themselves on opposite sides of the kitchen counter. They sat, perched on the tall chairs, Gabriel and Raphael on one side and Miranda and Terrence on the other. Gabriel sipped at his two drinks in front of him—first the coffee, then the Mimosa—knowing the combination would probably upset his stomach, and tried to follow the conversation. The chat turned, as Gabriel guessed it almost always did with this Miranda, to politics. He was uninterested, though, in the small talk. He was thinking of what fate his hosts had planned for him.

Miranda argued the side of the far left—big surprise—and Terrence took the side of the moderate left. Raphael sat silent with nothing to add and, at one point, even put a hand on Gabriel's knee. After a few more minutes of the mindless banter, Dustin came down the stairs from the guest room and called to Gabriel.

"Hey, Gabriel, it's time."

The political talk stopped instantly. The other three at the counter looked at Gabriel as if they were on pause, soundlessly excusing him before they continued.

Dustin's serious tone was ominous and suddenly Gabriel felt like he didn't want to leave the kitchen conversation so soon. He started to feel like maybe a slice of Raphael's frittata sounded quite tasty, perhaps another Mimosa was in order.

Dustin, this time with his teeth clenched, said, "Let's go, *Gabe*, I ain't got all day."

Gabriel, not wanting Dustin's anger to flare, hopped off the tall stool and, securing his robe, padded after him in his borrowed slippers. He followed him up the stairs and down the hall to the empty guest bedroom. Inside, the curtains were closed and it was dark. The only light came from a TV that sat playing the infinite static of no signal.

CHAPTER 18

After they'd crossed the Golden Gate Bridge, both the boys had fallen asleep. Bear drove Highway One in silence, preferring to concentrate on what lay ahead of him instead of distracting himself with his usual classic rock. The road began to wind as they got further into Marin County. Bear started taking the curves and corners faster than he needed to. He enjoyed hearing Rich's oblivious head bounce against the window with its dead little thump. He checked the rearview. In the backseat, Donny sat with his head straight back on the seat, his jaw hanging, a light snore whistling out of his nose.

When the road straightened and they reached the town of Stinson Beach, Bear pulled off the highway into a gas station. He drove around the back of the building and positioned the car beside a dumpster. He cut the engine and the sudden disappearance of its steady vibration woke the two boys up.

"Where are we?" croaked Rich.

"Stinson Beach."

"It stinks."

"That's the dumpster."

"It stinks like rotten fish," said Donny from the back.

"Oh," said Bear, "then that would be the ocean. I mean, it is called Stinson *Beach*. Must be low tide."

Bear got out of the car and walked around to the trunk and unlocked it. He took the blanket from the wheel well and looked at his weapon cache. First, he took his hunting knife and stuck it back into his right boot, then, checking that the safety on the Walther .380 was on, he stuck the gun between his belt and the small of his back. He took two clips and placed them into his jacket pockets, one on each side. He felt weighed down now, encumbered with metal. He picked up the .38, wondering where to put it, and decided it was fine to stick under the driver's seat. He returned to the car with the revolver in his hand and settled in behind the wheel.

Rich watched him hide the gun under the seat, gave him a quick fraternal nod and said, "Packin'."

To which Bear replied with a simple, "Yup."

Rich asked, "You got Donny's piece, too?"

"You meant the one he stole from Gilly? Fuck no. That thing is hidden away. You boys can have it back when this is all over," Bear lied. "We need something we know we can count on, which is why I brought what I brought."

Big Rich was disappointed, and his face showed it, but he knew better than to start arguing about it now.

In the backseat, Donny was reminded they were on a dangerous mission. It'd all been dangerous, he knew, but seeing the snub-nosed .38 being placed beneath the seat crystallized the situation for him. They weren't only going to get their phones back, they were going to rescue the old man. They had to if they ever expected to see a dime from him.

"What's the plan?" asked Donny. "Is there a plan?"

Bear made a sound that was half-sigh, half-growl, and said, "I guess the plan is to go find this house, see what the fuck is going on there, then make up the rest of the plan."

Big Rich clapped his hands together with excitement. "Sounds good to me. Let's go."

Donny, not sounding as confident as his friend, asked, "Bear, you ever done anything like this before?"

"Like what?"

"Like we're gonna do, rescue Gabriel."

"Fuck no," said Bear without even thinking about it. He reached into his jacket for his pack of Camels. "Nothing like it at all."

* * *

While Gabriel was upstairs with Dustin, the other three prepared for the big event. They moved from the kitchen counter to the large oak dining table. There, they spread out the necessary documents and papers. Miranda got herself ready by making sure her tools of the trade were in order, Terrence skimmed over the documents and placed them in their proper stacks, and Raphael set out glasses, empty ceramic cups for coffee, and a carafe of iced water.

When they were done, they sat quietly waiting for Gabriel and Dustin's return. They were patient. It was a somber moment for the three and they sat sipping at the water and fiddling with their empty cups. Raphael wasn't really sure what was going on, he only knew it was very important to Terrence and his guests. Miranda sat ready to do what she needed to do. She wasn't really sure why the VCR was necessary, but she told herself that it didn't concern her; she was here to do a job and that's what she was going to do. Terrence sat stone-faced. He was the only one at the table with any stakes involved and he knew exactly what was going on upstairs.

They all heard the upstairs bedroom door open and shut. They didn't look at each other; they only turned their heads toward the stairs. Gabriel came down first. He was pale and drawn; he looked exhausted, like a condemned man on his final walk to the gallows. Miranda wondered what in the world that boy had shown him on the video. Terrence, on the other hand, knew what was on the video, but he hadn't expected it to hit the old attorney so hard. He figured that Gabriel must have known, on some level, what was coming. But the look on the old man's face told him that Thaxton was caught by complete surprise.

Behind Gabriel, though, Dustin was absolutely beaming. He wore the first real smile of his stay there at Terrence's house. His normal pale, almost bluish pallor showed faint roses of blush on his cheeks. He looked both proud and triumphant.

Only Raphael said something, "Okay, who wants coffee and who wants a drink?"

No one answered but Gabriel. He said quietly, "I'll have one of those mimosas."

Terrence got up and pulled a chair out for Gabriel. He took him gently by the elbow, treating him with great sympathy and care. Gabriel took the chair and sat down with a grunt. Terrence went around the table to the other side and sat down directly across from the old lawyer. Dustin stood behind Gabriel, arms crossed, still smiling.

"Okay, Gabriel," said Terrence, changing his tone from nursemaid to businessman, "let's get down business. Miranda here is a notary. She's going to help us execute the transfer of a deed today. We have everything prepared, so this shouldn't take too long. Then, after, we can all have a drink and you can be on your way."

A second wave of realization swept over Gabriel. He blinked in astonishment and half-turned to Dustin and said, "*This*...this is what you want?"

Dustin stood silent and made no eye contact with Gabriel. His expression hadn't changed; the smile had only tightened on his face. His plan was on the verge of becoming a reality. He was having trouble holding back his excitement.

"We've done the necessary prep work," continued Terrence, "all you need to do is sign. Miranda will notarize them, I'll give you copies for your records and we'll be done." Terrence brushed his hands together, like he was wiping them clean. He was doing his best to keep it businesslike, trying to ignore that the old man was close to breaking down in tears.

Gabriel still spoke to Dustin, "How did you get these?" he said pointing to the papers.

"The only shit you kept locked in that fuckin' safe of yours was your cash and my speed; you never thought I'd want anything else. You never thought I was smart enough."

Dustin's word's came fast, nothing was holding him back now, he was glaring at Gabriel, "You think the shit we were doing was free? You think I liked that shit? No, I'm gettin' what's mine. Nothing in life is free, and it's time for you to ante up."

"What do you plan to do there?"

"Sell it. Maybe I'll live there for a few months and then I'll put in on the market. Sell it, pay my taxes like a good citizen, and get the fuck out of San Francisco."

"You realize who I am, you understand I know the law, I'm going to come after you for this." As Gabriel said this, out of the corner of his eye he could see Terrence shaking his head ever so lightly. He was letting Dustin know that it would be okay, that the deal would go through. Dustin had been coached from the beginning. Terrence had let him know that bank account transfers, living trusts, and wills, could be more complicated, leave a paper trail that could bring felony charges. The transfer of the deed was the simplest way of stinging him for millions.

Terrence interrupted again. "Okay, so here we have the Grant Deed. Gabriel, if you would be so kind as to sign as Grantor, I've marked the spots with the yellow stick-ums."

Gabriel looked down at the little plastic arrows he'd used thousands of times to help a client navigate through documents.

"Also, here's a letter, just a formality, which states you own the house and property in question free and clear." He turned his head to Miranda, "And sweetheart, what do you need from Mr. Thaxton?"

Miranda, who was looking more and more uncomfortable as the gears turned in her head, stammered, "I know you are who you say you are, but just as a formality, like Terry said, I'd like to get some information off of your ID."

"That's to smooth over any bumps down at the City

Recorder's Office, you understand," said Terrence.

Gabriel sat with the pen in front of him. He felt nauseated. He knew Dustin had painted him into a corner. His mind raced for tactics to prevent the transfer from happening.

Dustin put his cold, bony hand on Gabriel's shoulder and said, "You wanna take a minute and go upstairs and watch TV again?"

"No," Gabriel said. He picked up the document and began to read.

CHAPTER 19

The three were wide awake now. They'd left Stinson Beach and were on their last leg of the journey to the lawyer's house. Their anticipation had fueled a feeling of sobriety. Donny leaned forward in his seat; the morning's drugs had worn off enough to where his pain from last night's rape began to assault him all over again. Big Rich, nervous and not knowing what to do to prepare, pulled out a small glass pipe and took a quick hit before Bear could complain.

"What the fuck are you doing?" said Bear. "Blow that shit out the window, I don't wanna breathe it in. Fuck, can't you guys hold off for a few hours while we get this done?"

Rich said, "Sorry, man," but it didn't sound like he meant it. He then passed the pipe to his friend in the backseat. Donny took it gladly and repeated the same quick hit while Bear glared at him in the rearview mirror.

"Great, I'm going into battle with a couple of stone-cold junkie meth heads. This'll be fun. I should let you guys know, if there's any hostage taking, I won't be negotiating for your release."

"You don't even know if he's there," said Rich, lighting another cigarette.

"I already told you I think he is. Why the fuck would we be driving all the way up here if I didn't? What we're about to do is some serious recon shit, like they used to do in the Nam."

Donny finished blowing his hit out the opening of his window and asked Bear, "You were in Vietnam?"

"Fuck, no. I was a kid back then. How old do you think I am?" Bear shook his head. "Point is, we're goin' into a potentially volatile situation. We don't know what's up there, who's up there. All we know is that Dustin fucker is a homicidal psychopath. That's why we have guns."

Big Rich interjected, "I don't have a gun."

"That's why *I* have guns," Bear corrected. "I need you two to have clear heads. We're depending on each other to come out of there unharmed. We need to think like soldiers."

"You sure sound like you were in Vietnam," said Big Rich.

"Well, I wasn't, so stop askin'." Bear spotted the turnoff for McKenna Road and made a right. The two lane wound back and forth, forcing Bear to drive slowly. He saw several gravel roads on either side, but most of them looked like fire roads, unused and not attached to any residence. The farther they drove, the narrower the road became. Bear rolled down his window to see if he could hear any signs of civilization because he sure as hell couldn't see any.

They ascended a few more miles until Bear saw it. A lone mailbox perched on an oily wooden post. There was no name or marking on the box and it stood looking as unused as anything they'd already come across. The driveway beside it, however, was paved. Bear slowed the car down, then stopped.

"What is it?" asked Rich.

"I think this is the place," Bear keeping his voice low now. A sense of caution enveloped them all.

"How do you know?" asked Donny, also now at a whisper.

"I don't fuckin' know, that's what we're here to find out, remember? Now stop askin' so many questions."

Donny felt stupid for asking. He decided to stick close to Bear and follow his lead.

Bear put the car in neutral and rolled it back down the slope a ways, lodging it into some trees just a few feet off the road. It sat straddled in a makeshift ditch. He pulled the .38 out from under the seat and opened the car door.

"How come I don't get a gun?" said Big Rich. "If it's so

fuckin' dangerous up there, then I should have a gun."

"'Cause I don't need you shooting me. I trust your aim about as much as I trust his." He hooked a thumb toward Donny in the back seat. "Tell you what, I still got the stun-gun in my trunk, you can have it if you promise not to electrocute yourself."

"What about me?" asked Donny.

"You worried about stayin' safe? If your friend doesn't have a gun, then your chances of gettin' hurt just dropped by about seventy percent."

Bear walked to the back of the car, opened the truck and rooted around for the stun-gun. He found it and handed it to Rich with a serious look. "If you gotta use this thing, try to hit flesh with it. And hold it there till the fucker drops, he ain't gonna die, so don't be afraid to really zap him."

"Okay, I know what to do."

"Alright fellas, we're gonna go up to the house. I want you to stay behind me and stay quiet. Let's just see what the hell is up there. Don't talk to each other and watch for my signal."

As they moved up the tree-lined driveway, Donny was struck by the silence around them. The air was crisp and fresh. He could smell the ocean, the trees, everything all at once. The serenity belied his nervousness; it only served to make his senses more acute. He felt sharp, wide awake, and not the least bit high. He wasn't sick with withdrawals either. Donny felt alive.

They edged up the paved drive, Bear first, flanked by Donny and Rich. They heard nothing but the wind in the trees. Then they saw it, a huge house with shining windows reflecting the sky. It looked like the sheer face of a cliff, but it was glowing sun yellow and sky blue. Bear had to squint his eyes.

"There she is," he said.

"And there's the Bentley," said Big Rich, pointing to the black car parked in front of the house. It sat there, empty, unattended and sandwiched between a Jaguar and a Volvo. Further to the right sat a green Mazda with a bumper sticker that read "Goddess is my Co-pilot." Seeing the old man's car was a confirmation that they were indeed at the right place. It filled all three with a simultaneous sense of excitement and dread.

Bear turned and put his index finger to his lips, shushing the boys, but they were already quiet. He waved them back down the driveway where they could huddle and discuss a plan.

When they were out of sight and in the cover of the trees, Bear said, "I'm gonna go around back. Donny, you stand point, there on the right corner. That way, if anyone comes out the front, or if you hear anything at all, you signal."

"What about me?" asked Rich.

"You come with me. When I know it's clear, you'll take my spot and I'll go farther in, check out the back of the place. Donny signals you, you signal me. We'll have a line of sight all the way around the house."

The boys both nodded, although they weren't really sure what they were to do. Donny moved up to the mouth of the drive and watched the other two creep past him toward the back of the house. He chose a spot behind an untamed bush to squat. From there, he could see the front door and all along the right side of the house. If someone were to open the door, he'd still be out of sight. He crouched and waited there, keeping an eye on Rich who stood at the rear corner of the house while Bear disappeared around the back.

The first thing Bear saw was the big deck hanging from the back of the house; it was elevated on support beams and had just enough room for him to slip underneath. He had to crouch, but he could fit. The whole place was built on an upward slope so he figured the deck was still attached to the first floor. It would be just off the main living area, whether it was a kitchen or living room. Now, whoever was inside was probably right above his head, only a few feet away. He stood there a moment listening. He finally heard voices, too muffled to make out. All he could tell was that there was more than one. Several in fact, but there was no way to guess how many.

The glass door slid open above his head. He watched as two feet stepped out on the deck above him, then he heard the door slide shut again. Bear couldn't tell who it was; all he saw was the shadow cast down, breaking up the thin lines of light that shone between the boards. Whoever it was, they were a smoker. Bear heard the unmistakable sound of a disposable lighter being struck, followed by a cough. The sweet, skunky smell of high-grade marijuana wafted down followed by another round of coughing. Bear looked to the side of the house where Rich was supposed to be. He was nowhere in sight. The plan was already failing.

The person above him getting high moved to the edge of the deck and leaned on the rail. Bear could see the blue-grey smoke being blown outward to the sloping backyard. Bear took a silent step forward and looked up. Now he could see the chin, a young chin. It wasn't Dustin and it sure as hell wasn't the old man. From what he'd gathered about Terrence, it wasn't him either.

The smoker started to hum, quietly at first, and then it escalated to a singing. The words were in Spanish. That made three: Gabriel, Dustin, and this guy. Bear had to assume that Terrence was up there somewhere, too. That would make four.

He waited for the smoking and the singing to stop. It didn't. Bear figured it was now or never. He stepped out from below the deck and pointed his .38 straight at the head of the person standing at the ledge.

"Don't make a fuckin' sound."

Raphael made an audible squeak and dropped his roach. It landed right between Bear's feet.

"Now, c'mon down here."

"Who are you?" said Raphael, obviously terrified.

"I'm the guy who's got a gun aimed right at your forehead, that's who. Now walk to the stairs and come down here and talk to me. Don't turn around, don't shout or scream or nothin'. Otherwise, I'm going to shoot." Bear was nervous, but he held his gun steady. He knew the sliding glass door was shut; odds were whoever was inside wasn't listening or watching. "I'm only gonna ask once." He cocked back the hammer for added effect.

Raphael had a hurt look on his face, but he did what he was told. He walked stiffly to the edge of the deck and descended the wooden stairs. Once below, he took a deep breath for courage and faced Bear.

"Who is in the house?"

"*Que?*"

"Nice try, amigo. Who's up there, how many?"

"Look, if you came about the crop, there's nothing there. It's not ready yet."

"Crop? What're you talkin' about? You think I'm here to steal weed? I want to know who's inside the house, right now. Start talking or I start shooting, then I'm gonna go in and find out for myself."

Raphael broke down. He fell to his knees and began mock weeping. Bear wasn't buying it. First this guy pretended he couldn't speak English and now he was pretending to cry.

"How many? Is Terrence up there? Is Dustin? What about the old guy? Where is he?"

Raphael's shoulders shook and his chest puffed in and out with quick breaths. Bear realized he really was sobbing.

Terrence watched Raphael go outside for a smoke. When things got too confusing for the boy, he liked to smoke a little weed. It didn't help at all. Not ever. He inevitably ended up more confused than he started out. Terrence didn't blame him for wanting to step out. The tension around the dining room table was palatable. Gabriel was reading over the deed transfer slowly while Dustin paced around behind him. Terrence figured the old man was stalling, but it didn't matter, as soon as he signed the document the deal would be done. All they had to do was have it recorded in the city and there was no going back. Terrence leaned back in his chair and waited patiently.

When he looked back out at the deck, Raphael was gone from his view. He didn't think anything of it until a few more minutes went by. Usually Raphael only took a couple hits, then came back in. His young friend wasn't one for spontaneous nature walks. Raphael wouldn't leave houseguests unattended either—hosting was one of his only skills.

Terrence watched the empty deck and waited. His instincts started to kick in; he got up and went to the front of the house, pulled back a curtain, and peeked through one of the many glass windows. Nothing out there, no strange cars, no movement. He still felt unsettled. He went back into the kitchen and reached down to one of the bottom drawers beside the sink. From it, he pulled a Glock 17 and a fresh clip. He slapped the clip into the gun.

Miranda saw the gun in Terrence's hand and looked like she wanted to say something, but fear kept her quiet.

Not Dustin, he saw the gun and his senses immediately sharpened. "What is it?"

"Nothin'," said Terrence as he racked it and put one in the chamber.

Dustin told Gabriel, "That's enough readin', sign it *now.*"

Terrence stepped to the sliding glass door and pulled it open. Without going through, he called out to Raphael. No response. "Shit."

At the table, Dustin was hurrying Gabriel and Miranda up. "C'mon, c'mon, let's go. Sign that thing. Gather up your shit, we're going upstairs. Move it."

"Look," said Miranda, "I don't know what's going on here. But, if I were called to testify that the signor was under some form of duress..."

Dustin's face curled up like a gargoyle's. "Bitch, get your shit and move."

Miranda's eyes and mouth popped into the same oval shape. "I...I..."

Dustin reached across the table and took a fistful of her hair and gave it a sharp tug. She whimpered but didn't speak. She started stuffing papers into her floral briefcase.

"Raphael?" Terrence called again, louder this time. Still, no response. The clamor behind him at the table was making it hard to hear. He pointed the gun out the door, followed by one foot, then the other. He was studying the lines between the boards, trying to see if there was someone below him. There was no way to tell. Terrence edged closer to the railing, holding the Glock with both hands.

"Goddamn it, Raphael, if you're out here, say something."

"Something," answered a voice. It wasn't Raphael's voice.

At the edge of the wood, down the slope about twenty yards, Terrence saw Raphael being held from behind by a big, bearded man who was holding a revolver to his head.

"Put down the gun," the bearded man said.

"You put down *your* gun or I'll shoot you both." Terrence lifted his gun up and held it with both hands.

There was a long hanging moment when all they could hear was the commotion of people moving in the house.

Bear repeated himself, "Put down your gun."

Another few seconds went by and Bear decided that the man on the porch would not shoot. He added, "Put it down and send out Thaxton."

Terrence fired twice.

The first shot went right through Raphael. The force knocked them both backward. The bullet went clear through

Raphael's shoulder. Bear heard it hit a tree behind him. The second shot missed entirely, partly because the first one knocked them off of their mark and partly because the kick from the first shot forced Terrence to lose his aim. Still holding Raphael, Bear fired back once, but Terrence was already bent over, retreating back into the house.

"I am shot, I am shot," cried Raphael, then, "Don't kill me, don't kill me."

Bear left him laying there and moved toward the stairs of the deck.

As soon as he saw the guy smoking pot on the deck, Big Rich slunk down at the side of the house. He wanted to keep out of sight. He could still see Donny hiding behind the bush in front, but didn't know what he should do. Donny kept waving at him and Rich kept responding by shrugging his shoulders. He pushed his back up against the wall and kept static. He felt exhausted, his body crashing from the adrenaline he'd experienced when they'd come up on the house. He wondered if he and Donny's phones were inside the Bentley or inside the house. Holding still was making his mind drift, and before he realized he'd begun to slip into a nod.

Gunshots brought him out of it. Three of them.

Rich got up and ran toward Donny.

Donny stood up and shouted, "What the fuck are you doing?"

"Get down, they're shootin'." Rich slid behind the bush with Donny like he was sliding into third base.

"Where's Bear?"

"I dunno, last I saw he was walkin' under the porch."

"What do we do?"

"I dunno," said Rich, still out of breath. "Donny?"

"What?"

"You think our phones are in the Bentley?"

"You kiddin' me? I don't fuckin' know. Why don't you go check?" Donny wasn't serious, but to his amazement, Rich got up and ran toward the Bentley. He watched as Rich cupped his hands and peered into the car's window. Then, with a grin, Rich turned and gave him the thumbs up signal.

Bear entered through the glass doors slowly with his gun raised, just like he'd seen a million times on TV. He panned the empty kitchen space looking down the barrel of his .38. The place looked deserted. He could smell the food, saw the abandoned drinks, and noticed blood on the floor. He must have winged Terrence. He listened. The only thing he could hear was his heart beating in his ears and the distant cries of the wounded man he'd left in the back yard.

His mouth was dry with fear and he wanted badly to pick up one of the drinks left on the counter and have a swallow, but he kept the pistol raised, ready to fire. He stepped slowly through the kitchen till he could see the front door. A living room on his right—tacky white furniture—and a carpeted flight of stairs to his left. He saw drops of blood on the stairs. Like breadcrumbs, thought Bear.

They were up there, somewhere.

Fuck it, he decided, and reached out and grabbed a pint glass of orange juice off the kitchen counter. *Champagne, nice.* He took another big gulp and got ready to go up to the second level. But, when he set down the pint glass, he spotted his cell phone sitting on the counter. What d'ya know, thought Bear as he scooped it up and stuck it into his front pocket. He turned toward the staircase again and prepared to ascend. Where the hell were those boys? He took one step up the stairs and heard movement, someone was up there. He took another step and could have sworn he heard a woman's voice. Then, from outside, he heard the sound of glass breaking.

* * *

Rich was looking around for the biggest rock he could find. He found one, lifted it up, felt the weight in his hand like an oversized baseball, and pitched it at the Bentley's rear passenger window. The sound of the breaking glass shattered the silence in the air. Big Rich leaned into the car, reached down onto the seat, and grabbed both the phones. He pulled back out through the broken glass and triumphantly held the cells up to Donny.

Donny shuttered as the glass broke. It was like the sound of an alarm. He felt suddenly exposed as he watched Rich wave to him with the phones. Donny waved back.

"C'mere," he said in a whispered voice that only he could hear. Big Rich stood beside the Bentley, a phone in each raised hand.

A window opened on the second story of the house and a gun appeared. That's the way Donny saw it, no hand, no arm, just the gun. *Bam.* And Big Rich was down in a small cloud of dust.

It took a moment to register what had happened. Donny sat helpless waiting to see if his friend would move. He didn't. Rich lay still in the sun with the dust settling around him. Upstairs, the gun had disappeared back into the window, a yellow curtain waving there in its place. Donny sat frozen, looking at Rich's body, looking at the yellow curtain peeking out of the window. His mind raced. Was Bear still alive? Were those shots he'd heard from the back of the house fired at Bear—or by him? How would he get out of this place if the both Rich and Bear were dead?

He didn't know what else to do, so Donny got up and ran toward his friend. He got to him and squatted down, staring at the ugly gunshot wound in the middle of Rich's chest. Donny felt the sun on his back and wondered if the eyes of the shooter where on his back, too. The hole in Rich's chest was making a sound. Half gurgle, half whistle.

Donny told Rich, "You're alive." He wanted to reassure his friend, but instead it came out sounding as though he were surprised.

"Yeah, I'm fuckin' alive. Get me outta here, man. Take me to a hospital or somethin'."

Donny did the only thing he could do: he dragged his friend around to the back of the Bentley and positioned him in the shade. It seemed like it was the best place to avoid being shot. From where they were now, Donny couldn't see that yellow curtain, so he hoped whoever was behind it couldn't see him.

"Donny?"

"What?"

"I got the phones." The cells lay in the dust on the other side of the car. "I got 'em, Donny. Now we can get the money, right?"

"Right," said Donny, trying to sound comforting.

"Donny?"

"I don't think you should talk, try to hold still. Just hang in there till we can get you some help."

"There really are pictures of my kid in there. There's a bunch saved. I'm going back to Oregon, like I said. I'm gonna be with them again."

"I know, Rich, I know."

Donny couldn't help staring at the gunshot wound. It was red and meaty; blood was pumping out of it with every beat of Rich's heart. Whenever his friend took a breath, tiny red air bubbles would appear on the hole and make a wet, sticky pop.

"Donny?"

"Seriously, stop talkin', save your strength. I'm gonna go in back and find out what happened to Bear and get his keys. We'll drive you to a hospital and eveything'll be okay."

"Don't forget the phones. We gotta have the phones."

"I won't forget the phones."

"Donny?"

"What?"

"I'm not gay."

"I know you're not. Be quiet now, save your strength."

Donny held Rich's hand as his friend slid into uncon-sciousness and he wished more anything that he was higher than he was.

CHAPTER 20

Bear was only two steps up the carpeted stairs when he heard the gunshot. His heart stopped, only for one beat, but it stopped. He realized how scared he was.

"Shit," he murmured under his breath and took another step up the stairs. By the fourth stair he could see hallway. It was empty. He had his gun raised and kept his sight-line down the barrel. He felt the sweat on his palms against the grip. He wanted to call Gabriel's name, but instead took another step.

When he reached the hallway, he heard voices. He couldn't tell what room, not for sure. There were three doors on his right and he saw what he figured was a bathroom door on his left sandwiched in between two closets.

The door to the first room on his right was ajar. He could tell it was empty, silent. He looked inside and moved past. The second door was closed. He held his position at outside the door and listened. He could hear Dustin. He could hear a woman crying. Nothing else. Not Gabriel, not Terrence. He stood still for a moment, wondering what to do. Was Gabriel in there, was he alive? Did he kill Terrence with that shot on the porch? Bear reached down toward the doorknob and froze. He couldn't open it; he wanted to have both hands on his gun when it opened up. Five bullets, he thought. Should be enough. He moved and placed his back against the opposite wall and kicked the door as hard as he could.

The door swung open and he saw Dustin holding a woman in front of him. He held her by her brown dirty hair with his left hand and in his right he had a black semi-automatic pressed against her cheek.

"Don't fuckin' move," Bear said. He had his gun pointed right at Dustin's face.

Dustin didn't move.

In his peripheral vision he saw Gabriel in a chair with his head in his hands and Terrence splayed out on the bed, bleeding from the leg.

"Don't *you* fuckin' move or I'll shoot her," Dustin was sneering.

"Put down your gun."

"Fuck you, asshole. You piece of shit. You put down *your* gun."

Terrence started to get up off the bed.

"I said, don't move," said Bear, but Terrence kept getting up anyway—slowly, not because he was cautious, but because he was in pain.

"Get the shit, Terry," Dustin said.

Gabriel hadn't moved. He sat there with his head in his hands.

"You alright, Thaxton?" asked Bear. He kept his gun pointed right at Dustin's face. Gabriel didn't answer; he kept his head in his hands.

Bear watched as Terrence—Terry the lawyer—limped across to the dresser and pulled the floral briefcase off the top.

"Stop fucking moving or I'm gonna shoot," Bear repeated.

Terrence stopped. He was in the middle of the room now, closer to Bear than to Dustin and the woman. He stood there, still, waiting for instructions.

Dustin shot the woman. Right through the cheek. The shock of the gun blast was deafening. A huge splatter of blood and brain sprayed onto the ceiling, wall, and curtain. The second it happened, Terrence swung the briefcase at Bear. Bear ducked and fired at the same time. His shot went wild, breaking the window behind Dustin's head. He pulled back into the hall as Dustin let three more shots go through the doorway.

Bear retreated through the third door down the hall. He didn't bother to consider if someone was inside or not. He stuck his gun barrel out the door and waited for Dustin to make a break for the stairs. He was going to shoot that fucker right in the back.

But when Dustin came into the hall, he shot right at the door. The bullet splintered the doorjamb right beside Bear's head. Bear pulled his head back into the room and said, "Shit." He heard footsteps. When he poked his head back out, they were already down the stairs. Bear ran into the room where Gabriel still sat.

"Thaxton, are you okay?"

No answer.

"Thaxton, fuckin' talk to me. Say somethin'."

Gabriel lifted his head and said, "I'm okay." But he didn't look okay. He was pale and drawn, his facial muscles were slack. Bear figured he was close to being in shock.

"Get up, man. We got to go," said Bear. "Can you walk?"

Gabriel didn't answer, but he did try to get up. Slow and deliberate, looking like a man of a hundred years.

"Fuck, Gabriel, let's move. We gotta get you outta here."

"Did he shoot my friend?" asked Gabriel.

"I got no idea, let's get out of this room and find out."

As soon as Donny heard the shots and saw the window break, he started running to the back of the house. The first thing he saw was a man rolling and writhing in pain at the edge of the lawn. He'd remembered to grab the phones, but had forgotten the stun-gun. The injured guy wasn't going anywhere, but Donny still felt vulnerable with no weapon whatsoever. From somewhere in front, he heard car doors slamming, and he felt a pang of panic and regret that he'd left his injured friend laying in the dirt.

He moved up the deck's stairs and into the kitchen without

caution. The place was empty and quiet and felt like a crime scene.

"Bear," he called out. No answer. Donny could feel his heart beating in his chest.

"Bear!" he cried again. This time he heard an answer. From upstairs.

Donny bolted up the stairs, still calling Bear's name.

"In here, in here."

He heard a voice from inside the second bedroom and Donny went straight in.

Bear was helping the old man up, holding him by the elbow. There was a body on the floor, a woman Donny had never seen. She lay on her back with her eyes open wide, a pool of thick blood growing around her head. He felt the urge to vomit, but his throat was closed tight.

"What the fuck?"

"Don't look at her. You can't help her," said Bear. "Help me get Gabriel outta here."

But Donny couldn't help but look at her. She had a dark red hole under her right cheek and her open eyes bulged out at him. Her limbs were twisted like a broken doll's and she was bleeding. So much blood. It was still coming out of her, feeding that puddle around her head. Donny wished he could be sick.

"Where's your friend?"

Donny didn't answer; he gaped at the dead woman.

"Where's Rich?" Bear repeated.

"Somebody shot him. He's outside. I dunno if he's gonna be okay. He looks bad."

"Let's go find out. I think those assholes are gone. I heard a car. Did you see 'em?"

Donny shook his head, still looking at the woman.

* * *

"We're fucked," said Terrence. He sat in the passenger seat of Gabriel's Bentley while Dustin drove.

"No, we're not. This'll still work. We just gotta get this thing filed."

"We're fucked, Dustin. We fucked up. This is all bad. There's no coming back from this. I got bodies in my house."

"I know it's bad, but it can still work. We'll make up a story. Self-defense. We'll even get that old fucker to defend us. You'll see. We just gotta make it to the recorder first thing."

"Defend us? He's on the phone to the cops right now." Terrence turned his head toward the window. "My life is over. I got to get this gunshot taken care of. Where am I gonna do that? There's gonna be an investigation. There's no coming back from this."

"Roll down your window. I'm fuckin' boiling," said Dustin. Terrence rolled it down. Dustin pulled off onto one of the abandoned fire roads.

"What are you doing?" asked Terrence.

Dustin slowed to a stop when the gravel road degraded into a two track trail.

"This fuckin' gun is pokin' me right in the back." Dustin pulled the Glock from where it was wedged behind the small of his back. He pointed it at Terrence's head and pulled the trigger.

Dry click. No bullets.

"You piece of shit," said Terrence before Dustin clocked him in the temple with the butt of the Glock. Dustin hit him three more times and dropped the empty gun so he could use both hands on his throat.

Terrence fought back the best he could, but Dustin gripped and squeezed, digging his thumbs in to crush his windpipe. Terrence lost consciousness.

Dustin got out of the car, went around to the passenger side, and opened the door. Terrence's body fell out easily. Dustin dragged him a few feet from the car and climbed on top of him. He twisted Terrence's head around using all his strength, waited till he heard a crack, making sure he was dead.

He dragged Terrence's corpse back into the trees until the brush got too thick and he couldn't pull him any farther. It was hard tugging that dead weight and Dustin was winded and sweating. Finally he let go and let the body drop. He twisted the head back around from its unnatural position and listened at the mouth carefully to make sure there was no breath. Then he walked back to the car, got in, fired the engine, and backed out of the trail.

Before he hit the pavement though, Dustin reached into his jean jacket and pulled his glass pipe from his pocket. "Thank God," he said when he saw it still intact. He found his lighter, held the flame under the bowl and took a long, slow pull. He watched the yellow smoke curl in the bulb at the end and sucked it in. He then tilted the rearview down and watched as the thin smoke, now gray, exited his lungs. "This is gonna work," he told his reflection.

"Wait," said Gabriel. They were at the top of the stairs. Bear was holding his left elbow and Donny was holding his right.

"What? What is it?" said Bear.

"I've forgotten something," Gabriel said, "I'll be right back." He turned and went into the first bedroom on the right and shut the door.

Bear and Donny stood looking at each other while they listened to the sounds of Gabriel rummaging through the empty room. They heard him saying, *Damn it*, and, *Lord God*. Bear waited another thirty seconds before opening the door.

"Gabriel, let's go. There's no time to fuck around. We wanna get outta here."

"Just a minute," said Gabriel He rummaged through the dressers. He pulled open each drawer and slammed it shut. Then, he did it again.

"What the hell are you lookin' for?"

"He's got it. He took it with him," Gabriel said to himself.

"Took what with him?" asked Donny.

Gabriel looked at Donny with a crooked little smile. He looked wounded and absolutely distracted. "Let's just go," he said.

When they got to the bottom of the stairs, Bear let go of Gabriel's elbow and grabbed the unfinished mimosa from the kitchen counter where he had found his cell phone. He gulped and looked at it, trying to remember if there was anything else in the house he'd touched. He took another slug and decided to take the glass with him.

The front door was still open and as soon as they stepped through it they could see Big Rich splayed out in the driveway. Donny let go of Gabriel's elbow now and ran toward his friend. It looked as though Dustin and Terrence had run over Rich's legs in their hurry to escape. Rich lay twisted in the dirt, blue skin, blue lips, and a red, wet chest. Donny got down and leaned in close. He listened for breath, heard nothing, then put his head against Rich's chest hoping to hear a beat. Nothing. Donny sat up—Rich's blood covering the side of his face—and shook his head.

Big Rich was dead.

"Don't look at him, kid. If he's dead, he's dead. You can't do nothin' for him. Help me get Thaxton into the car."

The three hurried down the driveway toward the spot where Bear had hidden the car. Gabriel tried to keep up but was hobbling with an exhausted gait. Bear took him again by the elbow and rushed him along till they reached his Toyota.

Bear handed off Thaxton to the boy and Donny helped get him into the passenger seat. Before he got in, Gabriel turned his eyes back toward the house where his young friend lay dead in the gravel. He mumbled something about it being "all his fault." Donny pushed him into the seat and strapped him in.

Before they left, Bear pulled back up to the house, hopped out, and went around back to check on the other guy with the shoulder wound. He knew that Dustin and Terrence didn't have enough time to go back and fetch him. He half expected the guy to be gone, or be waiting for him, ready to fight. He wasn't. The guy was face down, dead on the lawn. He'd crawled halfway to the deck stairs and bled out. The grass around him was sticky and red. Bear nudged him with his boot. The guy was meat, heavy and lifeless. Bear headed back around to the car in front.

CHAPTER 21

Bear climbed into the driver's seat and started the car. He looked over at his passengers. Both Donny in the back and Gabriel beside him were deep in throes, silent, mourning the loss of their friend. Each had their head against the window and were lost in thought.

Bear broke the silence. "So, what's it gonna be, Thaxton? The hospital first? We can call the police from there."

"No," said Gabriel, still staring out the window, "No police. Not now. I want to call Beatrice."

"Bean? What for?"

"There are some documents I've stored at her apartment; I want her to bring them to me. I'll call and we can meet her in the city."

Bear thought the old man might be in shock. "Are you nuts? We can't leave a scene like this without calling the cops. They'll end up charging *us* with somethin'."

Gabriel turned his head toward Bear. He cleared his throat. "Bear, we have to. I have another deed to the house in Beatrice's possession, signed, notarized, and ready to go. I can transfer the possession of my home to her. If we can record that deed before Dustin records his, he won't be able to get the house."

"What the hell are you talking about? What deed?"

"That's what the boy was doing. He had me up here to sign over my house to him."

"Listen, Gabe, none of that matters now. The kid fucked himself. There are bodies all over the place. We need to get to the cops and stop that little fuck before he gets too far."

"He's not going far. I know him. He's going to the San

208

Francisco County Recorder's office. He'll be up all night waiting for them to open."

"No, I can't do this. We have to go to the cops. If that's what he's doing, then let the cops pick him up there. No way can the deed be good if he pulled this kinda shit to get it signed, right?"

Gabriel only said, "No police."

"Thaxton, think about what you're sayin'. You gonna tell me that it's okay to leave a crime scene as fucked up as this? You probably got fingerprints all over the house. They're gonna come after *you* when they find the bodies."

"I don't think so. I heard Terrence tell Dustin that they already had a clean-up crew ready. That's what they said. They were going to clean the house, wipe it down, hide the victims. They've allowed for this, planned for it. I don't want the police involved. I'll worry about Dustin after we've recorded the other deed."

Bear gripped the steering wheel and pushed himself back into the seat. He let the car sit and idle while he thought about what to do. Finally he said, "Gabriel, what the fuck does that kid have on you? Why aren't you doing the right thing here?"

Gabriel ignored the question, "Let's just call Beatrice and have her meet us at my office."

"No," said Bear, "I ain't movin' till you tell me what the fuck is goin' on."

Bear listened to the short, frustrated breath that shot in and out of the old lawyer's nose. Gabriel was wrestling with the truth, his conscience, and the result was audible.

"Fine. Dustin has a tape, an old VCR tape. I think he has it with him. I need the tape back. Then we can let the chips fall where they may. But first, I need to have that tape."

"What's on the tape, Gabe?"

"Something that could ruin me—destroy everything I've built."

"What's on the tape?" Bear repeated.

"It could even land me in prison."

"Fuck, Gabriel, where do you think the shit here at this house is gonna land you? Leaving the scene, tampering, I don't even know what. You got to get your head straight, man. This Dustin is a goddamned psychopath; he needs to be put away for good."

"I appreciate your concern, Bear, but I'm the attorney here. I'm the one qualified to hypothesize about the risks and results." Gabriel was regaining some of his eloquence. "I'm grateful for your attempt to rescue me, but I have to examine the situation for all its potential. There are consequences greater than you can calculate."

"Attempt? Yeah, you're fuckin' welcome." Bear reached into his jacket for a smoke, lit it, and said, "Bullshit. Total bullshit."

"Terrence said that the clean-up crew was on their way. I don't want to be around when they get here."

"That also sounds like total bullshit. You need to clue me in, Thaxton, or this is gonna be one short fuckin' ride."

Bear threw the Toyota into drive and the tires gave an abrupt squeal as he peeled out of the driveway.

"Donny," he said. The boy was near catatonic, staring out the window. "Put your seatbelt on. God forbid we break any laws."

They were winding down the asphalt road as fast as it would carry them. Each of their minds focused far ahead of the car, to the city, where their fates would thrust them into another confrontation—if not prison. Bear gripped the steering wheel so tight the tips of his knuckles appeared white. Gabriel kept his eyes straight ahead and both hands placed flatly on each knee. The gears of his mind churned away while he calculated possible outcomes of the day's events. He tried to conjure ways to do damage control. Beads of sweat grew on his upper lip as he thought.

Only Donny in the backseat was pulled back into the moment. The sadness and shock of seeing his friend blown away was quickly being quelled by the immediacy of his withdrawals. Nothing kept you in the moment quite like dope sickness. He was cold and felt goose bumps rising on his skin. His stomach began to churn. After a fit of sneezes he leaned forward and said, "I gotta go to the bathroom."

"Hang in there, kid. We'll be back to civilization soon."

A few more turns. The fading sunlight through the tall trees cast shadows across the windshield that appeared to Donny as a strobe light, making him nauseated. The lack of sleep combined with the events of the day was making the sickness come on faster than usual.

He leaned in between the front seats again. "I really gotta go."

"I'll pull over," said Bear. "You can piss on a tree."

"No, I need a bathroom. I gotta shit."

"You got to be kiddin'. After all this?"

"I got to go," repeated Donny.

"The closest place I can think of is the shitter at that gas station we stopped at on the way up. Can you hold on that long? Pinch it up, man."

Donny flopped back into the rear. He began feeling his jacket pockets to make sure he had all his gear intact. Spoon, lighter, rig—there were two of them, good—and the dope, two small balloons tucked into the change pocket of his jeans. He didn't think to grab Rich's dope before they left. Stupid. He decided he'd shoot a whole balloon when he got to the gas station. He deserved it, he needed it. Even thinking about getting well, the dope in his pocket had a way of making the sickness recede. He was feeling better already, he just had to wait.

He rocked back and forth a little in his seat until he saw

Bear watching him in the rearview. He stopped moving. Letting his nervous hands fall to his sides, he touched the two cell phones on the seat beside him. Their importance seemed ridiculous to him now. He hated looking at them. He didn't care about the plan, the movie, he only wanted to get high and figure a way to get out of this car, away from this day, the memory of it. He'd rather be back on the corner than in the situation he was right now.

They eventually reached the main road and took a left on Highway One toward the city. The gas station was only a few more miles. Donny got ready.

Before they'd even come to a complete stop Donny's door was open. Bear coasted the car into the same spot as before, behind the dumpster and out of sight.

Donny said, "Be right back."

Neither Bear nor Gabriel answered.

Bear waited until the boy had shut the restroom door before telling Gabriel, "Alright, Thaxton, out with it. What the fuck is on that tape? I'm not driving another inch until you tell me what's really going on. I wanna know why a man like you—a lawyer, a so-called officer of the court—would defy common sense, would break the fucking law—like we are—risk everything and put yourself, and *me*, further into the jackpot. What are you doing? What are *we* doing?"

"Bear, I'm sorry, but..."

Bear watched as the old lawyer tried to gain composure, to act like he had any credibility.

"But you just need to trust me on this. It's going to be okay."

"You gotta be kidding me."

"I know it sounds terrible, but, as your attorney, I assure you that your actions in helping me can be explained later. If you act on my advice, I can promise you that you will not jeopardize your freedom."

"What happens when it comes out? And it will. You think

212

what happened back there will just go away?"

"No, but I'm advising you that we have no choice, this is the only way we can hope to bring this murderous villain to justice. It is imperative that we meet him before he slips away."

"What makes you think he hasn't slipped away already? You know what's coming out of your mouth is bullshit. Anyone can understand that. The world is gonna wanna know why we didn't go to the cops right away. *I want to know*, goddamn it. You need to tell me why the fuck I would follow you down this hole, Gabe. You need to spill, before I go any further. Otherwise you can just get the fuck out and me and the kid will drive to the nearest police station and deal with what comes."

Gabriel gripped his knees.

"I mean it. Start talkin' or start walkin'."

Gabriel sighed and glanced over at the closed restroom door.

"Bear," he said, his voice quiet now, "how much do you know about Mr. Dustin Walczak and his history?"

"I know what I dug up on the Internet. I know about the killings, three of them. I know that you're the one that sprung him."

"Yes, it was me who won his reversal. No small task either. It took years and some manipulation of the original evidence to secure his freedom."

"You tampered?"

"Well, that's one way of putting it."

Bear was astonished. He'd known Gabriel to be a man of the law, a wizard at bending it, but never breaking it. In all his experience with Thaxton, Spreckle, and White, never had the idea of doing something as outrageous as tampering ever even been broached.

"Why? Why for him?"

Gabriel's eyes finally met Bear's. "The tape. He's always

had it. I've known it and I've gone to great lengths to keep it hidden. The tape would be the end of me, I'd be ruined. My career, my family, even my freedom."

Bear had known Gabriel long enough to think there was nothing he couldn't quash with his legal talents. He found it hard to believe that there could be something so threatening that would break a man like this.

"What's on it?'

"You know, there was a thread connecting those murders Dustin committed. A thread we kept hidden from discovery, hidden from the prosecution." Gabriel paused now to see if Bear was following where this was heading. "That thread was me."

"You? How? What do you mean?"

"I knew all three of those men. I didn't know them well, but they were acquaintances. We were part of a social circle. I guess that's what you'd call it. We saw each other at parties and other select events. We were a group of men who kept our secret lives obscured from our families. We were homosexuals, yes, but we were also family men—successful family men—who felt it was our duty to protect our loved ones from the truth. Every one of us felt that our success would be threatened if the truth about our sexuality came out. It sounds silly, I know, what with the way society views these things today, but, when you're on the other side of the fence, it can be quite intimidating, I assure you.

"This was during the late nineties; the dot-com boom was still in full swing. Many of our group had gone from being wealthy to super-wealthy. With our increasing fortunes, the importance of keeping our secret grew."

"So you knew 'em. So what? What does that make for, a conflict of interest?"

"There's more to it than that. These parties we threw, they often, well not often, *always* had a sexual theme. They were designed as a sort of safe outlet for our more decadent desires.

We would have entertainment provided, and the entertainment was usually younger men. The parties would be held at one of the member's households when his family was out of town. The young men were to be provided by another member." Gabriel cleared his throat and went on, "One such party took place at the home of Ronald Gower. You probably remember his name from the articles, he was victim number two. That night at Gower's home, I was to be the one providing the entertainment. I'd done so before, but this time I'd thought of bringing an old friend of mine, someone new to that circle, a young man who'd just been released from prison. You see, years before I'd started up an improper relationship with a client. A foolish indiscretion, I know, but I'd always been attracted to what we used to call rough trade."

"Dustin," interjected Bear.

"Yes, Dustin. Anyway, I knew it was wrong, but it was one of those things. It kept going long after it should have stopped. Dustin and I had brief, clandestine dalliances that were eventually interrupted by one of his short stints in prison. But when he was released, I was usually one of his first calls. Anyway, at the time of this party I was still involved with Dustin. He was different then, to some extent anyway. The drugs hadn't done to him what they've now done. Perhaps they had and I just didn't see the signs, I don't know. But, I offered him some money to escort me to this party and befriend some of my associates there. He did. You see, I introduced him to the victims, all three of them. I was the one who brought him into their lives. It was me."

"How's the tape figure in?"

"I'm getting to that. Dustin did what he does; he slept with the men, the victims, and began a passing relationship with them as well. However, as I say, this was in the height of the dot-com era. Silicon Valley was simply floating in cash. I, too, wanted to be in on the cash. My extravagant lifestyle—my dual lifestyle—had taken a toll on my bank account. I'd backed off a bit at my practice and there was simply more money going out than coming in. I'd been enamored with some of the figures my associates had bragged about earning and I decided to invest in a few projects with them. At first, things were going well, then came the bust. If you remember, the end of the dot-coms came fast and sudden. There were a lot of people left scratching their heads, wondering where the money went.

"That was when Dustin started pushing me to exact revenge. He repeatedly told me that I'd been screwed, that these men had taken me purposefully. He kept at me, saying that I was to get what I was owed. I brushed this off at first, believing myself to be just another soul who'd lost big at the wrong time. However, after a time, his logic began to make sense. I don't know if I ever really believed if they'd set out to take my cash, but there was a convenience in thinking I was a victim. Part of me, I suppose, only wanted to recoup. I'd used more of the firm's money than my own in the ventures and I'd made the mistake of keeping it a secret from my partners. Investing in online startups would have been a laughable idea at the office. With good reason, too, I came to find out. I'd lost a bundle and only wanted to go on living the way I had been with no consequences. It was foolish, I know that now, but it was the selfish way I was thinking.

"Eventually, Dustin hatched a scheme to get back some of my losses. I, of course, was against it. It was illegal and I wanted no part, but Dustin was going to proceed with or without me, telling me it didn't matter what I said or did. When he'd achieved success, he promised he'd give me my money back. I suppose I secretly hoped he would succeed and I turned a blind-eye to his activities. By this time I was deep in denial about the strange turn our relationship had taken. He was calling too many shots, and I, I'm sorry to admit, was letting it happen. It was a bit like being under a spell. Not love, but something different.

"What started out as a grand scheme to blackmail and extort these men quickly turned into torture, then murder. Of course, the money never came; I don't doubt that Dustin got it. He simply moved into these men's lives, like some sort of super-parasite, and within weeks they started turning up dead."

"Jesus," said Bear.

"Indeed. Dustin is a sick, but deceptively bright and manipulative young man. He latched onto these men, took what they had, and then destroyed and killed them."

"You still haven't told me what's on the tape."

"Yes, the tape. Ronald Gower had a dangerous fetish for men of our ilk; he liked to videotape his sexual conquests. A bit akin to a serial killer keeping bits of evidence to enjoy later. Against my advice, he made several tapes at these parties, tapes that Dustin discovered while he was taking over the home of Mr. Gower. On these tapes, besides other things, there is videotaped evidence of me introducing the killer to his victims, all three of them."

Bear asked, "What *other* things?"

Gabriel looked at Bear as though he'd lost his train of thought, so Bear repeated the question, "You said 'besides other things' on the tape. What else is on there?"

"Me, Dustin, Gower, all in the same room, caught in a compromising situation. A sexual situation. In it, I'm engaging in sexual activities with both the victim and his killer, at the same party where I introduced the killer to his other victims."

"A sex tape? All this trouble over a fuckin' sex tape?"

"It's more than that, Bear. It implicates me in the crimes. Beyond accessory, I would be charged with murder—probably all three. They would see me as the connection they failed to find the first time, they would dig deep, destroy my family, my life. Dustin has the luxury of double jeopardy; the murders would come to rest on me. It goes beyond only me.

After being disbarred, they would attempt to retry some of my clients, uproot their lives. The ripples of this muddy water would keep spreading out. I can't let it happen. I just can't." Gabriel's voice trailed off. He fought back sobs because he didn't want to appear weak, he didn't want to beg, but that was exactly what he was doing. Gabriel wanted his logic to hold up, to convince his friend in the same way he had convinced so many juries. He desperately needed Bear's help.

Bear took the uncomfortable break in the story to light a cigarette. He cracked his window, blew out a plume of blue tobacco smoke, and said, "Shit, that kid's been in there a long time."

Gabriel ignored Donny's absence and carried on.

"Bear, I can assure you, that even in the worst case scenario, you'd have the best counsel out there."

"Next to you, of course," said Bear.

"Next to me," said Gabriel, completely missing the sarcasm. "I've thought this through and thought it through. There's no way around it, ours is the best course of action to take."

"You mean other than me turning all your asses in and walking away from the whole mess."

"Bear, please, we've been friends a long time. I've seen you through some rough times. I need your help with this. You'd be protecting more than me. You'd be helping protect the firm, its clients, my family—*my grandson*."

"Don't lay it on too thick, Gabe. I know who I'd be protecting." Bear took another drag off his Camel. "What about the bodies at the house? You don't think there'll be an investigation when somebody notices that woman missing."

"We have our own investigators, the best in the business. We can be on top of this, control the information, guide the police."

"Control the information? Listen to yourself. Isn't controlling the information what got you into this fucked up mess in the first place?" Bear tapped his cigarette ash on the edge of the open window. "You think that kid is alright in there?"

"Bear, I need an answer. I need to know that you are with me on this."

Bear didn't answer; he opened his car door, got out, and walked up to the restroom door and gave it a sturdy knock. "Hey, what happened? You fall in?"

Bear listened but there was no sound.

"Donny, you okay?" He pressed his ear up against the chipped white paint. "Hello, kid? Say something." He tried the knob, but it was locked. No surprise. Bear looked back at Gabriel in the car and said, "Shit." This is all he needed. After all they'd been through, for the whole thing to unravel because this dumb fucker overdoses in a gas station john. Bear began to pound on the door, slamming up against it with his shoulder.

Gabriel opened his door and stood beside the car. "What is it, what's wrong?"

"I think the little shit is turning blue in there."

Gabriel's face registered panic with the realization that they could be tripped up. "What do we do?"

"Goddamn it, Thaxton, I don't know," said Bear, then loudly to the door, he added, "But if Donny doesn't open this thing up, we're gonna have to leave him here."

Bear listened—the sound of a toilet flushing. Bear's face turned crimson. If the kid did come out of there, he was going to punch him in the face. There were a few more signs of life in the bathroom and, finally, the door opened.

Donny squinted at the fading sunlight, then looked at Bear, surprised to see him angry. "What's wrong?" his voice croaked.

Bear grabbed him by his jacket, spun him around, and shoved him back against the car. "You dumbass, what the fuck do you think you're doing? You junkie fucks ever think about anything else but gettin' high?" His fists were clenched. He blew air through his nostrils hot and fast. His urge to hit the kid was quelled only by the pathetic shape the boy was in. Probably wouldn't feel it anyway, thought Bear. "Get back in the goddamn car."

Donny scurried around to the other side of the car and quickly returned to the backseat. "Sorry, I went as fast as I could."

Gabriel looked at Donny in the back seat and frowned paternally. Donny seemed to have no idea why they were so angry. His pupils were constricted, his eyes glassy and lidded, and he was having trouble holding his head up. Bear and Gabriel re-entered the car, slammed their doors, and they pulled out from behind the station.

CHAPTER 22

They wound back on Highway One toward San Francisco. Bear took the turns more cautiously this time, checking the rearview for police every few seconds. Gabriel sat beside him patiently pressing redial on Bear's cell. There was no signal. The mere fact that Bear had let Gabriel try to use the phone told him that he was willing to help. Grateful, Gabriel promised him that they'd all eat and rest when they reached Beatrice's apartment in the City.

"Who's Beatrice?" croaked Donny from his half-slumber in the back.

"She works for me. I need to take care of some paperwork at her home. You'll both be able to relax there while we figure out what to do next."

Donny didn't say anything; his chin was bouncing off his chest.

"He's plenty relaxed already," said Bear. "Fuckin' dope fiend and a pervert. I'd be doing the world a favor if I drove this car off a cliff right now."

Gabriel glanced over the edge of the road. The sheer drop provided no chance for survival. "I don't mean to sound trite, Bear, but let he who is without sin cast the first stone."

"Not for nothin' there, Thaxton, but you quotin' scripture right now is kind of demeaning to the Good Word, and it's definitely not what's gonna keep me from hangin' a hard right and taking us all on a short flight."

Gabriel ignored the comment and asked, "Perhaps it's your phone, Bear. Maybe it's lost its charge. What do you think? Do you have a car charger?"

"The charge ain't got nothing to do with it. Look where we are, for Christ's sake. We'll get in range soon enough."

"Are you sure it's not your phone?"

"Yeah, I'm sure, I'm sure. Donny, let him try your phone, would ya?" He turned his head toward the back. "Donny, you got your phone, don't you? Didn't you guys get your precious phones?"

"My phone is dead."

"What about the other one?" asked Bear.

Without missing a beat, Donny said, "No, it's dead, too."

Now Gabriel turned. "Are you sure? May I try them, please? It's very important."

"They're dead. They don't work. There's no point. Just wait till we get there, will you?"

Both Gabriel and Bear caught the defensive tone in Donny's response. Bear took it to mean he was full of shit. Junkies lied on instinct.

"What the fuck was so important about them phones anyway? You and your friend acted like they were the most important thing in the world yesterday and you haven't said a word about 'em."

"I got 'em back, that's all."

"Y'know, I think I have a charger in the car after all. Let's charge up Donny's phone. Thaxton, take a peek in the glove box, would you?"

Gabriel unlatched the small door and began to search though the napkins and old tickets stuffed into the tiny space.

"I think they're busted, a charger won't help," said Donny.

"Busted?" said Bear, "Both of 'em? I call bullshit, Donny. Maybe it's time you told us what's really on those phones. Why a couple of junkie kids put their lives on the line—on the line, shit, your friend is *dead* 'cause of that damn phone of his—for a phone, *a goddamned phone*. Now tell us what the deal is."

Donny's chest caved in. He looked like he was deflating,

imploding into himself. "The phone didn't kill Rich, that fucker Dustin did."

Bear stayed quiet and let that one go—letting Donny's guilt do the work for him.

They came round a curve and caught a glimpse of the Golden Gate Bridge. The city lay beyond it, looking like a postcard still. A short blanket of fog was receding, pulling itself back out to the ocean. The view of San Francisco looked the same as it always did. Constant, reassuring. The city meant something different to each of them, but, after the day in Marin, it looked like a safe haven to the whole car.

Gabriel dialed again as soon as he saw the tall, red, rigid towers of the Golden Gate. This time he got through. Beatrice answered quickly, probably wondering why her boss was calling on a late Sunday afternoon. Gabriel explained what he could, told her that he'd divulge more when he got there, and then, as an afterthought, mentioned he had Bear and a "friend" with him.

When he hung up, he told Bear the cross streets where Beatrice lived and said, "Let's go."

Bear said, "I'm going, I'm going."

Beatrice lived in an apartment building not far from Gabriel Thaxton. It was a tall, overpriced art-deco number in the Russian Hill district. It featured all the amenities of a modern big city apartment—except for parking. Once Gabriel had pointed out which one it was, Bear circled the surrounding blocks endlessly looking for an empty space.

"Christ, Gabe, what's she pay for this joint?"

"On the salary I give her, I'm afraid to ask."

They finally found a spot and hiked back to the building. The climb winded all three by the time they reached the building's lobby. Gabriel located her name on the bank of buzzers and pressed. They waited, three mismatched men thrown together by terrible circumstances, and an uncomfortable silence fell between them. The wind whistled and the cold bit and finally the front door buzzed.

On the sixth floor, they found her door cracked open with a warm smell and soft music emanating from within.

"Beatrice, you remember Bear," said Gabriel.

"Of course," said Beatrice blushing noticeably.

"Bean, what smells so goddamn delicious?"

"It's the sauce for the pasta. I hope you're hungry. I never get to cook for anyone but myself."

"Hungry? You know we are. I haven't had a home-cooked meal since...since I don't know when."

"And, Beatrice, this is our friend Donny," said Gabriel, still effecting his most polite tone.

Donny only nodded hello, so Gabriel added, "Donny's not been feeling well."

"Awe, I'm sorry to hear that, Donny. Is there something I can get for you?"

Donny shook his head this time. He was pale and looked sickly. He moved across the room slowly and slumped down on a corner of the couch.

"He'll be fine after some dinner," said Gabriel. "Listen, Beatrice, there are some papers that I had you store; is there any way you could retrieve them for me?"

Beatrice furrowed her brow. The request was only to be made in the case of a serious problem—like a sudden divorce—or in the event of Gabriel's unexpected death. It was designed as a covert defense against Mr. Thaxton's wife or her attorneys.

"Is everything alright?" asked Beatrice.

Gabriel let out a long sigh, "No, I'm afraid not. I've run into some trouble and I need to have the documents. We may have to proceed with the plan we'd discussed."

Beatrice said nothing more and hurried to her bedroom to find Gabriel's papers. After a few minutes, she reappeared with a short stack of legal documents in both hands.

Gabriel accepted them gratefully and sat down at the small table by her kitchenette and began sifting through them, methodically laying each out before him.

Left mostly to themselves now, Beatrice offered Bear a glass of wine.

"Vino? You got anything stronger? It's been a hell of a day."

Dustin Walczak sat alone in Gabriel's Bentley. The cold night air poured steadily through the shattered window in back. He sat huddled into himself, trying to stay awake. The chaos of the weekend had left him drained and in a near stupor. His head weighed heavy and his chin rested on his chest. He needed desperately to rest, but he was afraid that the police might roll up and roust him. The missing window was a dead giveaway the car was not his. That combined with the fact he was sitting in a Bentley. A guy like him in a fucking Bentley. The high profile car was going to be a magnet for both police and the homeless. He tried to stay vigilant.

He was wedged into a spot in an alley off Larkin Street. He didn't expect much foot traffic—it was far enough up the hill from the Tenderloin that there wouldn't be many street people prowling—but the cops would be a different story.

His eyes burned and he closed them for a few minutes at a time, telling himself it was enough rest. His cigarette would burn down and singe the hair on his knuckles and he'd wake back up. A few more hours, he told himself, just a few more hours.

Gabriel, Bear, and Beatrice sat around the small, round table that bordered the kitchenette. Donny had passed out where he sat on the couch and no one had the heart to wake him.

"He needs his rest," said Gabriel.

"He needs a hell of a lot more than that," said Bear.

They fell back into the happy ritual of eating. They passed plates, sprinkled parmesan cheese, poured wine, and buttered bread without saying a word. Other than the sporadic, "*Mmmmn,*" directed at Beatrice, they ate on in silence.

When the meal was done, and only the wine glasses sat before them, Gabriel tried to explain to Bear the importance of the deed he'd squirreled away.

"Originally, I thought I might need the Grant Deed because of my wife—soon to be ex-wife—and I never thought I'd need it in a situation like this, but I'm damn glad it's here." Gabriel tapped his index finger on the deed before him. "You see, the law considers the transfer of the property the minute the deed is recorded, not when it is signed. If one has another deed, signed and notarized, one only has to record that deed first. Not too long ago, I had a Grant Deed drawn up transferring the asset to Beatrice. It sits waiting, notarized and ready to record. The property can reside in her possession for as long as I need it to, then she can simply grant it back to me. You see, there'll be nothing to grant to Dustin once this deed is recorded."

"We just gotta get in line first?" asked Bear.

"Exactly."

"You think Dustin knows you have another deed?"

"I doubt it, but he is being advised by Terrence. That means he's got one of the best snakes in the west guiding him through the grass. I think it would be best if we were at City Hall when they open the doors."

Bear thought about it. The city had cops stationed at the doors of City Hall ever since Mayor Moscone had been assassinated way back in '78. It should be safe, should be a breeze. They'd follow Gabriel's plan to save his precious mansion, then worry about how to capture Dustin. Maybe let the cops nab him right there at City Hall.

Beatrice threw a blanket over Donny. He hadn't moved since he'd passed out. She then went back to the kitchen and poured herself another glass of wine. Bear asked if he could smoke in the house and Beatrice guided him to the balcony where she joined him outside in the cool, fast-moving air. There was an ashtray already in place between two lawn chairs.

"Bean, I'm surprised. I didn't know you smoked."

"A girl's got to have some vices. Besides, there're a lot of things you don't know about me. Things that Mr. Thaxton doesn't know either."

"Ooh, really? Well, I guess it's high time I found some of these things out. You've always struck me as the mysterious type."

They chatted on, flirting back and forth until their glasses were empty and Beatrice went inside to refill them. Gabriel had fallen asleep in the recliner with his legal papers on his lap, so she covered him with a blanket too and returned with two full glasses to the balcony.

It was refreshing for Bear to let go of the last few days and just be with someone. It was only flirting, after all, and he only thought about Sheila once or twice. Bean was the polar opposite of Sheila. Where Sheila was brass and bold, Bean was shy and quiet. Sheila was seasoned and full of sass; Bean was sweet, naive, and young. Too young for Bear, he thought, till after a few more glasses of wine.

The night grew cold and eventually they moved inside. Not wanting to wakeup Gabriel and Donny, they positioned themselves in the bedroom and continued their talk. She told Bear about growing up in Nevada, how she hated the heat and the whole state. Bear revealed a little about his own history and Bean surprised him by already knowing more about him than he cared to divulge. She'd peeked at his files at the office, she said. Then she admitted having a long-standing crush on him.

"Hmmn," he said, "must be a Daddy complex. I gotta be old enough to be your father."

"No, you are nothing like my dad. He's a straight-arrow, button-down conservative."

"Is he still around?"

"Yeah, but if he knew I was sitting in my bedroom talking to someone like you, it might kill him."

They both laughed about that, and, then, without warning she kissed him, a long, sloppy drunken kiss on the mouth.

Bear held her by the shoulders and said, "Be careful. I may be old, but I'm not dead."

She kissed him again. This time he kissed her back. She fell slowly back onto the bed, pulling him with her. Before long they were under the sheets and the lights were off.

It didn't last long, but it was as passionate as anything Bear could remember.

Soon after, he found himself deep in a dreamless sleep.

There was a banging on the bedroom door. It was Gabriel, shouting that it was time to go. Bear tried to focus on the clock beside Bean's bed. Five-thirty a.m. Jesus Christ, thought Bear, what am I, a farmer?

He sat up, hoping Bean would remain in her slumber, and he pulled himself out from the warmth under her comforter. His head was pounding louder than the door. He opened it.

"What?"

Gabriel said, "Bear, we've got to get ready. We want a jump on Dustin. I fear he may be already camped out, waiting." Then he looked over Bear's shoulder at his sleeping secretary and said, "Really, Bear, my receptionist? You couldn't contain yourself?"

"What was that you said yesterday? Oh yeah, let he who is without sin ..."

Gabriel cut him off, "Yes, yes, yes. Let's just focus now on getting ourselves down to City Hall on time, shall we?"

Bear found Donny in the kitchen slowly stirring a pan of scrambled eggs with a spatula. Donny's pupils were constricted and he boasted a sleepy, relaxed smile. He'd clearly already spent some time alone in the bathroom this morning.

"You okay?" asked Bear.

"Oh, yeah, I feel great. I'm really a morning person anyway. I'm ready to go."

"You can't keep doing this shit, you know. At some point," said Bear, "you're gonna have to get your life together."

The smile dissipated from Donny's face. "I know," he said, "I'm going to...I plan to." Then after a moment of contemplation, he said to the frying pan, "I have to."

"Don't forget to butter the toast."

While Gabriel moved into the bathroom for a quick shower, Bear scoured the fridge for a beer. Nothing. "Goddamn wine. I woulda been better off with whiskey," he mumbled to himself. He gave up his search and decided to wait out the hangover and moved himself outside to the balcony for the day's first cigarette. It was cold and windy still and he stubbed it out after only a few puffs and returned to the comfort of Bean's apartment.

The sky outside was growing a pale blue by the time Gabriel emerged from his shower. Donny and Bear already had their shoes and jackets on and looked impatient.

"What the hell did you drag me out of bed for, Gabe? If I hadda known you were gonna shower, shit, and shave, I could have stayed in bed an extra hour."

"I wanted to make sure you were ready—*really* ready—to do this. If I know Dustin, he's been awake this whole time trying to figure out how to beat us to the punch."

"It's not even seven o'clock, when does that joint open anyway? We got time for a coffee at least, don't we?"

"Eight a.m., sharp. We'll be there, at the front door, waiting."

"What if he's on the other side? Don't they open the Van Ness doors and the Polk Street doors at the same time?" asked Donny.

"The kid's got a point, Thaxton. How we plan to stake this place out?"

Gabriel pursed his lips, thinking it through. "We'll have to put Donny on one side—the Van Ness entrance. He can guard that door and let us know if he sees Dustin."

"How am I gonna let you know?" said Donny.

"Use your cell phone. Call Bear if you see anything, anything at all. We'll be waiting at the other side with the paperwork."

Bear interrupted, "He can't call me. My cell is dead. It sat there in Marin for almost two days. That call you made to Bean killed it. I wasn't kidding yesterday when I said I hadn't charged it."

"Donny, let Bear use Richard's phone."

Donny's face blanched. "No, I told you guys, it ain't workin' either. It's broke. It ain't got no charge."

"Which is it?" said Bear. "Is it broken, or does it have no charge?"

Donny hesitated only a second before Bear lit into him, "I'm sick of this shit. You been jerkin' me around about the goddamn phones for three fuckin' days now. Before we go into goddamn battle, I wanna know what the deal is with those phones. What's on 'em you had to have 'em back so fuckin' bad? And don't tell me about no goddamn kid pictures this time."

Gabriel looked confused. He had no idea what Bear was talking about. He had no idea why Donny was looking like he wanted to disappear into the carpet. "Donny, what is it? Just tell us. This far along, I don't think there's any need to keep secrets."

Donny felt all at once exhausted, sick of the whole thing. He didn't care anymore. He didn't care about the money, getting off the street; he was tired, pushed to his limits. He thought about his dead friend, he thought about the freak raping him in the motel room. He thought about the plan to extort the man standing right in front of him, a man who was waiting for an explanation with his big, watery blue eyes. A man that had been only kind to him. Donny gave up.

"There's a video on Rich's phone. A movie. We shot it at the hotel last week."

Both Gabriel and Bear waited.

"It's got you in it, Gabriel. You, me, and Rich. We were gonna tell you we'd put it up on YouTube if you didn't pay us off. That was it, our big plan. We just wanted enough dough to get off the streets and now," he almost choked up, but held it in check. "Here we are. Rich is dead."

Bear held up a finger and said, "Don't forget about that poor woman upstairs."

"Oh, Jesus," said Donny. The image of her dead body flashing through his mind again before he continued, "Dustin's stealing your house, and...and I'm probably going to fucking jail."

Bear and Gabriel only let the boy talk.

"I don't know, I went along with it. I just wanted to get clean and get outta here, outta San Francisco. Rich told me again and again it would work, even when I knew it was never going to. Then, it was too late, we'd gone too far."

Beatrice's tiny apartment was silent. They heard a toilet flush in another unit, then the creaking of a neighbor's footsteps upstairs. Still, no one said anything.

Then Bear said, "I don't think they even let you put that kinda shit on YouTube."

Gabriel smiled. Bear was right. It didn't take a lot to maintain damage control on a scheme like that. There were entire firms whose sole function was to root out slanderous Internet posts. It would be particularly easy for someone who was not a movie star, someone that nobody wanted to see naked—someone like himself—to quash a plot like that before it got out of hand. *Outed.* When he thought about it, it was the least of his worries.

Donny looked visibly relieved. When he'd gotten it all out, he took a couple of deep breaths and lifted his head to face Gabriel. He felt foolish. He felt like a dumb kid, caught with his hand in the cookie jar.

Gabriel said, "I'm going to help you, Donny, but not because of the film. I'm going to help you get off the street, off the drugs, because I think you deserve that. I'm going to help you because you're helping me." He paused a moment, then said, "And because, regardless of what you two were up to, I considered Richard a friend."

"Alright, enough of this shit. I don't want to watch an *Afterschool Special.* Jesus. I'm gonna say goodbye to Bean and then we're out of here."

CHAPTER 23

They'd reached the car, got in, and started to pull out before Gabriel asked Bear, "What did she say?"

"Nothing," said Bear. "I couldn't wake her up."

It was an unusually clear morning, crisp and cold. There weren't too many other cars on the street either, only taxis, Muni buses, and early morning commuters. All three of them kept their eyes peeled for the black Bentley.

They rolled down Polk Street and when they'd reached City Hall they went around the block a few times, looking for Dustin and trying to find the right parking spot with the best vantage point. They finally settled on a spot perpendicular to the sidewalk on Grove Street across from the Bill Graham Civic Auditorium. They pulled in and could see the doors of City Hall from where they sat. Civic Center Plaza was designed to offer a sense of classical antiquity. A hodge-podge of different themes from different eras, there was Roman and Greek architecture mixed in with City Hall's Parisian dome. The whole place gave one a feeling that its best days were behind it. The plaza laid out in front of the grand buildings was dotted with homeless people—in tents, in sleeping bags, or curled up around their battered shopping carts.

Bear struck up a Camel and cracked his window. "What time is it?"

Gabriel didn't even have to check. "Seven-twenty."

Bear leaned back. "Donny, you got that phone?"

Donny passed it up, and with it the video, the failed plot, and his hopes of extorting Gabriel. "You got another one of those Camels?"

Bear shook one out for the boy and passed him the lighter.

"Now remember, kid, when you walk around to the Van Ness side, keep an eye out. We figure he's gotta be near here somewhere, waiting, just like we are. If you see anything, anybody that looks like him, you call. Let's make sure we're the most recent dialed number in your phone to speed things up."

Donny scrolled to Rich's number and hit send. The phone in Bear's hand rang once before Donny hung up.

"Good luck, son," said Gabriel as Donny got out of the car.

Donny walked around to the driver's window and Bear rolled it down. Donny said, "One more, for the road?"

Bear sighed and shook out another Camel for the boy. "You know, kid, they sell these things in stores." Donny took the cigarette and Bear added, "Remember, be smart. Use your head, Donny. Be smart."

Donny turned and walked away, still limping with the pain from his last time on the corner.

"We should discuss any weapons you might have." Gabriel spoke without taking his eyes off the ornate golden doors in the middle of City Hall.

"Why? I know there're metal detectors. I'll leave what I have in the car."

"When we do see him, he'll be away from the vehicle. We've got to get into that trunk. He won't have the VHS tape with him, I don't think. It'll most likely be in the trunk."

"Don't worry, I haven't forgotten about your precious tape."

"Getting this deed recorded is the easy part, Bear. It's getting that tape back I'm worried about."

Bear asked, "You think the kid is over there yet?"

"You could call him."

"Nah, I'll wait."

Just as the words left Bear's lips, they spotted the black Bentley. It rolled slowly down Polk Street, from McAllister toward Grove, right past the front steps of City Hall. They could see Dustin behind the wheel, alone in the car, with his neck craning toward the building's entrance.

Gabriel said, "Good Lord."

And Bear said, "Holy shit."

The car moved through the light at Polk and Grove and continued on toward south of Market.

"Where the fuck is he going?" asked Bear.

"Pull out, Bear. Follow him," Gabriel said excitedly. "Quickly, before he gets too far."

Bear started his Toyota and threw it into reverse. They made the light and turned left onto Polk. They could see Dustin in Thaxton's Bentley stopped at the light up ahead of them.

"He's in a stolen car, Gabe. Call the cops. Tell 'em where he's at."

"The car has not been reported stolen. It will only complicate things. Please, just stay close and keep an eye on him."

"Jesus Christ, what the hell do you think I'm doing?"

They now sat two car lengths behind Dustin. They watched his head turn, bird-like, from side to side, either looking for a place to park or the usual paranoid jerking motions he always made. Bear got a chill just seeing the back of his head. The light changed and they followed the Bentley across Market onto 10th Street. Dustin was moving away from City Hall.

"You think he sees us?"

"I doubt it," said Gabriel. "But I'm not sure what he's doing either. Maybe he's looking for parking. Maybe he's not even sure where he's going. Stay close, Bear. This is our chance."

"To get the tape, you mean."

* * *

Dustin drove ahead for three more blocks, then, without signaling or slowing, took a hard left on Folsom Street. By the time Bear made the same left, Dustin was halfway up the next block. The Bentley was moving fast. Dustin caught the next two lights and showed no signs of slowing.

"Shit, I think he spotted us."

Gabriel pointed at the corner ahead. "He's taking a left on 7th. Hurry, Bear, stick with him. He's going back to the Civic Center."

Dustin crossed Market Street again, hooked a right, and zipped into the Tenderloin District. Gabriel started to get nervous. They were dangerously close to a high speed chase. This could only go on for so many minutes before they attracted the attention of the police. They followed Dustin, zigging and zagging over the one-way streets of the city's skid row. Then, he was gone.

"I don't see him," said Bear. "What time is it?"

"Seven thirty-three," said Gabriel.

"Call Donny and let him know he's coming his way. We gotta get back and cover the other entrance."

"We've got to find him," Gabriel sounded desperate now. "He's probably pulled into one of these alleys. We still have time, let's find him, please. Turn here at Larkin."

Bear turned.

"Left here, on Willow, slow down," Gabriel commanded. He knew the alleyways of the Tenderloin well, having prowled here when picking up young men. He was sure Dustin would be hiding somewhere near.

Before they'd made it halfway down the alley, they were hit from behind. The jolt shocked them both and Bear stopped the car. He looked in the rearview and saw Dustin's smiling face behind the wheel of the Bentley.

"Son of a bitch," Bear growled. He watched as Dustin

threw the Bentley in reverse and began to back out of the alleyway. When Dustin reached the mouth of the alley, he reversed into traffic. Horns sounded and there was another metallic crash. There were more horns followed by a squeal of tires. Bear watched as he saw the Dustin's vehicle flash past the entrance to Willow Alley. It was a hit and run; the Bentley was gone.

Instead of following him in reverse out of the alley, Bear put it in drive and moved forward to Polk. There was no point in getting tangled in the destruction Dustin had created. Larkin was a one-way street; the Bentley had to be moving north now.

Bear took a right on Polk and moved north too, hoping to spot the Bentley on one of the cross streets. There was an unbearable rubbing sound where the fender had been pushed into the right rear wheel. He was sure several citizens had called 911 by now. The police would soon be scouring the Tenderloin for the Bentley.

"He's dumping the car," said Bear.

"How do you know?" asked Gabriel.

"He's got to. Hear the sirens? He's gotta dump the ride if he's gonna make it to City Hall."

Then they saw him, walking quickly out of Cedar Alley. He had a shoulder bag wrapped around his neck and he was moving fast, trying to act nonchalant. Bear's eyes met Dustin's. Bear yanked the Toyota over. The right front tire jumped the curb.

Bear started to jump out of the car, but he was caught by his seatbelt. While he fumbled with it, Dustin broke into a sprint. He was running down the gentle, sloping blocks toward City Hall. Bear, remembering that all his weapons were still in the trunk, said, "Shit," and got back into the driver's seat and pulled his battered car off the curb.

He tried a clumsy three-point turn and got the Toyota facing the same direction as Dustin was moving.

"Get him, Bear. We still have time," Gabriel cried, his voice high and excited now. He was torn between chasing Dustin or finding his Bentley and searching the car for the VHS tape before the police discovered it. "Did you see where he left the car?"

Bear made the decision for him and sped after Dustin.

Donny sat on the stone steps leading up to City Hall on Van Ness Avenue. He twirled the second Camel Bear had given him between his fingers. He wasn't watching the sidewalk for Dustin. His mind wandered. It played over the scenes of the last three days. He felt sick when he thought about Rich. Not dope-sick, but a sour queasiness in his stomach. He kept flashing back to Dustin, too, that jailhouse tattoo on his chest, the deranged look in his eyes. Donny wondered if that's what was in store for him; if he, too, was to become an animal like Dustin.

"Pull over, pull over, there he is," Gabriel shouted as they watched Dustin slip into another alleyway.

Bear yanked the car over along a section of the curb painted red beside a fire hydrant and hopped out of the car. The Toyota was hanging in the street with its rear end damage visible to anyone who may drive by. He ran around to the rear of the car and opened the trunk. He reached into the wheel well and got his gun.

"C'mon," he said to Gabriel, but Thaxton was already crossing the street to reach the mouth of the alley.

Dustin had reached the alley's halfway point when Bear shouted, "Freeze, motherfucker!"

Dustin didn't freeze; he darted behind a large dumpster and grabbed the nearest thing he could find, a half-conscious homeless woman slumbering there with her man. Dustin wrapped his arm around her neck and pulled her up on her feet. She protested, grumbled, not really sure what was happening, perhaps thinking that she was being arrested. He pulled his gun from behind his back with his free hand and stuck it into her cheek. He peeked out from behind the dumpster and saw that Bear and Gabriel had slowed to a cautious walk.

Bear had his gun out in front of him, aimed at Dustin's head. "Dustin, you fuck, let that woman go. You're gonna get her killed."

"Fuck you," said Dustin, "You're the one that's gonna get her killed. You back off, go back the other way and I'll let her go."

Gabriel pleaded with him. "It's gone too far, Dustin. They'll never let you record that deed. They're watching for you at City Hall. You won't even make it into the building. Give this thing up before someone else gets hurt." Then Gabriel said something that astonished Bear, "Dustin, I can still represent you. What have you done? A hit and run is all you'll be charged with. Please, it's not too late."

"Hit and run? That was your car, old man. You fuckin' deal with it." Dustin's voice was venomous, hissing. His glassy eyes lit up with glare.

He reminded Bear of some kind of angry reptile, cornered and about to get a swat.

"It's your problem; it's all your problem. I have the tape and you know what that means. I'll always have the tape, you old fuck."

The woman in Dustin's clutches was making unintelligible gurgling sounds. She knew now she was not under arrest, but she still looked wild and confused.

Bear had his gun aimed right at Dustin's head. "You want me to shoot him, Gabe? I think I can do it. It's an easy shot."

Sirens rose, several of them, the sound was getting louder and louder. Gabriel said to Bear, quietly and out of the side of his mouth, "Can you do it, can you hit him?"

"I think so." Bear kept his hand steady, his sights on Dustin's forehead.

"Please, Dustin," said Gabriel. "Where is the tape?"

"I got it. I got it right here. And you're never gonna get it."

"Shoot him," said Gabriel.

From behind Dustin, a great, dirty, meaty paw rose. The homeless woman's man, or husband, or boyfriend, rose up and was going to swing at Dustin. "Leggo uh her," he said with a slurred growl.

Dustin swung around, the woman still clutched with his left arm, and shot the man in the face. The sirens blared on Larkin Street and the noise of the gunshot was lost among them. A red mist flew up from the back of the man's head before he disappeared, dropping out of Bear and Gabriel's view like a dirty puppet.

Dustin returned the gun barrel to the woman's cheek and said, "You see? You see what you made happen? You're the ones. Now fuck off. I have the tape, I have the house. It's all mine. I earned it, every last bit of it. I deserve it. You get nothing, you old fuck, *nothing*."

"Shoot him," said Gabriel.

Bear expelled his breath and squeezed the trigger. The shot went high.

Dustin fired into the woman's cheek, just as he had the notary, Miranda, back in Marin. The shot tore through her skull in the same fashion. She was instantly dead. He dropped her lifeless body and pointed the pistol at Bear and Gabriel.

"You fucks, you shits, goddamn you, I'll kill you both." He began firing.

One, two, three shots. Bear heard them ricochet all over the alley, off cement, off brick, off cars. Bear dropped to one knee and emptied his gun into Dustin. This time, with Dustin's gun pointing straight at him, Bear did not miss. Not one shot. Dustin's body danced backward as he contorted to the impact of the bullets. When he finally fell, it was backward over the homeless couple's up-turned cart.

Gabriel ran to Dustin, flipping open the satchel that hung from his neck. He searched it and squeezed it, and found no tape. Gabriel squeezed his jacket and there, smashed by the bullets, was the VHS tape. Gabriel quickly pulled the tape out. It looked like it had been run over. It was smashed and shattered and utterly destroyed. He then lifted the edge of the dumpster and threw in what remained of the tape.

Bear stood watching. He'd already gone too far; he wasn't tampering with evidence, too. As soon as Gabriel let the lid of the dumpster fall back down with its deep metallic slam, police cars began to fill up the alleyway, both ends. The sirens were deafening now. Bear dropped his pistol to the ground, put his hands behind his head, and dropped onto his tired knees.

When Donny had heard the first siren, he stuck that Camel in his mouth and lit it. As the sirens increased, both in number and in volume, he knew somehow they were on the way for his friends. He looked at the phone in his hand and waited for it to ring. When he'd finished his smoke and the phone still hadn't rung, he stood up, dug his fingernail into the plastic cover on the back, popped it open and took out the battery. He walked down the steps of City Hall toward the trashcan on the corner of McAllister and Van Ness and tossed the phone and battery in. Then he kept on walking.

CHAPTER 24

True to his word, Gabriel got Bear the best representation he could find. Just as good, in fact, as the attorney he retained for himself. Eli Schnabel arrived with a smile on his face and an outstretched hand. He reassured the biker over and over that this was going to work out in time. Patience and prudence were his key phrases.

Bear was relieved not to have to waste his one phone call on a lawyer and used it to call Sheila instead. She told him she loved him, that she couldn't wait to see him. It wouldn't be long, she told him. It made Bear feel like he was going to get out of there; he *was* going to see her soon. It gave him some hope. It turned out Sheila and the lawyer were both right. Bear was held for seventy-two hours at the Hall of Justice. Much of that time he spent being interrogated by an endless stream of detectives.

The investigators didn't seem to have much of the story yet, so Bear offered up as few details as possible. They didn't ask about any VHS tape. They didn't have any idea about it. Because all the guns were recovered, nobody bothered to look in the dumpster for evidence. To the cops, it was more cut and dry. A case of self-defense—in the alleyway, at least. Dustin wasn't alive to complicate matters with his version of the events. As for the details from Terrence's house in Marin, there was clear evidence that Gabriel was held and tortured by the madman. In fact, with Gabriel and Bear being the only available witnesses to the carnage there, it played more like Dustin had held them all hostage: Gabriel, Terrence, Raphael, and Miranda the Notary. They were all victims of a speed freak's psychopathic rage. There were plenty of bullet holes and spent casings to back up the story. Dustin had used Terrence's gun to kill the woman and Terrence himself. The same gun as Rich was killed with. It was the same pistol Terrence shot Raphael with while aiming at Bear. Then Dustin brought that same gun into the city and used it to kill both the homeless people before unloading bullets all over the alleyway.

As much as the cops hated Gabriel, he was still a respected member of the community. He knew how to lay his story out in a manner that would be believable. He was a master at manipulating the flow of information. The press viewed Dustin as a mass murderer. There were headlines like, *Meth-Fueled Mayhem In Marin* and *Crystal Killer Had Killed Before*. They called him the *Speed Slayer* and the *Meth Murderer*. Gabriel was made out to be a victim, an attorney whose tireless efforts on behalf of his client came back to bite him. Dustin's known criminal history only underscored the story. Little was known about the hero, the man who came to save Gabriel from the clutches of Derek "Dustin" Walczak. All involved worked hard to keep it that way.

Donny spent the first twenty-four hours holed up in his hotel room. He sat watching the door, expecting a phalanx of police to come bursting in at any moment. He pounded old cottons and rinsed dirty spoons to stay well. There were enough scrapings in his drawer for him to get by—barely. After he'd exhausted those, he decided to call Gabriel's office. He wanted to know if Gabriel was going to keep his word about helping him off the streets.

He ventured out into the daylight and realized as soon as he hit the sidewalk how sick he really was. The sun was bright and the streets were warm, but Donny shivered all the way to the only payphone he knew had a phonebook attached. He found Gabriel's office number and popped in two quarters.

A friendly, familiar voice answered the phone. "Thaxton, Spreckle, and White."

"Bean, I mean, Beatrice? Is that you?"

She knew instantly who it was; she'd been expecting his call. "Donny? How are you? Are you alright? Where are you calling from?"

Donny told her he was at the BART station at Market and Powell and reassured her that he'd not spoken to any police. He told her he was sick, but couldn't go back to what he was doing for money. He needed help and wondered if Gabriel was there.

"No, I'm afraid that both he and Mr. Mayfield are still being held at the Hall of Justice."

"Mr. Mayfield?"

She corrected herself. "Bear, honey, that's his name."

"Oh, well..." Donny's voice trailed off.

Bean listened to the background noise a moment, the trains, the people, and over it all she heard a quiet sob.

"Donny, Mr. Thaxton has left me with a set of instructions in case you were to call." There was silence. "Donny, are you there?"

"Yeah, I'm here."

"He asked me to write out a personal check for you to take to the methadone clinic. The check is to be made out to the clinic, though. You understand? He wants you to begin a detox. He also wanted to make sure that your rent was paid for the duration of your treatment. At the end of the treatment, he wanted to give you the opportunity to go back home."

Donny listened.

"Do you have a place to go, Donny? A place that is out of the city?"

Donny thought about his home, his family. There was no

going back there. He lied and said, "Yes."

"Okay, good. All you need to do is come down here to the office and we'll get you squared away."

There was more silence on the phone. Bean listened close to see if she could hear anymore sobbing. Finally she heard Donny say something that sounded like a yes and then the line went dead.

On the bus over to Thaxton, Spreckle, and White, Donny discovered a discarded newspaper on the one free seat he found toward the back of the bus. The headline caught his eye. *No Charges For Gabriel Thaxton.* Donny picked it up and started reading. It told some of the tale, not much though. It said that, although he was still being held, it was unlikely that the famous lawyer would be charged with any wrongdoing, even though he'd failed to notify police of the murders in Marin before tracking the killer back to the city. Likewise, his mysterious companion—the one who'd actually shot Derek "Dustin" Walczak—would probably not be charged. It praised the man known as Darrel Mayfield as a hero. He scanned the rest of the article. There was no mention of him anywhere. The closest thing he saw to any information about Big Rich was a one-line description of his friend as "another victim found at the gruesome scene."

A victim, thought Donny, a nameless victim. That's an understatement. He watched the city go by as he rocked back and forth in his bus seat. He was downtown now, in the financial district. It was a place where Donny had never spent much time. It was lunchtime now and the sidewalks were crowded. The people looked different, sounded different. It seemed like they all had somewhere to go, somewhere to be. Donny envied them. They had lives to attend to.

It would be a long time before Donny stopped feeling like a victim himself.

ACKNOWLEDGMENTS

There's a lot of people I'd like to thank for helping me through the writing of this book. First and foremost, my wife, Cheryl, and my children, who put up with my obsessive behavior during the actual writing. Brian Stannard for the excellent painting and Eric Beetner for his talents and patience putting the cover together. Thanks to Michael Mohr for the editorial input, and Liz Kracht for believing in the story—even though it was too damn sleazy for the big boys. Also R. for speaking to me so honestly about his life in the "trade." Brian Lindenmuth at Snubnose Press for initially taking this book on without blinking. And last, but not least, Eric Campbell at Down & Out, for breathing new life into the book and caring about it enough to offer it to his readers without giving a shit about how much it had sold or how many it would sell—or how damn sleazy it was. You're a class act, Eric.

Tom Pitts received his education firsthand on the streets of San Francisco. He remains there, writing, working, and trying to survive. He is the author of two novellas, *Piggyback* and *Knuckleball*. His shorts have been published in the usual spots by the usual suspects. Tom is also an acquisitions editor at Gutter Books and Out of the Gutter Online.

Find out more at TomPittsAuthor.com.

OTHER TITLES FROM DOWN AND OUT BOOKS

See www.DownAndOutBooks.com for complete list

By Anonymous-9
Bite Hard

By J.L. Abramo
Catching Water in a Net
Clutching at Straws
Counting to Infinity
Gravesend
Chasing Charlie Chan
Circling the Runway
Brooklyn Justice

By Trey R. Barker
2,000 Miles to Open Road
Road Gig: A Novella
Exit Blood
Death is Not Forever
No Harder Prison

By Richard Barre
The Innocents
Bearing Secrets
Christmas Stories
The Ghosts of Morning
Blackheart Highway
Burning Moon
Echo Bay
Lost

By Eric Beetner and
JB Kohl
Over Their Heads

By Eric Beetner and
Frank Scalise
The Backlist
The Shortlist (*)

By G.J. Brown
Falling

By Rob Brunet
Stinking Rich

By Dana Cameron (editor)
Murder at the Beach: Bouchercon Anthology 2014

By Mark Coggins
No Hard Feelings

By Tom Crowley
Vipers Tail
Murder in the Slaughterhouse

By Frank De Blase
Pine Box for a Pin-Up
Busted Valentines and Other Dark Delights
A Cougar's Kiss (*)

By Les Edgerton
The Genuine, Imitation, Plastic Kidnapping

By A.C. Frieden
Tranquility Denied
The Serpent's Game
The Pyongyang Option (*)

By Jack Getze
Big Numbers
Big Money
Big Mojo
Big Shoes

(*)—Coming Soon

OTHER TITLES FROM DOWN AND OUT BOOKS

See www.DownAndOutBooks.com for complete list

By Richard Godwin
Wrong Crowd
Buffalo and Sour Mash (*)

By William Hastings (editor)
*Stray Dogs: Writing from
the Other America*

By Jeffery Hess
Beachhead

By Matt Hilton
No Going Back
Rules of Honor
The Lawless Kind
The Devil's Anvil

By David Housewright
Finders Keepers
Full House

By Jerry Kennealy
Screen Test (*)

By S.W. Lauden
Crosswise

By Terrence McCauley
The Devil Dogs of Belleau Wood

By Bill Moody
Czechmate
The Man in Red Square
Solo Hand
The Death of a Tenor Man
The Sound of the Trumpet
Bird Lives!

By Gary Phillips
The Perpetrators
Scoundrels (Editor)
Treacherous
3 the Hard Way

By Tom Pitts
Hustle

By Robert J. Randisi
Upon My Soul
Souls of the Dead
Envy the Dead (*)

By Ryan Sayles
The Subtle Art of Brutality
Warpath
*Swansongs Always Begin as Love
Songs* (*)

By John Shepphird
The Shill
Kill the Shill
Beware the Shill (*)

By Ian Thurman
Grand Trunk and Shearer (*)

By Lono Waiwaiole
Wiley's Lament
Wiley's Shuffle
Wiley's Refrain
Dark Paradise

By Vincent Zandri
Moonlight Weeps

(*)—Coming Soon

Made in the USA
Charleston, SC
25 May 2016